TWO NOVELLAS

THE

MAN

AND

IN THE WAKE OF

Gerard R. D'Alessio

The Man
and
In the Wake of Love
Two Novellas

Copyright © 2016 Gerard R. D'Alessio

Books may be ordered through booksellers or lulu.com.

ISBN: 978-0-692-77712-1

This book is dedicated with all my love and appreciation
to my wife, Susan, whose inspiration, encouragement, and helpful
insight and advice have made it possible for me
to engage and persist in my writing endeavors.

Novels by Gerard R. D'Alessio

Dr. Cappeletti's Chorus
The Giantonios: Family Matters
Iraq Dreams

Acknowledgments

I cannot thank Wendy Bernstein enough for her invaluable suggestions, excellent advice, and enormous help in guiding this project to completion.

Table of Contents

The Man 1

In the Wake of Love 121

THE
MAN

THE
MAN

A NOVELLA

Gerard R. D'Alessio

Introduction

My cousin lived a very colorful life. Born in 1952, Vittorio Putino went on to serve in the Pennsylvania attorney general's office and, in 1992, he labored vigorously for the Democratic Party and received credit for helping Bill Clinton win the state with a substantial majority. The Clinton administration rewarded Vittorio by making him an assistant U.S. attorney for the district of Eastern Pennsylvania and, almost immediately, my cousin was thrust into the center of the famous trials of the Philadelphia mob in the 1990s. Around this time, he began keeping a journal, which, he told his wife, would form the basis of a book chronicling his life. For as long as I knew him, my cousin harbored a powerful need to be regarded as consequential. Many of his exploits, however, were done in private and required concealment. Vittorio's notes reveal that he hoped one day to expose his noteworthy accomplishments to the world. Then, he knew, everyone would recognize how illustrious he had been.

My clearest memory of Vittorio is as a young teenager. Even then, he was known as a tough guy. There were three or four boys who followed him around, eager to please. Although he had a reputation as a bully, I don't know that he actually got into fights himself, preferring instead to egg on his supporters (too few to call a *gang*) to physically intimidate others. I once heard Vito and his friends singing a racist song to humiliate one of their classmates. My personal impression is that he was cruel. Even his own father didn't like him.

I never expected him to achieve anything of note. He was not a good student and he didn't participate in school sports. I don't recall his ever doing anything to call attention to himself. He was neither a class clown nor, certainly, a class leader. To tell the truth, I was surprised when he graduated from high school. But he did graduate, and even went on to Temple University, where he also managed to graduate. You can imagine

1

my surprise when Vito entered Temple law school — and graduated! That was in 1977. It only added to my bewilderment when he obtained a position in the office of the state attorney general and, later, became an assistant U.S. attorney.

I've never understood how he managed to accomplish these feats, and I've come to realize that, in spite of having known Vito and his family for my whole life, I really knew nothing about what made my cousin tick. Obviously, my one-dimensional idea of him as a sadistic bully of average ability and limited social skills was not a complete picture of him — and possibly wasn't at all accurate. How this person ended up employed as an assistant U.S. attorney was beyond my comprehension.

After Vittorio's death, his wife made his writings available to me. I read them with eagerness, curious to learn more about who my cousin was and how he thought of himself. Sometimes he wrote of his current experiences. Often he wrote about past events, including those of his childhood. I became privy to his feelings, thoughts, and observations, as well as details about personal relationships, affairs, and illegal activities. His entries included accounts of significant events in his life and many remembered — or imagined? — conversations.

Needless to say, I cannot vouch for the veracity of his recollections or the credibility of his writings. We all have our own subjective bias, of course. What was clear was that he wanted to tell his story, and to celebrate what he believed was a life of extraordinary achievement — and a brilliant exploitation of governmental authority.

Vittorio's widow and two daughters have given me permission to write this book. Based largely on his journal entries, it is supplemented by interviews with his family and by my own experiences with him. I chose to write the book because it affords an insight into the mind of a man obsessed with the acquisition and abuse of power.

In the process of compiling my cousin's written material, I took the liberty of making a number of changes. For example, I eliminated or changed most proper names in order to preserve the privacy of certain individuals, to avoid defamation of character, and to preclude potential lawsuits (or acts of vengeance).

During the final year of his life, Vito suffered from depression and significant emotional distress, and his writing became increasingly disorganized. While attempting to preserve Vittorio's point of view, I have eliminated much of what constituted irrelevant meanderings, unnecessary profanity, and repetitive accusations blaming others for his misfortunes. In addition, I attempted to improve the grammar and syntax in order to make the book more readable and, where possible, to bring an organization and coherence to his writings.

Although I have made every attempt to retain his voice and perspective, I chose to present Vittorio's story in a novelistic form, instead of the memoir that my cousin anticipated writing. Here, now, is the story of Vittorio Putino, *The Man*.

— Vincent Putino
December 2015

i

It was Wednesday, Nov. 4, 1992, the day after George H. W. Bush lost his bid for re-election to Bill Clinton. I was at the condo I'd bought for my parents in Philadelphia. I was deep in thought as I sipped a vodka and tonic and gazed out the floor-to-ceiling window at the city below. Standing there always gave me a thrill. I felt powerful, as if I were standing astride the city, with all of it beneath me — and at the same time teetering at the edge of a precipice. Exciting. Intoxicating.

My parents were sitting behind me, whispering to each other. I say whispering — they were both so hard of hearing that their whispers were loud enough for me to hear. Maybe they wanted me to hear. How should I know?

It was late afternoon; the overcast sky was losing its light, and I could see their reflection in the darkening glass in front of me. Mama sat on the stiff, old-fashioned couch and Pop, as usual, in his plush wing-backed chair. They had brought some of their old furniture and sentimental mementos with them to the condo, so being here was like going back in time. Photographs of them when they were younger and posed graduation pictures of me and my daughters adorned their walls. Faded lace doilies protected the tops of antique end tables that looked even more old and fragile here in the stark, sterile, modern condo.

My mother whispered to my father. "Silvio, I don't know when I've ever seen him this nervous."

"Then you haven't paid attention."

"What do you mean? I've never seen him like this."

"Whenever things don't work out for him," my father tried to placate her, "he always freezes up and withdraws into himself."

"But that's not what happened. He won big. He should be ecstatic. Instead, he looks worried."

"Maria, he's worried that he's going to be screwed, that he'll be left standing at the alter, looking like a complete fool."

"They wouldn't do that to him!"

"Ah, what do you know? When it comes to him, you've always been blind. You think your son is so precious that nobody would dare disappoint him. They don't give a shit about him, Maria. Everyone is out for himself. Of course he's worried. His problem is that he doesn't know what to do about it."

My father was right.

"Ah, yourself," my mother shot back. "You think you're always right, and your opinion is the only one that matters. There's no reason for him to worry. Everything will work out just as he's planned. He's too intelligent for them not to want to reward him. You'll see. He's going to go far. To the top, just like he said he would."

I had spent the previous year working for the Democratic National Committee, and was actively involved in Clinton's presidential campaign in Pennsylvania. I was able to get time off from my job in the state attorney general's office in order to serve as a deputy chairman of the state campaign committee. I worked hard and helped deliver the state to Clinton with a margin of almost 10 percent. I helped Ed Rendell win his race for mayor of Philadelphia. I delivered exceedingly well on everything I'd been asked to do.

With the Clinton and Rendell victories, I expected to be appointed to a position in the Department of Justice in the new administration — as I'd been promised. I had already come quite far, but I was 40 years old and, if I didn't continue to advance, I might very well be condemned to a mid-level dead-end job for the rest of my life. That might be much better than any of my peers would achieve, but it wasn't the goal I was seeking. I wanted to be at the top.

Now it was a matter of waiting until I heard from someone on Clinton's transition team whether I would actually be appointed to a position in the Department of Justice. It was time for my reward. But what would it be and when would I know? I was hoping for an appointment to the U.S. Attorney General's office, but I didn't trust that it was a done deal. Promises are made to be broken.

6

Pop adjusted his glasses and returned his attention to the newspaper as Mama pushed herself up awkwardly from the sofa and walked stiffly to the kitchen. She spread a bit of Gorgonzola on a slice of Italian bread and brought it to me.

"Here, eat something."

Hobbling slowly back to the sofa, she grimaced slightly as she sat down adjacent to her husband, who sat pontifically in his big chair. As usual, he wore a shirt and tie, the collar stiffly starched; instead of his customary vest, he wore a light grey woolen cardigan.

"He's so worried," Mama whispered, picking up her book.

My father nodded. Putting his paper down, he turned to her. "He's reaching too high. He's going to get hurt when he falls."

"It's not too high. He's ambitious. It's good that he has a goal. At least he wants to make something of himself."

Pop looked at her, then shook his head. "You don't know what you're talking about," he said. "I'll tell you what his ambition should be. He should want to be a better husband and a better father to our granddaughters. That should be his ambition. Where the hell did he ever get it into his head that he had to be a big shot?"

"Why shouldn't he be? You think Clinton is better than him? Or more clever or ambitious?"

"Listen to yourself, Maria. You and Anthony Savona put these crazy thoughts in his head. You're insane. Be reasonable. The next thing, you'll believe he can fly."

"Your problem, Silvio, is that you don't have any faith in your son. He can do whatever he sets his mind to."

"I'll agree that there's one way he's a match for Clinton. Neither one of them can keep his dick in his pants."

Watching their reflections in the window, I saw my mother scowl and pick up her book.

"I hope he's at least giving Lydia her share," Pop muttered.

"Shut up with that stuff. If Vittorio's seeing other women, I'm sure he has good reason. Lydia's far from a perfect wife."

"No one is," my father said. "But not every man tries to fuck the world into submission."

Mama laughed. "Oh, you! With you everything is about sex."

Pop put his paper down. "At least it used to be."

"It still would be if you had your way."

It was touching, that they still enjoyed bantering about sex.

"You're right about that," Pop admitted. "But we're not talking about me. We're talking about Vittorio. I'm only saying that he's going to get himself in trouble one of these days. He has an arrogance about him, as if he thinks he can get away with anything and do whatever he wants without ever paying a price. Contrary to what you may believe, I am concerned about him. I don't want to see him destroy himself anymore than you do."

Their bickering annoyed me.

"I have to go," I said, looking at my watch. "Lydia is expecting me and I've got a thousand calls to make."

Mama pushed herself up and kissed me on the cheek. I picked up my overcoat from the back of a chair.

"Don't forget your hat and gloves," she said.

I forced a smile as I removed the black calfskin gloves from my coat pocket and showed them to her. My mother was 81, the same age as Pop, and I tried to overlook her constant, suffocating attempts to mother me.

At five-foot-seven, I tower over my parents. Even with her hair pulled up on her head and wearing low-heeled shoes, Mama is barely five-foot-two. As I observed my mother caressing me with her gaze, I recognized that, although we have the same blue eyes, on her face, with her fine features, they appear warm and gentle. On me, with my father's narrow straight nose and small mouth, they look cold and piercing. But I was glad I had inherited their slim, wiry body builds.

"And give my love to Lydia and the girls," Mama said.

My father was watching me with his characteristic lack of expression. I nodded toward him, then I turned back to my mother. "I'll call tomorrow," I reassured her.

Mama paused a moment, absently fingering the cross on the thin, gold chain my grandmother had given her.

"And relax, Vittorio. Everything will work out for you."

My mother always told me that. It was her favorite saying.

"Right," I said, and left the apartment.

8

I knew my mother better than she knew herself. I knew she was obsessed with my welfare. She had lost two children, my brothers Alberto and Giancarlo, before I was even born, and I was the center of her life, Christ reincarnated. I knew she continued thinking about me after I left their apartment. I can see her as clearly as if I were there, her book on her lap but her eyes unseeing.

She's watching her life from almost 50 years earlier. My older brother, Giancarlo, was nine years old in 1943, when my father was serving on a submarine in the North Atlantic. Mama and Gianni were living with my grandfather on Second Street, while she worked at the Philadelphia Navy Yard. Giansalvatore Putino — my father's father — was not in good health. He drank too much wine, smoked too many cigars, and complained too much about everything. Mama recounted how unhappy she had been living with the angry bastard, but she had no family of her own. At least Giansalvatore provided a roof over their heads.

But Gianni suffered from chest colds and asthma, and the cranky old widower was not the best person to take care of him when Mama was at work. Giansalvatore was impatient with the boy, always finding fault.

On one occasion, Mama came home from the Navy Yard to find Gianni in the grip of a severe asthma attack, wheezing and coughing, gasping for breath. Giansalvatore was asleep in his chair, anesthetized from wine, the room thick with stale cigar smoke. Dead tired from a long day at work, she grabbed her son and had her next-door neighbor drive her to the emergency room. Gianni was in the hospital for three days, and all the old bastard could do was complain that she had taken the boy without notifying him. He accused her of a lack of consideration and respect, arguing that she had caused him to worry when he awoke and found the boy missing. Gianni died from pneumonia two years later, shortly after my father returned from the war.

And here was Mama, almost 50 years later, living in an expensive condominium provided by her third son. Gone forever was the poverty of her childhood and bitter hardships of the war years, the austerity of living with my grandfather and raising Gianni by herself. Now, thanks to yours truly, she and Silvio were basking in luxury. How could she not be proud of me? How could Silvio even entertain a critical thought about me? She'd shake her head, unable to understand the tension that had always existed between father and son. Why did Silvio have such difficulty appreciating his surviving son?

In the elevator, I took out my cellphone and punched in Anthony Savona's number. There was no answer, so I left a voicemail. I was in the cab, on my way home, when Anthony returned my call.

"How are you?"

"I'm fine," I said.

"You doing anything later?"

"Not really."

"Then come over after dinner," he said. "Around eight would be good. I'll have some people here and we can talk about what's next."

"Sounds good. I'll see you then."

"Ciao," said Anthony.

When I arrived home, I paid the taxi driver and climbed the front steps to my house on Delancey Street.

"Vittorio, is that you?" Lydia shouted.

I hung up my coat in the hall closet and sat down in the living room. I was scrolling through my cellphone messages when Lydia came in from the kitchen.

"I thought it might be you," she said. "Why didn't you answer me?"

Glancing up at her dismissively, I brought the phone to my ear and began talking. Lydia stared at me for a few moments, then turned and left the room.

When I finished making my calls, I went to the kitchen, where she was preparing dinner. We could easily have afforded a cook and a housekeeper, but Lydia insisted on being an old-fashioned housewife. She enjoyed cooking, and thought grandiosely of herself as a gourmet.

"I wish you wouldn't ignore me like that," she said.

"How would you like me to ignore you?"

I thought I was being funny. Wry.

"You know what I mean."

"I'm busy, that's all."

10

"Yes. Busy with other people and too busy for your family."

"I'm here, aren't I?"

"Are you?" she asked.

"Don't be tedious."

"Oh. Excuse me."

"By the way, I'm going to Tony's after dinner," I said.

"Tonight?"

I looked at her. Lydia could be so obtuse.

"I should have figured." She opened the refrigerator and poured herself a glass of white wine. "I assume you forgot that my sister is coming to dinner tonight."

I took the bottle of chardonnay from her and poured myself a glass as well.

"You never told me that you'd invited Lisa for dinner tonight."

"Jesus, Vito. You're incorrigible."

"I'm incorrigible? I'm not the one who screwed up. How could you invite anyone for dinner *tonight*? Don't you realize we just had an election? Do you think I'm a nobody? That who gets elected has no meaning for me? That it's unimportant to me?"

Lydia turned and marched into the living room, where she sat on a loveseat and put her glass on the small table beside her.

I followed her.

"You complain that I ignore you, but I don't turn my back and walk away while you're talking to me."

Lydia raised her eyebrows and smirked.

I knew she recognized the critical way I was scrutinizing her — thinking that she was gaining too much weight, that her hair color was too blond, her lipstick too red. I also perceived that she was deriving pleasure from the fact that her smirk had annoyed me.

"Lydia, do you realize what happened yesterday?"

"Yes, I understand. Clinton won — by over 200 electoral votes. Bush got his ass kicked."

"You say it like you're unhappy about it."

"No. Of course I'm happy. I'm ecstatic."

"Why are you being sarcastic?"

"Oh, come on, Vittorio. Of course I'm happy Clinton won. And Rendell. I'm thrilled. I'm proud of you. I'm just not sure what it might mean for you. For us."

11

"It'll be a good opportunity for us, a move to DC."

"That's what I'm afraid of, Vito. The girls and I don't get to see you enough now. If you get a position in the attorney general's office, then what? Are we going to see you at all?"

"Stop complaining, for Christ's sake. We're talking about my career. The more successful I am, the better it is for all of us, especially for you and the girls. Don't be selfish."

"Oh, Vittorio, that's not what I mean. I'm not saying I don't want you to be successful. Of course, it'll be wonderful if you get what you want. We're so proud of you already. It's just that we love you and don't want to lose you. That's all I'm saying."

I was standing over her, with my head lowered, looking at her from under my eyebrows. It felt like I was standing there a long time, but it was probably only a few seconds. I was wondering if what she had just said was really true.

"Trust me, you'll be happy when it comes to pass," I told her.

Lydia returned my look. "You know, Vittorio, even when you're attempting to say something reassuring, you often come across as menacing."

I scowled at her. "I have some more calls to make. What time is Lisa coming?"

"Dinner is at seven, but Lisa and Daniel will be here around six or six-thirty."

"All right, but I have to leave right after dinner."

"Of course," she answered. "I understand."

I was already halfway out of the room, on my way to my office.

During dinner, I sat at one end of our long dining room table. I love this table. The rich, burled wood looks as expensive as it was, and it can seat 12 people without adding leaves. I felt like a king sitting in my upholstered chair.

Lydia's younger sister, Lisa, and her husband, Daniel, sat on one side, and our daughters, Marie and Catherine, seven and six, sat across from them. Lydia sat between me and the girls. They were mostly silent, as I had taught them to be in the company of adults. I contributed minimally to the conversation, which I'm sure Lisa and Dan thought was impolite.

12

The two adult sisters engaged in inane conversation about celebrities and gossip, avoiding any talk of the election and my accomplishment. As soon as we were finished with the main course — broiled scallops and risotto — I excused myself and left the table.

Lydia later told me about the conversation that ensued after I had left. "Vito had a meeting he had to attend," she explained. "It can't be helped." Lisa looked at Lydia, who briefly glanced toward the girls and then shook her head slightly.

"Vito has a lot of meetings," Dan commented.

"Yes," Lydia said. "That's his life now. It's just the way it is."

Lisa smiled at her nieces, and said to Lydia, "I know it must be hard on you and the girls. Vito is away in Harrisburg so often and then, even when he's home, he's either on the phone or off to meetings."

"Of course we miss him," Lydia said, "but that's the nature of his work. He wants very much to do well for us and make us proud of him. This is who he is. It's our job is to accept him as he is. Besides, it won't always be this way." She turned to our two daughters. "One day, we'll have Daddy all to ourselves, won't we?"

————————————————

At least that's what Lydia told me happened. But Lydia has always had her own agenda, and I think making me look bad has often been at the top. To hear her tell it, she loved me. She often said so. She'd tell me how she got hot for me during the day, while she was doing laundry, washing my socks and underwear. But talk is cheap and people are born liars. Not just women — everyone.

A few days later, she said to me, "We have this magnificent house, two beautiful girls, a luxurious lifestyle — and still you're not satisfied. Nothing is ever enough for you. It's always more, more, more. Washington, Georgetown. What will be enough? When will you stop? When will we be enough? When will I be enough? When will you pay more attention to me? Or have I lost you already?"

Doesn't that show how little she understands? Lydia has no fucking idea what I'm about: the importance of getting ahead, of achieving something, of being respected, of being a person of stature. And it's not as if she doesn't appreciate the perks that came with my advancement. Oh, she loves the perks — the closets full of clothes and shoes, the expensive

13

jewelry, the mansion on Delancey Street, the cleaning lady, the entertaining and luxury vacations and gambling trips. She loves the perks, all right. But Lydia thinks she's entitled to them. She never connects them with my needing to put work first.

I entered Anthony Savona's condominium, which occupied the entire 20th floor of a building in Center City. My former law professor, Anthony was the senior partner of a prestigious law firm and a member of numerous boards of directors. Three other men were in attendance for tonight's meeting. One of the men, Fred, I later determined was from the intelligence community, probably FBI. Jules was a typical corporate executive, a tall, good-looking WASP whose tan probably resulted from frequent golf and tennis. The third guest was a heavy-set man named Carmine, who I later learned was mob connected. Anthony introduced me to them by my first name.

"You know where the bar is, Vittorio. Help yourself."

After pouring myself a weak vodka and tonic, I joined the others in Anthony's expansive living room and sat down on one of the plush loveseats where I could easily observe the others. Apparently, they had already started discussing what the next four years might hold for the new administration in Philadelphia.

"There's one thing I'd like to clear up before we get too engrossed with politics," said Fred. "I'm thinking of Joey Brachitta's attempted assassination of Emelio Meninzani last year, which led to Johnny Scafuzzi being made the new boss in Philly. Ever since, there have been rumblings of a turf war between the rival factions of the Philadelphia mob — Scafuzzi and Brachitta. Does anyone know what we can expect during the next couple of years?"

I noticed Tony glance in Carmine's direction and watched as Carmine took his time formulating his answer. Carmine was a large, burly man with a fleshy face and thick, wavy, black hair. Like Anthony, he was in his mid-50s. He maintained a serious look, but every once in a while he flashed a smile that was surprisingly boyish and appealing.

"The situation is unpredictable," he said. "That's the bottom line. Joey Brachitta is a hothead. He's not called Joey Hotdog for nothing."

"But what's your best guess?" Fred asked.

"My best guess is that things could blow up. It could easily erupt into open warfare between them and things could get very messy. You know what I'm saying?"

"You realize," Fred countered, "that if a war breaks out between those two, the feds would have no choice but to become even more actively involved in everything going on here in Philly."

"Carmine," Jules added, "if Scafuzzi and Brachitta start a bloodbath, it's no good for anybody. It'd be very bad for business. Isn't there something we can do to stop this?"

Carmine shrugged. "I have no idea."

"You're Scafuzzi's *consigliore*," Fred pointed out.

Aha!

Carmine frowned and glared briefly at Tony, who lowered his head and shook it wearily. I suppressed my urge to grin. It was obvious that Fred wanted everyone to know he was aware of Carmine's role in the mob, but I was shocked by the news. What would a mob player be doing at this meeting? Did Tony know? I glanced over at him. Of course he knew. What the fuck was going on?

I decided to play it close to the vest and not let my surprise show.

"That may be true," Carmine agreed, "but as our host here will tell you, advisors aren't always listened to."

Anthony chimed in. "Hypothetically speaking, isn't there some way to head off a turf war? Would it be helpful if it were known — perhaps in New York or Atlantic City — that important people here in Philly are on one side or the other? Do you think that might make a difference?"

"As of now," Carmine said, "The Columbo family — publicly — is unwilling to take sides. But they've also let it be known that they don't want this situation to explode. They want it settled peacefully. Behind the scenes, of course, everybody knows they're backing Scafuzzi. After all, they installed him after Meninzani was shot last year." He took a sip of his drink, then continued. "But I don't really think Brachitta is going to hold back."

"So you're saying we can probably expect the shit to hit the fan during the next couple of years?" Fred leaned forward in his chair and waited for a reply.

"It's very possible, yeah."

I spoke up. "If a war does break out, as Carmine predicts, it could be an opportunity for the law-and-order people to bolster their standing and demonstrate how much society needs them."

Actually, I saw the whole scenario as an advantage for me. I wanted to move up in that world, and a mob war in Philly would be a great opportunity.

"You almost sound glad there might be a gang war," Jules spoke up. "You don't have any idea what terrible damage that could do. It would be extremely bad for business."

I was annoyed. I thought to myself: *I don't understand. Are these assholes so hard up for cash that they can't afford to pull back for a couple of years? So they take a hit. So what? Eventually, either Brachitta or Scafuzzi will win out and, in two or three years, things will be back to normal.*

"It's Jules, right?" I said.

He nodded.

"Jules, you're wrong," I told him with a straight face. "I wouldn't be at all happy to see a gang war. What I'm saying is that, if it's inevitable, then deal with it. If it happens, so your business will suffer for a while. Whatever you lose, it's peanuts. I'm just guessing, but I bet Anthony could lose three hundred, four, five hundred grand a year for the next two years and he wouldn't break a sweat — and you're probably even better off than he is. You and your friends can afford to have a bad year or two if that's what it comes down to. Look, all I'm saying is if that's what's going to happen, I'm sure you can deal with it."

Jules glared at me. "*Millions* ain't peanuts." He paused for emphasis and I saw the utter contempt for me in his eyes. "I still say it would be better if we could head it off."

"Jules," Anthony said, "we all agree on that. But Vito has a point. If Brachitta and Scafuzzi go after each other ..."

"We'll have bodies in the streets," Jules said.

Uncrossing my legs, I leaned forward and glared at the asshole. "Then the new Rendell and Clinton administrations will have an opportunity to look tough on crime."

I turned to Carmine. "Carmine, you could be in a position to be helpful to Fred. You wouldn't want the FBI to be stepping on the wrong toes." He nodded. "If it comes down to a war, New York will be very unhappy. Maybe I can get the Columbos' cooperation."

Anthony turned to me. "Where do you see yourself in all this?"

I was surprised by the question. Anthony had practically promised that if I helped put Pennsylvania in Clinton's column, I could be assured of a significant appointment in the Justice Department. So what was he asking me? Was he distancing himself from that promise? And another thing — I didn't know these people. One of them was a fucking mob boss. I had to be careful.

"The Democratic Party won big in Pennsylvania yesterday and I had something to do with that," I reminded him. "If that gets me a position at Justice, then dealing with organized crime would be a convenient — and helpful — place for me to be."

Carmine cocked his head and looked at me. "What are you saying, Vittorio? That you can't wait to come after me? Is that what you're saying?"

I leaned back in my chair. Jesus, these guys were touchy. I felt my temper rising, and resisted the urge to hit him. "Hey, what are you getting so hot about? What would make you think I'd get any pleasure from going after you? On the contrary, I'm saying that being in a position where I might have some influence over who the feds go after would appeal to me. Wouldn't it appeal to you? Just think if you could have control over who the feds target — and who they don't. Think about it. I could be the best friend you ever had."

Carmine scowled and looked at Anthony. Anthony's expression was noncommittal, as was mine.

Finally, Carmine said, "You saying that you gonna be The Man, Vittorio? That my friends will have to come to you?"

Carmine turned to Anthony for confirmation. "Is that what's going on here? Vittorio setting himself up to be The Man?"

"Come on, Carmine. I didn't hear Vittorio say anything approaching that. I asked him a question and he answered it."

"Yeah, well, I don't think I like the answer."

Carmine glared at me. I stared at my shoes. Glancing up from under my eyebrows, I gave him a cool look of bored disdain.

Later, when the evening was coming to an end, Anthony asked me to stay behind. I let him say good-bye to the others while I lingered in the living room. After pouring another drink for himself and for me, Anthony looked at me questioningly.

"You think you might be jumping the gun a little?"

"Is that what you think?" I asked.

Anthony sought a comfortable chair and lowered himself into it. "Nothing is definite yet, you know."

17

"I know that. You asked me what I wanted, so I reminded you — a position at Justice that gives me opportunities for advancement. Having responsibility for targeting organized crime, especially here in the Philadelphia area, would be in all of our interests. I've got to get out of Harrisburg and back into civilization. I've got to get somewhere, stand out from the crowd. You know that. So I'm confused why you asked me the question."

"I was just checking. That's all."

"Checking how it would go over with the others if you delivered on your promise?"

"Come on, Vito. You know better than that. There's no such thing as a promise. I'm doing what I can, but the decision is out of my hands. I'm not saying you won't get what we talked about. I hope it comes through for you. You know that. I'd love to see you advance in the way you deserve. We all would. And I agree it would be in all our interests to see you succeed. But we'll simply have to wait and see what Clinton's brain trust decides. Be patient."

"Let me change the subject. After tonight, I'm a little concerned about you."

"I'm not sure what you mean," Anthony said.

A brief flicker of anxiety flashed across his face, and I remember feeling pleased.

"You had a couple of people here tonight: Fred — who the hell is he? CIA? FBI? And Carmine? A mob guy? I wonder if you're protecting yourself adequately. I don't know how far I'd trust him. He's a fucking snake. I hate to see you exposed to people like that. I don't want to see you hurt. As far as I can tell, they're only trouble."

"Thank you, Vito. Yes, I know what you mean. Don't worry about it. My eyes are wide open."

"Good. So, who is Fred?"

"You're right, he's in the intelligence community. Just leave it at that."

"But ..."

"Vito, you don't need to know more than that."

"I'm sorry, Tony, but that's not fair. He knows who I am. He knows we met with Carmine. I need to know who has that kind of information about me, about us."

Anthony shook his head. "Vito, you're getting ahead of yourself. Right now, to them, you're nobody. As far as they're concerned, you're a friend of mine, somebody who worked on the campaign, somebody on the way

18

up. That's all. Right now, you're no threat to anybody. You're not on their radar, OK?"

"What do you mean I'm nobody?"

"Cool it, Vito. There's no need to get hot with me, all right? I only meant you don't yet have a position that warrants anyone feeling threatened by you. You know how I feel about you. Don't question that. I've never let you down, have I?"

"No. You haven't."

Not yet, anyway.

I paused and took a breath.

"Maybe you're right. Maybe I was jumping the gun. I guess I was already seeing myself as a U.S. attorney or something."

"Well, you have to be patient about that. Like I said before, there are no promises. I'll do everything I can, but ultimately it's not under my control. Shit, I don't even know what's in the cards for me."

"You don't have to worry," I told him.

Tony gave me one of those condescending smiles that implies: *You idiot, you have no fucking idea what you're talking about.*

"In a way, Vito, you were right before. I did want to see how you would react and how they would respond to you. Don't worry, you did fine. You're going to be moving up, and there will be more opportunities for you — and for us. You've already had a chance to see how your current office can be used to your own advantage, by doing favors for friends — who, in return, are able to do favors for you."

Tony was reminding me that he and I had crossed an ethical and legal line a long time ago. This is how you got ahead, accumulated wealth, and protected your turf — by doing favors for the well connected and cashing in on them.

"I understand," I said.

"I'm not sure you do, Vito. If you get into Justice, it's going to be a whole new world. You'll be dealing with people at a different level. You follow me? You'll be in a position to do very well for yourself. I needed to see how the chemistry was between you and them."

"You mean Carmine?"

"Yes."

"You mean organized crime, the Mafia?"

"Let's just say you'll have different clients. It can be very profitable for us."

19

I thought about what he'd said. I don't know if I should have been shocked or not. I wasn't. I was surprised, but not shocked.

"I know I'm new to this, Tony. I gather you're not. But am I justified in being concerned? What am I getting into? What are you exposing me to?" As I asked the question, I was aware that I suddenly felt clammy. My trousers stung against my calves and I felt simultaneously hot and chilled — like a young child entering a dark cellar.

"Vito, it's always justified to be vigilant, suspicious even. Yes, we both have to watch our step. Don't worry. You'll be protected."

I noticed he said that I'd be protected — he didn't say who'd be doing it. I'll admit I felt some trepidation, but I was also excited. I knew Tony was right: There'd be tremendous opportunities. Besides, it was too late to turn back, even if I wanted to. We'd already crossed the line a long time ago.

On my way home, I pictured Tony locking the door and returning to his living room, with its sublime view of the night lights of Philadelphia. He'd probably pour himself a nightcap and bring it onto his balcony, leaning against the railing to admire the panorama. There was a time when Anthony's ambition was to be mayor, to have the power to control one of the country's major cities, to command the respect of hundreds of thousands of people. But now his ambition was much greater.

At this point in his life, governing Philadelphia wouldn't be sufficient. Now Savona's sights were set on Washington. With the reputation he'd earned and the contacts he'd made — powerful people with significant amounts of money — there was no telling how high he could go. Major politicians consulted him. His opinion mattered. He was trusted. He was respected. People relied on him to get things done. DC was the center of the universe, and he was positioning himself as one of its most important players.

I knew I needed to be careful, but what I didn't know that night was that Carmine Belloni was an old and valued friend of Anthony Savona's. Their fathers had been neighbors in South Philly long before Tony and Carmine had been born. Carmine's father had only a peripheral relationship to the mob, but enough to give his son a foot in the door. The boys had become friends and had maintained that friendship, as had their fathers, even after the Savona family left the neighborhood.

20

Tony's father eventually became a successful attorney, and Carmine often secretly consulted him. Anthony followed in his father's footsteps. As Carmine rose in the ranks of the mob, so Anthony rose in his profession. When Anthony's father passed away, many of his clients — including Carmine — came to him. But on the night I met Carmine Belloni, I knew none of that history.

The downstairs lights had been left on for me, but everyone was in bed. Lydia never bothered to wait up for me. Pouring myself a glass of ice water in the kitchen, I sat down to think about my future, my allies — and my enemies.

That sudden urge to punch Carmine rose up in me again, and I recalled the first time I'd felt angry enough to strike someone. I was in seventh grade. We lived on Eighth Street and my father was working for Mayor Tate. He'd gotten his job from the previous mayor of Philadelphia, Richardson Dilworth, after his service in World War II and years of grunt work as a committeeman in the Democratic Party.

On my way home from school, a priest from St. Paul's on Christian Street ran up and grabbed me by the shirt. For no reason, he started slapping me across the face, calling me a little guinea and accusing me of throwing eggs at the parish house. At first, I was shocked and frightened. It wasn't until later that I became enraged, humiliated at having been falsely accused. I wanted to pummel the fucking priest with a baseball bat. Still shaking when I got home, I told my mother what the priest had done.

That evening, my father questioned me about the incident. Without a word, he went to the gym at St. Paul's, where Father Mike was coaching a basketball team. Pop marched straight up and punched him in the face, knocking the bastard right on his ass in front of everyone. With a menacing glare, he leaned over Father Mike and told him that if he ever laid a hand on his son again, he'd kill him. I was so proud of my father. I admired his courage and his physicality, and I was honored that he was willing to do that for me.

It was then that I started taking judo lessons and, later, joined the neighborhood boxing and judo teams. At the time I was still a skinny little kid, the subject of ridicule and name-calling — like Weasel and Rat Face. But once I learned how to fight, everything changed. Winning a few significant fights cemented my reputation and eventually built my confidence. And I learned that simply by remaining silent and stone-faced, I exuded the appearance of unpredictable danger. I discovered that I could manipulate others through fear — without actually having to prove that I was fearsome.

The confrontation with Father Michael also marked another turning point: I began to align myself with my father's atheism, and renounced my mother's pious Catholic beliefs.

The day after the meeting in Tony's condo, I left the campaign trail and returned to my regular job in the Pennsylvania Attorney General's office. It was a monotonous, mid-level shit job, but somehow it felt good to be back. Working on the state election campaign had been stressful, but it made me realize that being a politician — having to kiss ass to garner active support and money — was definitely not my strong suit. I had too much contempt for people to be good at brown-nosing. For six months I had faked it, manipulating, threatening, and persuading people with surprising aplomb — but I wouldn't want to do it for long.

An appointed position, obtained through behind-the-scenes politicking, was more to my liking. I had no doubts about my ability or willingness to do what was necessary to succeed. The image of myself as attorney general of the United States crept into my consciousness again. I relished the idea of heading the Department of Justice: FBI, ATF, DEA, Immigration, Marshal's Service, and so much more.

Carmine had been right. I did want to be The Man.

My mind whirled as I calculated the enormous riches I could gain with that kind of power. Already I had succeeded in acquiring a small fortune. People with insider knowledge of the stock market and real estate market appreciated the favors I did for them in the Pennsylvania attorney general's office. Imagine the favors I could do — and the gratitude that would be shown — if I were in a position of *real* power. Of course I realized that some would regard the use of power for personal gain as a form of corruption. Therefore, the exchange of favors had to be done with discretion. It takes brains to make power work to your own benefit.

The thought made me feel immensely satisfied, as if I'd already become the attorney general of the United States. I could taste the power — and it tasted rich.

22

Five weeks later, in December of 1992, Anthony called and arranged to meet me at the bar in the Bellevue Hotel. He ordered a Rob Roy on the rocks and I had my usual vodka and tonic.

"Vito, I've got news," he said seriously.

"From Clinton's people?"

"Yeah. I'm sorry. The DOJ is not in the cards."

"Nothing in Justice? Nothing at all?"

Tony looked morose. I could see that he truly regretted having to give me such discouraging news. I almost felt sorry for the prick. He'd promised me!

"I'm sorry, Vito. They said it was a matter of supply and demand. There were just too many others in front of you."

"Fuck!"

"I know. I did everything I could."

I felt like shit. My whole life's plan had depended on this. I stared into my glass and saw no future.

"Didn't they offer anything? Clinton won the state by 10 fucking points. We did that. They should come up with something besides *Thank you very much*."

Tony paused and sipped his cocktail.

"Well, they did mention something. They wanted me to ask you to think about it."

"Well?"

"I know you won't be interested, so I told them to forget about it."

"Tell me anyway," I mumbled. I wanted the whole shitty turd then. I couldn't bear to hear more bad news later on.

"Actually, it is in Justice, but it's not in DC."

"Stop breaking my balls, Tony. What is it?"

Savona started to grin and lowered his head.

"What, goddamnit?" I almost shouted.

"They want to know if you'd be interested in being an assistant U.S. attorney for Eastern Pennsylvania."

"Assistant U.S.? You're shitting me."

Tony kept a straight face. "No, I'm not shitting you. But I told them you wouldn't be interested and they should give it to someone else."

"You cocksucker. You did not."

He broke out laughing and embraced me.

"You're serious? It's done? You're sure?"

"I'm sure, Vito, they really want you aboard. They were apologetic that the spot in DC didn't come through. But this is right up your alley. Hanratty, the current federal prosecutor, is retiring within the next couple of years and things will open up. It's looking good for you, my boy. Before you know it, you'll be the U.S. attorney for Eastern Pennsylvania. And then, who knows? Onward and upward."

"Thanks, Tony. Christ, you had me going there for a minute."

"You realize, of course, that — technically speaking — this isn't an appointment. Your 'application' is being moved to the top of the pile."

"I understand."

"Now listen. Eastern Pennsylvania is one of the most important districts, so it has one of the largest offices."

"I know."

"There's something like 130 assistant U.S. attorneys there."

"Christ, I didn't realize there were that many."

"Not a problem," Tony said, smiling at me. "They're divided up into three divisions. The Criminal Division is the largest, and that's where you'll be going. The criminal chief is a guy named Mulligan. He's been there forever and isn't going anywhere. He loves his job and wants to hold on to it. The 90 or so assistants in the Criminal Division under Mulligan are divided into eight teams, one of which is organized crime."

Anthony paused and gave me a long look.

"And?"

"And guess which team you're on."

"Organized crime?"

Anthony smiled. "And the team leader of the Organized Crime Strike Force is an old war horse named Josie Panterra."

"A broad?" I was incredulous.

"Exactly. You see my point. When Hanratty retires as U.S. attorney, the Panterra broad isn't going anywhere. She's been there for ages and can't get higher than where she already is. When a new U.S. attorney is chosen from within, it's almost always from the organized crime unit. Not always, but usually. So if you play your cards right, you've got minimal competition.

"There's also this," Tony continued. "Most of the assistant U.S. attorneys there are young kids, fresh out of law school. Almost no one in your division has the kind of experience you have. Nobody will expect you to remain at that level. As soon as you start, Panterra will probably make you her chief assistant. It's just a stepping stone for you — assuming you can handle it."

I understood what he was telling me. It was up to me to make the most of this opportunity. Nothing was guaranteed, but I had a very good shot at moving up. I felt relieved. After sipping my drink, I turned to my friend and mentor.

"What about you, Tony? Did you get something for all your troubles?"

"Yeah, Vito. I came out all right. Better than all right. I'm going to be in the Department of Justice, too."

"No kidding? That's great. Doing what?"

Tony smiled. "I'm being appointed to the Office of Legal Counsel."

I nodded as I digested the news. The OLC is one of the government's most important divisions in the Justice Department. Eventually, this appointment would put Tony in line for some of the country's major positions, including the Supreme Court or even the attorney general's office. Once again I marveled at the power and influence of my former professor. And I realized that his good fortune was potentially my good fortune.

"Fantastic," I congratulated him. "I'm very happy for you. You must be very proud."

"Yes. It's been a long climb, but I guess it's true that good things come to those who wait."

"At least it's been true in your case — and mine. I want to thank you again, Tony, for all you've done for me. I know I couldn't have done it without you."

"Vito, from the first time I saw you in my class at Temple law school, I took a liking to you. I recognized that you had something special: a relentless drive to be on top. And you've never disappointed me. I'm glad I've been able to help you move along your career path. I'm very proud of you."

A warm glow of satisfaction spread through me. Being in Tony's good graces meant a lot to me. I hadn't been the brightest student — and let's face it, Temple is a good school, but it's not Harvard. But I worked hard. Tony was right. I was ambitious. I was hungry.

I wondered how my father would react to the news. Mama, I knew, would lavish me with praise. But my father? If I'd failed to get any recognition for my campaign work, Silvio would have ridiculed me for my poor judgment and naiveté. But eliciting any praise or approval from him was like pulling the proverbial hen's tooth. When I was younger, it was much easier to get a slap in the head than a smile from the old man. *Tough old bastard.* But maybe this time he'd recognize that I did something laudable. Assistant U.S. attorney. Not fucking bad!

I went straight home after my meeting with Tony. Lydia looked surprised to see me. "What are you doing home so early?"

I gave her a brief smile. "I thought we'd all go out to dinner. I had my secretary make a reservation for the four of us."

"Are you sure? I have everything all ready. But we can have it tomorrow night if you want. What's the occasion?"

"Tony heard from Clinton's transition team."

Her face lit up. "Then it's good news? Something came through for you?"

"Yes," I said. "Pour us a glass of wine and I'll tell you about it."

Lydia hurried to the kitchen and came back to the living room, where I had taken a seat in one of the plush chairs.

"So tell me the news," she said, putting down a tray carrying a bottle of prosecco and two glasses.

"I'm going to be an assistant U.S. attorney for Eastern Pennsylvania. It's not what I'd hoped for, but it's good. There's an excellent chance that, within a couple of years, I'll have the opportunity to move up and become *the* U.S. attorney. This is a huge break for me."

"Then we'll be staying here in Philadelphia? We won't have to move to DC?"

Jesus, I'm getting a leg up from the president of the United States and all she can think about is not having to move?

"That's right. I knew you'd be happy about that."

"Oh, Vito, that's wonderful news! You must be so relieved. I know how worried you were ..."

"That's not true! I was never worried. I always knew something good would come through, I just didn't know what it would be."

"That's what I meant. Of course you weren't worried. That's not you at all."

"So," I announced, "I had my secretary make reservations for us at Le

Bec Fin. I know you and the girls enjoy it there."

"Wonderful," she said. "As soon as the girls get home from school, I'll let them know. They'll be so pleased. What time is the reservation?"

"Seven o'clock."

"Excellent. We'll be ready."

I went into my office and called my mother to tell her the good news. Impulsively, I invited them to join us for dinner. Mama was thrilled. Of course she was proud of me. I deserved it — and more! She would tell Pop.

At some point, long after the actual event, my father told me what had gone through his mind when he heard the good news. He said he'd been watching television when Maria sat down on the sofa with a broad, self-satisfied grin on her face. He knew right away that it was something good about me. Not much else could put that kind of delighted smile on her face.

"That was Vittorio on the phone. He has wonderful news. President Clinton is appointing him to be an assistant U. S. attorney for Eastern Pennsylvania."

Silvio nodded and smiled, pleased that Anthony had delivered on his promise. He told me that he'd felt proud, and that he felt some ownership in this positive turn of events. After all, he was my father. His input — discipline, values, example — had influenced my success.

In a flash, he recalled my early childhood, teenage years, and young adulthood. He saw the skinny little boy the other kids teased and called names until — at his urging — I started taking judo and boxing lessons, and earned their respect. He saw the wise-ass kid in high school, surrounded by loyal followers — a real alpha dog. And then, finally, he saw me knuckling down and using my brains in college and law school. Pop said it brought back memories of his own youth, his life in the navy, and the injury that turned him back into a civilian.

My father was 18 when the crash of 1929 turned the world upside down. His father, Giansalvatore, lost his job and became a drunk. Silvio decided to join the navy and, when World War II broke out, he was assigned

27

to submarine duty in the North Atlantic Theater. In 1943, he suffered a crushed right ankle when a torpedo fell on him during a depth-charge attack from a German destroyer. But he didn't let the injury crush his spirit. Even when my older brother died, he kept pushing forward.

"Always do what has to be done," he said. "Never give up or give in." Obviously, my father took pride that I had learned the lesson from him.

Lydia briefly made a face when I told her that I'd invited my parents to join us for dinner, but she quickly covered it up with a smile. She knew my parents would be very pleased, and the girls would be happy to see their grandparents. When Marie and Catherine came home from school, they were delighted to hear that I was taking them out to one of their very favorite restaurants, and that Grandma and Grandpa would be there as well.

At the restaurant, I ordered champagne for the adults and Shirley Temples for Marie and Cathy. Lydia was the first to mention my appointment.

"So, Mom and Dad, what do you think of your brilliant son?"

Beaming at me, Mama said, "I can't say I'm surprised, except that you should have been made the attorney general, or the U.S. attorney, at least — not assistant."

I closed my eyes briefly in embarrassment, then looked at Pop questioningly.

"We're both very proud of you, Vito. Your mother is right that we're not surprised. You've always been ambitious and hard working. We expect that you'll continue to be recognized for your accomplishments, and that ultimately you will reach your goals. Nothing can stop you as long as you continue to push forward."

"Thank you. That means a lot."

Silvio patted me on the shoulder and I wondered how much of what he'd said was sincere, and how much was meant to satisfy my mother.

Lydia explained to the girls that the new president of the United States was giving their daddy a very important job, and that's why we were celebrating. The girls looked at me in awe. The president was giving their father an important job? Initially, they were full of questions, but soon their attention turned back to the little umbrellas in their cocktails. Kids.

"Does this mean you'll be spending more time at home?" Lydia asked. "I'm assuming you'll work out of an office here in Philadelphia, and you won't have to keep traveling to Harrisburg the way you do now, working for the governor."

I told her I didn't know. I might have to travel a lot to DC or New York, maybe Harrisburg, too. I didn't really have any idea. But I thought she was right — I expected that mostly I'd be working out of the Federal Building on Chestnut Street.

"What kind of work, exactly, will you be doing?" my father asked.

I'd been a lawyer for almost 20 years, and this was the first time he'd ever asked about what I actually did. Even when I first got hired by the governor's office a few years ago — thanks to Anthony — Pop never showed an interest, even though he'd worked at City Hall for years until he retired.

"That's hard to say exactly, Pop. There may be some important federal cases coming up that I hope to be part of. It's too early to say. I haven't even officially been given the job yet. Nothing will happen until after the inauguration in January, so there's plenty of time to find out the details."

"But you're sure? You've got the job?"

"Yeah, I'm sure. Tony said it's a done deal."

I sat back and let the others think I was absorbed in watching my daughters pretending to be adult women out on the town. While Lydia and Mama discussed the social and financial implications of my new position, I was thinking about major indictments of Philadelphia mobsters and the role I might play as an assistant federal prosecutor. In my mind, I was compiling a to-do list. I was sure I could use my position in the Pennsylvania Attorney General's office to gain access to classified information, and I planned on getting a good head start. I'd be well prepared when my time came.

2

Lydia and I often invited Tony to dinner at our home on Delancey Street. Sometimes he joined us for lunch or a leisurely weekend brunch. He was practically a member of the family. Catherine and Marie adored him because he often brought little presents and showered them with attention.

"I don't have any children of my own," he once told me, "and I think of your little princesses as my nieces or even my own daughters."

He was more effusive with them than their grandfather was, and they responded to that — sitting on his lap, tugging at him, and demanding that he play with them. So it was on this occasion, during the Christmas holiday season of 1992.

Lydia embraced Anthony and kissed his cheek.

"The girls love seeing you, Tony. If it were up to them, you'd be here all the time."

"But you spoil them," I said, taking Tony's coat and hanging it in the hall closet.

Watching Anthony interact with our girls, Lydia asked why he had no children of his own.

"Sadly, my wife wasn't able to have children," he confided. "We thought about adoption or in-vitro fertilization, but we never pursued it. When she died, I didn't want to marry again."

Lydia regarded our friend. Anthony Savona was an attractive man in his 50s. His thick, gray hair was combed straight back, giving him a sophisticated, European look.

"That's a shame. Such a waste. I know you'd make some woman happy."

"I hope I'm making many women happy," he smiled. "Everything is fine as it is."

Meanwhile, Cathy and Marie were clamoring for Anthony's attention.

I gave them a stern look and they toned down their behavior, but couldn't entirely stop themselves. Eventually, out of satisfaction or resignation, they left him alone and we adults sat in the living room with our cocktails.

Lydia took Anthony's arm. "We're very excited about Vittorio's new position. And Vito told me about your good news, too. We should celebrate. Here's to the two of you and your new careers. I know both of you will be spectacularly successful."

"Thank you, Lydia. You're too kind. But yes, we were fortunate. The gods were smiling upon us."

"May they continue to do so," I added.

"Look at you," Lydia exclaimed. "My atheist husband invoking the gods?"

"Merely a figure of speech."

Lydia raised her eyebrows. "Really?"

She turned suddenly to Tony. "And you? Are you a non-believer, too?"

"Life is too treacherous not to believe in something," Anthony replied.

"It's because life is so treacherous that it's foolish to believe in anything," I countered.

"But you're a Catholic," Tony said. "I know your mother is quite devout. And you went to Catholic schools — as do your children."

I sipped my vodka before answering. "It didn't take. I lost my capacity to believe when I was still a boy. All we've got is ourselves — and sometimes, not even that."

"Vito, cheer up. You sound so gloomy," said Lydia, trying to lighten the mood.

"I'm not gloomy. Reality is what it is. I can't be like you and my mother, believing in fairy tales. All we have is ourselves," I raised my glass to Tony, "and our friends."

"Friends with power," Lydia said.

"With even more powerful friends," Tony added.

After we each sipped our drinks, Tony continued. "Vito is right, Lydia. No one gets ahead in this world without making it happen. Each of us has worked extremely hard to get where we are. Still, part of our success comes from being able to cultivate powerful friends who can be helpful to us."

He turned to look directly at me. "If I can be blunt, my friend, that's the single area where I believe you come up a little short."

Although Tony cultivated a lightness to his voice, his arched eyebrows and pointed gaze set off an alarm in my brain. I suddenly felt very alert.

Was he implying something specific?

"What area is that?" I asked, feigning calm.

"In making friends. You could put more effort into it."

"I suppose we could all put more effort into everything," I said offhandedly.

"Anthony is right," Lydia jumped in. "Sometimes you're too outspoken. I've told you before that you get more flies with honey than with vinegar."

"Sometimes flies are even more attracted to bullshit," Anthony joked.

"So you think people are flies, just looking for a sugar fix?" I asked my wife.

"I'm not saying that," she softened. "Of course I don't believe people are flies. But yes, you should learn to be nicer. You never know who could end up doing you a favor."

"It's more likely that people will want me to do favors for them."

"Stepping on people's toes never helps matters," Tony put in.

I took another sip and put my drink on the table. "I hear what the two of you are saying. Sometimes, Tony, I watch you massaging people's egos and I truly admire your skill. Of course I know what you're talking about. But it's not in my nature. I don't have the patience for bullshit. I can't sweet-talk some asshole when I know he's an idiot. If the truth offends him, so be it. I think, in the long run, people will trust me because I'm honest. They know I'm not lying to them. Their trust, and their respect for whatever power I may hold, will get me what I want. I think friendship is highly overrated. People operate out of self-interest, not friendship."

"I still think you could make more of an effort to pay attention to people, to at least feign a little bit of interest. No one likes to feel unimportant," Lydia said, casting me a sideways glance as she spoke.

"Maybe you're right," I said, attempting to give Lydia a sarcastic smile. "I'll try to make more of an effort."

Lydia rolled her eyes. "Oh, you!" she said. "Let's go in to dinner, shall we? I think we need some food to soothe this savage beast."

3

I remember sitting at my desk in Harrisburg, mulling over the list of names in front of me. Johnny Scafuzzi and his archrival, Joey "Hot Dog" Brachitta. Joey's father, Charlie "Ciucci" Brachitta. Mel Meninzani Sr. and his son, Emelio Jr. Roland "Rollo" Navarro. Steven "Rocco" Marrone. Carmine Belloni — the man I'd met at Tony's condo, the *consigliore* to Johnny Scafuzzi.

Once again, I asked myself why in hell Tony had held a meeting with somebody this high up in the mob. Tony had hinted that he wanted to see if Carmine and I could work together. Would I be expected to work with (for?) Carmine? I realized at that moment that my future was going to be complicated: working to aid the federal prosecutor while probably having to protect some of the mob. I felt anxious and excited. I sensed that I might be in a very important position, a link to each side.

As I'd indicated to Carmine Belloni, the mob might have a say in who would be indicted and who would avoid federal prosecution. I didn't much care — as long as I had the opportunity to establish my reputation as a tough, skilled prosecutor, which would provide justification for future appointments to higher offices.

The confidential FBI records I'd accessed indicated that, two years earlier, in 1990, while Joey Brachitta was in federal prison, he'd concocted a plan with his cellmate, Rollo Navarro, and Carmine Belloni to take over the Philadelphia organization. And just recently, in Tony's living room, I heard Belloni predict that Joey Brachitta might soon challenge Scafuzzi for control of the Philly mob.

I sat back in my chair in deep thought. Although Belloni was acting as the *consigliore* for the current don, Johnny Scafuzzi, he had made a secret deal with Brachitta to help him take over the Philly operation. Don Scafuzzi had the backing of both the Giganti and Columbo families in New York, but Navarro and his cronies had strong ties to the Lamatta family, which had been a major presence in Atlantic City for the past 10 years or so.

I saw the pieces coming together. I suspected that Belloni would have a stake in instigating a war and having the feds play a role in weakening the Scafuzzi organization, allowing Brachitta, Navarro — and himself — to rise to power. The Columbo family would blame the feds, not Belloni, for Scafuzzi's downfall. So be it. Participating in the takedown of Scafuzzi and weakening the Giganti and Columbo families would add significant luster to my résumé.

You would think that when a man gets noticed by a newly elected president and rewarded with an important position, he would get some recognition from his own wife? Maybe this conversation didn't take place exactly as Lisa described it to me afterward, but I'm sure it's pretty damn close.

Lydia and her sister were having lunch in our kitchen on Delancey Street. Lydia was multi-tasking: drinking wine, picking at her tuna salad, and making cookies for the girls. Lisa, more focused on her lunch, chatted about her teaching job and her anxieties about Dan finishing his law studies.

"Dan is a sweetheart," she said, "but he lacks ambition. He's always coming up with excuses. Sometimes I wish he were more like Vito. Look at him: He's worked in City Hall and the governor's office and now he's going to be an assistant federal prosecutor. Dan can't even get his butt out of law school. I don't understand him. It can't be that hard."

"Be careful what you wish for, sis. Vito has more ambition and is more single-minded than anybody I know. I wish he could relax a little and spend more time at home, but the only thing he cares about is getting ahead."

"I know," Lisa conceded. "You're always saying how he's in and out like a boarder."

Lydia paused to sip her wine. "It's not so much his physical absence. It's much more than that. The only thing he truly cares about is his god-damned career."

"What are you saying — that he doesn't care about you? About the girls?"

Lydia's eyes welled up.

"Oh, come on. Of course Vito loves you and the girls." Lisa spread her arms and turned to survey the spacious kitchen, the high-end appliances, sleek fixtures, and granite countertops. "Look around you. Is this indifference?"

"Bullshit! You know that this house, his gifts, the clothes and jewelry, all of it, don't mean he loves me. Most of it's for him, for show, to impress everyone with how successful he is. It's a trophy house and I'm his trophy wife."

I admit it. She has a point.

"Uh-uh, Lydia. You're wrong," her sister protested. "You're more than that to him. He really loves you. I can see the way he looks at you when we're all together. He looks at you with such intensity in his eyes, like he could devour you right there on the spot."

"I wish."

"Lydia, it's true. I see it. Dan doesn't look at me like that — at least not in public."

Lydia softened a bit. "Yes, there are times when he is attentive — when he wants to have sex — and I do feel wanted. But it doesn't last long, so I don't trust it."

"Lydia, he's incredibly busy. My God, look at who you're married to, for Christ's sake. He's not a nine-to-five shoe salesman. He's got a lot on his mind."

"Maybe you're right."

"I mean, maybe he does take you a little for granted. Shit, Lydia, you've been married for nine years. What do you expect? Moonlight and roses 24-7? If he doesn't make you his priority, it's because he has other things on his mind. It doesn't mean he doesn't love you."

But even as Lisa offered this reassurance to her older sister, she recognized the puffiness in Lydia's cheeks, the bags under her eyes, the slight slur in her speech. They both drink too much wine, she knows. Maybe that's part of the problem, why Vittorio might be losing interest, seeking out other women, having affairs. Maybe it isn't just sex, the thrill of the conquest and a perk of power. Maybe Lydia's excessive drinking and weight gain turn him off.

Lisa was right — although, when she shared that conversation with me a few days later, I didn't say anything. Maybe I didn't want to badmouth Lydia behind her back, especially to her sister. Maybe I simply didn't want to give Lisa any leverage, something that might be used against me later on. After all, what were her motives for talking to me about Lydia behind her back? Lisa was a hot number and I wouldn't have minded a quickie with her — if I trusted her to keep her mouth shut about it.

After I'd graduated from Temple law school, Anthony helped get me a job with the Philadelphia mayor's office. Pop had just retired from his job at City Hall and was also able to put in a good word for me — not that he had to go out of his way to do it. I was doing all right, making a nice salary, not working too hard. When I met Lydia in 1978, she was a sophomore at Temple. Looking back, I think I was seduced by the fact that she really seemed to like me. Until then, not many women liked who I was, but Lydia was different. I'm six years older and I impressed the hell out of her. We met at one of the clubs on Delaware Avenue. She was into dancing and I wasn't too bad, plus I was older, working, and had money. The sex was fantastic.

Lydia had a great body then, and I foolishly thought she'd stay that way. Unfortunately, she let herself go — especially after she had Marie and Cathy. Now she drinks too much and it doesn't do any good to say anything to her. It only starts a fight. So the hell with it. If she wants to destroy herself — and turn me off in the process — then let her. Be my fucking guest. There are lots of other women out there who appreciate me and don't give me any agita at all.

Of course, that's not the way Lydia sees it. She swears that I never cared about her, that I was only in it for the sex. She claims that my work and my friends and my mother always came before her, and justifies her eating and drinking as a way of coping with my rejection — not the other way around. Typical. Lydia never takes responsibility for her behavior. It's always somebody else's fault — like it's my mother's fault that Lydia is a wino and a fat slob. Give me a break!

4

During a typically busy day in my cramped Harrisburg office, a phone call had just come in from the office of the federal prosecutor in Philadelphia. I was to start work there in two weeks, and U.S. attorney Philip Hanratty wanted to meet with me in his office at my earliest convenience.

It was January 1993 and I had been having some doubts that my new job would really come through. I had completely suppressed my anxiety, but suddenly I realized how tense I'd been for the past couple of months. I immediately made the appointment with Hanratty's secretary and then went to tell the attorney general that in two weeks I'd be leaving. For the rest of the day, there was a bounce to my step and the hint of a smile on my face. I let the world see that Vittorio Putino was in a rare good humor.

After telling my wife and mother the news, I called Anthony Savona to thank him once more for his help in obtaining the position. Anthony was pleased to hear that I'd be starting in a couple of weeks, but he sounded distracted and I cut the conversation short. Lydia had suggested a celebratory dinner for just the two of us and I agreed. I'd plan another dinner to share my success with my parents and daughters.

The following week, on a blustery February day, I went to the Federal Building at 615 Chestnut Street in Philadelphia. I understood that the interview was a formality and that the job was secure. Still, I admit I was a little nervous. After a short wait, I was ushered into the spacious office of Philip Hanratty, the U.S. attorney for Eastern Pennsylvania. I was surprised to find a fit and vigorous man of my own age behind an expansive desk covered with folders and papers. Hanratty was all business. After a pleasant get-to-know-you 15 minutes, we were joined by first assistant U.S. attorney

Matthew Garrett, a younger, dark-haired man. At six-feet-four, Garrett towered over me. In my eyes, he was a typical good-looking, outgoing Irishman, and I took an instant dislike to him. The younger man invited me in to his office so we could get to get to know each other. He explained the workings of the office, gave me some orienting information (procedure manuals, job descriptions, makeup of the various teams, etc.), and then escorted me down the hall to my team leader.

I'd expected Josie Panterra to be an older Italian woman who'd "been there for ages," but I was introduced to an attractive Asian woman not a day over 40. My look of puzzlement must have been obvious; she smiled and said, "My husband is Italian; everybody gets thrown by that. They assume I must be the secretary."

That's exactly what I had assumed.

Panterra immediately impressed me. Young and attractive, her body language and manner of speaking exuded decisive assertiveness. My plans to circumvent the team leader and carve my own pathway to the top office were obviously ill conceived. A no-nonsense leader, she made it clear that — once I got up to speed — she would soon be giving me assignments and expected me to hold up my end.

I felt totally disoriented. Nothing was as I'd expected. Everyone was young, bright, energetic. I had imagined an easy journey through placid waters, where everyone was lazy or incompetent and I would quickly be recognized as the savior who would lead them to glory.

Panterra had her secretary show "Mr. Putino" to his desk in an immense, common area that housed the Organized Crime Strike Force and their secretarial and investigative staff. It was a slap in the face. My step up felt like a step down.

The man at the desk facing mine stood up to welcome me to the team. He introduced himself as Arnie White. Arnie was about my age, African American, with a pudgy build and winning smile. I shook his hand and he took me around the office to meet the rest of the OCSF team. Tom Mulligan, chief of the Criminal Division, was out of the office, but Arnie told me what I needed to know about him. By the end of the mini-tour, my head was spinning and I was glad I had another week to adjust to my new reality before starting my new job.

When I arrived home, Lydia was in the kitchen as usual. I suggested that we have a drink in the living room. I knew she'd want to hear how the meeting with Hanratty went, and I was so angry and disappointed that I needed to spout off to someone. Still, I wasn't in the habit of opening up to Lydia. I made myself a stiff vodka and tonic and poured Lydia a glass of chardonnay. Sinking into the chair, I resisted swallowing the drink in one gulp. I was uncomfortable at the prospect of letting Lydia know how demoralized I was. I didn't want to expose myself or appear vulnerable, which would diminish me in her eyes.

"Well," Lydia said, settling herself on the couch and toasting me with her wine glass, "tell me all about it. How did it go?"

"Fine. The people seem fairly well qualified."

"And your bosses? Who will you be working for? And what about your office? What's it like?"

I was too ashamed to tell her that I didn't have an office.

"My bosses? Sharp. They seem sharp, very professional. My immediate boss, Panterra, is Asian. At first I thought she was the secretary — I was expecting an older Italian woman. I'd pictured someone like my mother. It's a good thing I didn't say anything and make a fool of myself."

"I'm sure they're glad to have you."

"Hopefully, that's how they'll come to feel. Right now, I'm just a new face squeezing myself in. Anyway, it's an easy commute. I can walk it whenever I want to."

After sharing some details about Hanratty, Mulligan, and Garrett, I told her about Arnie White's assertion that this would be a very busy couple of years for our team.

"I wouldn't be surprised if I end up working a lot of overtime," I told her.

Of course, I knew there would be no office in my near future — not until I moved up and took someone else's spot in the hierarchy. And I could see that the time frame would be longer than I'd anticipated. Jumping over my team leader, Panterra, wouldn't be easy. She was sharp and well organized. Arnie confirmed my impression that she ran a tight ship and was well respected by the Organized Crime Strike Force.

Then there was Matt Garrett, the tall first assistant U.S. attorney, who served as Hanratty's chief of staff and was also reputable. And finally, there was the chief of our Criminal Division, Tommy Mulligan, who had been there a long time and, as far as I could tell, had no higher aspirations.

41

Bottom line: I'd probably remain an assistant USA for a long time. But I put on a brave face and told Lydia I was optimistic that, within a couple of years, I'd be able to move up. I'm sure she believed me.

Soon after I started work, Hanratty called the entire OCSF into his office and informed us that we were to start preparing for major indictments of Philadelphia organized crime figures. Panterra divided us into four teams. She would be heading the group focusing on Johnny Scafuzzi and his top leaders; Arnie White and I would work with her. When she called us in to the conference room for our first meeting, she handed out some materials, including the list of people we'd be targeting. I was not surprised to see Carmine Belloni's name listed right after Scafuzzi's.

In addition to Arnie and me, we would be working with two investigators — Marvin Uretsky and Victoria Belladonna. Three legal assistants — Selma Green, Carol Reynolds, and Jorge Villanueva — would do research and help put our case together. We would be coordinating with teams targeting Brachitta and his crew, or those lower down on the food chain — capos and soldiers. Hanratty wanted us to be ready to move forward by the end of the year.

It was still too early to tell exactly what role I might play when it came to the trials. I assumed Panterra would take first chair — or maybe even Hanratty himself. I couldn't worry about that. My first priority was to demonstrate that I knew what I was doing, that I was competent and ready. As time went by and we began to develop a working routine, it became obvious that Arnie's laid-back nature allowed me to shine. Although he had been in the office for five or six years, I became Panterra's de facto second in command. When Panterrra asked for a progress report, Arnie hung back and I grabbed the opportunity. When tasks needed to be delegated to one of our assistants or investigators, I was more likely the one to do it. This didn't escape Panterra's notice — or anyone else's. Before long, team members came to me with questions or ideas, rather than to Arnie — and Panterra began to call me in to her office to pass on orders from Hanratty. All in all, I felt pretty good.

About once a week, I was sent to DC to confer with FBI agents or other members of the Department of Justice. A legal assistant would accompany me and, more often than not, it was Selma or Carol. That's how Carol and I started seeing each other.

Carol, a voluptuous, big-boned girl, was in her late 20s and newly married. Bright, competent, and very conscientious about her job, she was a delight to work with. She also had a kooky sense of humor and the most melodious voice I'd ever heard. There was so much to appreciate about Carol; I couldn't point to any particular trait, but over time I began to idealize every detail about her: the crooked incisor tooth, the big, curvy hips and wide thighs, the round, brown eyes — everything.

"No, Vito, I'm not going to your room. I'm married and I love my husband. You're just a horny bastard. Go jerk off, or wait until you get home to your wife." She'd say these things with such affection, such good-humored acceptance of my lust, that I was certain she'd relent if I persisted.

Although I behaved myself at work, I think it was clear that Carol and I had an affinity for each other. We became a team within a team, and it wasn't long before Selma or Jorge would switch off with Carol so our trips to DC became a regular occurrence. But even then, it was weeks before she let her guard down and accompanied me to my room after dinner. By then I'd built up a huge reservoir of fantasies of how explosively passionate we would be together.

She accepted my offer while we were still at the restaurant, and from that moment I had an erection that wouldn't quit. Swooning like a 16-year-old, I was glad to be wearing a suit jacket that covered my embarrassment. In the elevator, self-conscious and bursting with excitement, I admitted I'd be lucky if I didn't come in my pants before we got to the room. She laughed her musical laugh and rolled her big, brown eyes.

"Please don't get it caught in the elevator door," she joked. "I've got some fantasies of my own."

In spite of our eagerness, that first time our lovemaking was surprisingly leisurely, and we spent most of the night exploring, enjoying and pleasing each other. It was the first time in my life that sex was not just about fucking and coming. How did I get to be 41 years old, having fucked dozens of women, without discovering that making love could be such a soul-shattering experience? Lying on top of Carol after coming, I could have died happy.

We spent many wonderful moments together. At work, I appreciated her efficiency and creativity — and her discretion. But during our DC trips, after-work dinners were joyful and relaxing interludes. Carol was fun. Her laughter was infectious. I enjoyed every moment with her and, even now, when I think of her, I smile. In spite of exquisite tenderness and an over-powering desire to please and pleasure each other, our lovemaking could also be hungry and physical, fierce and sweaty and urgent. We stuffed our mouths with each other as if we had only seconds to live. Our urge to consume each other, to fuse, was as insatiable as our desire to arouse joy.

But in addition to our passion, we shared a familiar warmth and comfort. I felt at home in her embrace. I still have the letter she wrote to me around that time. I'm not sure why I've kept it.

> *Dearest V,*
>
> *I've been thinking about our last weekend and how you responded when I told you that I love you. You pulled back and frowned. And then you said, "Be careful, Kiddo." I was too caught up in our love-making to think about it at the time, but ever since then I've been wondering about it.*
>
> *I can't believe you didn't know that I love you. It couldn't really have come as a surprise when I said it out loud. I think I'd made it quite clear when you first started to pursue me that I wouldn't have sex with you just for the fun of it, or for the thrill. I was perfectly content with my sex life with Alan. I'm sure I told you that I don't do things in half measures, that if I went to bed with you, it would be for love, it would reflect a commitment on my part. I know I made that clear.*
>
> *Then I wondered if you had trouble believing that I love you. Do you? How sad. If you wonder why I love you, "let me count the ways": I admire your strength. You have a natural way of dominating whatever situation you're in. You're a natural leader, full of confidence and authority (and everyone in the office recognizes that). And despite your height (am I taller than you? With my high heels on, I am), you convey a dominating physical presence as well.*
>
> *Then there's that poker face of yours, your unwillingness to let anyone know what you're feeling or thinking. I admit I'm not so enthralled with that aspect of you; it makes you seem cold and uncaring.*

But I have also seen the vulnerable side, when you're lying beside me, snuggled comfortably in my arms. I've experienced your tenderness as well as your passion. I know — you don't need to tell me — that you love me.

Still, that air of self-restraint gives you an aura of mystery that I do find sexy. There's an element of inscrutable danger that others find intimidating, but acts like a magnetic force that pulls me in.

Did I mention your sexual passion? God, you are a bull! I can't believe your sexual stamina or the depth of your need. It's deliriously and wondrously glorious. It's the icing on the cake — but it's not what pulled me to you. I was drawn in by all the things I mentioned above — but mostly, it was how loved and wanted and cherished you make me feel.

I know Alan loves me and I do love him (yes, I do). But he has never made me feel so treasured, so necessary. Oh, Vito, I do love you. And right now, I'm so wet for you. I can't wait until we're together again.

I'm going to give this to you at work, I'm afraid that, if I mail it, someone else might open it up. Once you've read this, you can destroy it. I know how concerned you are that someone might discover us.

K (for Kiddo)

Every couple of weeks or so, Tony called to see how things were going in my life. I told him about Carol and he was happy I'd found such a compatible playmate — not only a fun companion, but someone who understood and appreciated the work I was doing. I knew it didn't bother him that I was cheating on Lydia, even though he had great affection for her.

After all, this wasn't the first time.

I was flattered that Anthony was still interested in my career. He expressed great satisfaction that I was on Panterra's team investigating Scafuzzi and Belloni. I wondered if he'd had anything to do with arranging that. I really had no idea as to the extent of his power. He did say he wanted to be kept up to date on the development of the case against them. About three months into preparing the indictments, Marvin Uretsky, our top investigator, got transferred to St. Louis and it disrupted the efficient way our team had been functioning. After Uretsky left, we discovered that some of our key files had been misplaced; we assumed he had screwed up and been transferred. Due to budgetary constraints, Uretsky's place on the team was never filled and the files — mostly focused on Belloni — were never found.

Then there was this: On one of our jaunts to DC, Carol and I were having dinner at a romantic little place in Georgetown, drinking our wine and waiting for our dinners.

"I guess I'm going to have to stop doing this," she said.

My stomach dropped to the floor and I felt a yawning sense of dread.

"Stop what? Seeing me?"

"No, silly. Drinking wine."

"Why?"

"Because I'm pregnant."

"You're what? What are you telling me?"

"That I'm going to have a baby."

I looked at her incredulously.

"And — it's ours," she told me.

"You're sure? It's ours?" I was stunned. How could this be?

"I'm sure."

"Carol, how could you have gotten pregnant? You're on birth control, right?"

"Of course I am."

"Then how?"

"Vito, I don't know. But no contraceptive is 100 percent. It just happened."

"Nothing just happens. You're sure you've been taking the pills like you're supposed to?"

"Of course I'm sure. Vito, please don't question me like I'm a stupid schoolgirl. Christ, I've been taking them for 10 years. Don't question my ability ..."

"It's a natural question. I'm surprised, that's all."

Of course I wondered if she had stopped taking the pills in order to deliberately get pregnant. Women do these things.

"So what do you want to do?" I finally asked her.

46

"You mean am I going to abort it?"

"Yeah. I guess that's what I mean."

"No. I want to keep it. I want to have our baby," she said excitedly. "Of course I won't tell my husband — or anyone else for that matter. Alan will assume it's his. It won't be a problem."

I slumped back in my chair. The idea of Carol carrying my child was a pleasant one, but I saw complications. Everyone in the office knew we were close. I'm sure some people were already gossiping about us, even though no one had anything to go on. Once her pregnancy became apparent, they might put two and two together. It could become problematic.

"Maybe hubby won't suspect, but the office could be a different situation."

"What are you saying?"

"Only that people are probably talking about us already. Once they know you're pregnant ..."

"Well, I am married. Married people do have children together."

"I know. I'm simply saying that there will be talk, conjecture."

"So what if there is?"

"Somebody could bring a sexual harassment suit."

"Against me?"

"Don't be ridiculous — against me. Technically, I'm your superior. If I'm having a relationship with a subordinate, that constitutes sexual harassment. But now that you mention it, we could both be fired."

"Wouldn't I have to make a complaint?"

"No. Anyone could bring the complaint against us — Selma, Vicki, Jorge, anyone."

Carol sat back and took a long sip of her wine. "I'm not having an abortion, Vito. I'm glad I'm pregnant. I want to have your child — *our* child. I'm not getting rid of it."

"I'm not asking you to. I'm just thinking out loud. I like the idea of you being pregnant with my baby. But it could present us with some problems."

"Well, I'm only a few weeks pregnant. We still have some time before I begin to show. We'll figure something out. Meanwhile, I'm content thinking about being a mommy."

When I told Tony, I asked him if it was possible for him to arrange for Carol's husband to get downsized and, soon after, to receive a good job offer in the DC area. Tony said he'd be happy to see what he could do. Within a few weeks, Carol asked for a transfer to Washington to be with her husband, where his company had moved him. We never saw each other again.

Carol sent a birth announcement to our office letting everyone know she'd had a baby boy. She named him Walter — which, I guess, was as close to Vittorio as she dared to name him. I know Carol planned to go back to school and get her law degree. Just what Washington needs — another lawyer. But I know she'll be good at it.

5

The year after Clinton was inaugurated, Johnny Scafuzzi and his main rival, Joey Brachitta, went after each other like two pit bulls. It wasn't only about money and power — they wanted to disembowel each other. Scafuzzi ordered at least a dozen hits on Joey and it infuriated Scafuzzi that Brachitta survived every single attack. In August of 1993, Scafuzzi did manage to kill Joey's second in command. That same month, Brachitta retaliated by having Scafuzzi's son shot. Although severely wounded in the face, the son survived, but he never fully recovered emotionally.

In 1994, Hanratty and our Organized Crime Strike Force indicted Scafuzzi and 23 others for racketeering, extortion, loan sharking, and murder. As a result, the Columbo family withdrew its support from Scafuzzi, and Rollo Navarro was installed as the new don. The trials lasted for the second half of 1994 and into 1995. Hanratty was the lead federal prosecutor against Scafuzzi and some of the other big names. Panterra was his assistant, and Arnie and I backed her up. Although I never got to present in court, Hanratty and Panterra told me how valuable I had been in the preparation and organization of the evidence. Arnie and I were assigned to try a number of the underlings, and I presented evidence then — my 15 minutes of fame.

The team was successful in getting convictions and stiff sentences on most of our cases, but we lacked sufficient evidence to convict Belloni, Brachitta, or Navarro. Those fucking missing files! Anthony never told me directly, of course, but I assumed that every bit of information I shared with him regarding our case against Belloni was passed on to the defense team. And I have no doubt that Scafuzzi's defense counsel left him twisting in the wind. The defense did little things, missing an opportunity to object here or there, a certain flatness in a presentation. It would be hard to prove, but anyone looking for it, as I was, could spot it.

In 1995, when the trial was over and Scafuzzi and the others had been sentenced, Hanratty resigned. He had a job waiting in a major firm, where he'd make out like a bandit. Clinton appointed Garrett to the position of U.S. attorney in his place, and Babat "Lucky" Chaudhary, from the Terrorism and National Security section, took over as first assistant U.S. attorney. I didn't receive a promotion then, but I knew I'd proven myself. It would only be a matter of time.

Although it took another five years before Josie Panterra left, I was confident that I would be in line to take over her position as deputy chief of the Criminal Division and leader of the Organized Crime Strike Force. If I could choose, I decided I'd make Arnie my right-hand man. We worked well together and he accepted my authority.

During those five years that Panterra was still the team leader, we set upon harassing Joey Brachitta, Rollo Navarro, and the rest of his crew for petty shit: violation of parole, associating with known gangsters, failing to report to a parole officer on time, etc. The sentences were usually short, but they interfered with their ability to conduct business. More than one of them decided it was too much trouble to remain a dedicated criminal, and went straight just to get us out of their lives.

Joey was granted permission to move to Florida to serve out his parole. We had done such a thorough job ridding Philadelphia of mobsters in 1994-1995 that the leadership of organized crime actually moved to southern New Jersey. Technically, they were under the jurisdiction of a different federal district.

Our office's involvement with Carmine Bellino effectively ended after the trials. As far as the public knew, Carmine was an honest Philadelphia businessman. He joined a local, family-run corporation headed by Paul Romano, whose family was on good terms with the larger Mafia families in New York and New Jersey, but remained unconnected to them. For the most part, the Romanos loaned money to businesses that were in financial distress and ended up running them, laundering money, skimming profits, and paying themselves big salaries. In other words, they weren't that different from a lot of so-called legitimate takeover companies. At any rate, Carmine was apparently untouchable — making money and living the good life. We never received any orders to move against him.

I kept Tony abreast of anything going on in our office that might have impacted Carmine — directly or indirectly — because of his connection to the Romano family. Any time our office would develop an interest in the Romanos, it seemed as if we were diverted to something else that was of a higher priority. I still have no idea how Tony managed it or who he worked through, but he never failed to make it happen.

After the trials were over, things settled into a quiet routine in the office and I found myself feeling irritable. Maybe I was missing Carol; maybe it was the lack of a big case and the opportunity to shine again in court. Maybe I'd become an adrenaline junkie. But for whatever reason, Panterra called me in to her office and chewed me out for being too hard on the rest of the staff. Staff members had complained that I was too officious, insulting and ridiculing people in front of others. She told me to clean up my act or she'd send me for counseling to learn how to express my anger appropriately. I practically told her to go fuck herself but managed to keep my mouth shut. I was raging with anger at her. Who did she think she was, criticizing me, scolding me as if I were a child? I had been doing my best to make our strike force work even more efficiently. If she wasn't going to take responsibility for improving her staff's work habits, then it fell upon me. Who else was going to do it? The easygoing Arnie White? Give me a break!

Tony's response to my reprimand surprised me: He told me to learn from what Panterra had said.

"I'm telling you, Vito, you can't keep doing this to people. Jesus, don't you realize how you piss people off? It's going to come back on you. You're only hurting yourself."

"She's a stupid chink bitch, Tony. No wonder she's never advanced beyond team leader in all these years."

"She's a stupid bitch? She's the fucking deputy chief. Who the hell are you? You've been on her team now for over five years. Where the hell are you going? You've got a fucking attitude, Vito, and it's hurting you."

"I'm not kissing her — or anybody else's — ass," I spat back. "If that holds me back, then so be it. I don't need her fucking approval."

"You do if you ever want to move up. You need her approval if you want to be a lead prosecutor, if you want to work on the major cases," he reminded me. "But hey, if you're content to push pencils and paper clips around and just collect your pension, then fine. You don't need me. And listen to me, Vito — if this is where you're content to hang out until you retire, then I don't need you either."

51

I looked at Tony. He was furious, but his deadly calm demeanor confirmed that he was willing to terminate our relationship if that's what it came down to. I realized suddenly that my position in the U.S. attorney's office was just as valuable to him as it was to me. As sharp and clever as I'd thought I was, I hadn't understood until that moment how much I'd been used. Of course I'd known it wasn't only a as favor to me that I'd been placed there. I knew I could be useful to him — and others. But what I hadn't appreciated was that it might not have had *anything* to do with me. It was *all* about him having a source of information in the federal prosecutor's office.

Granted, I benefited from it, too. I made out very well during these five years. Most of the perks came by way of Tony, usually as investment tips, which I thought of as gifts to a favored protégé. Money rarely changed hands. Of course, I had been making my own deals on the side and doing what I could to nudge the cases in one direction or another in return for considerable compensation. Now I saw my relationship with my mentor more clearly for what it was: I was on his payroll. Period.

"You're right, as usual, Tony," I said. "I don't know why I let her get under my skin. I'll apologize to her tomorrow. I'll turn over a new leaf. No more Mr. Nasty. Don't worry. I'll smooth it over."

"Vito, I hope you're not saying that just to shut me up."

"No. I'm serious. I know you're right. You and Lydia have been preaching to me for years about how I should pay more attention to people's feelings, make more of an effort to make them feel important. Sometimes that's hard for me. I'll just have to try harder with Panterra, that's all."

I vowed then and there to either get Panterra fired or persuade her to quit.

Panterra finally resigned in 1999. I like to think that my efforts at sabotage had something to do with it. Garrett delayed naming Panterra's successor for a few weeks and Lucky Chaudhary filled in as interim leader. Then they made the announcement: Arnie White was named as the new deputy chief of the Criminal Division and head of the Organized Crime Strike Force.

I was shocked. Fucking devastated. I asked Chaudhary and Mulligan about it, but they only mumbled something about seniority. That sounded reasonable, but it had to have been clear that I was far better suited for the position.

6

My mother died in the spring of 2000. She was 89, and had been diagnosed with cancer about two months earlier. I'm glad it was quick — for her sake, and for mine — but it didn't give me much time to prepare. There were things I wanted to say, although she knew how I felt about her.

We had the funeral at her church, and she was buried in the cemetery where she and Pop had bought burial plots some years before. After the service, Pop had a small, catered lunch at his condo. There weren't many people: Lydia's sister, Lisa, and husband, Dan, came, and Anthony Savona flew in from DC. A couple of my superiors — Garrett, Mulligan, Chaudhary, and Arnie White — came from the U.S. attorney's office, and that was about it, aside from Lydia, Marie, and Cathy.

After everyone had gone, Pop and I sat quietly in the empty condo. We made a fair attempt to finish off the booze and some of the food. Until then, I'd never spent any time alone with him. I don't think he'd ever been as intimate — certainly not with me — as he was that evening. He asked if I knew how he and Maria had met. It struck me that he always referred to her by name, never as Mama.

"No," I said. "I know it was after World War I, but I don't think Mama ever told me the details."

Pop was sitting in his chair, the top buttons of his shirt undone, a glass of whiskey in his hand.

"My father was a famous chef, you know."

"Was he?"

"Oh, yes. He once cooked for the president, Woodrow Wilson."

"No shit."

"I'm serious. Giansalvatore was the head chef at a big restaurant in New York, The Rose Room at the Hotel Algonquin. Famous people went there just for his cooking. The restaurant was very popular and your grandfather was well known. Then the fucking Great Depression came and we were out of a job. I say *we* because, when I was 16, I started working in the kitchen of the Rose Room with him. Christ, Vito, you think I was tough on you? I was nothing compared to my old man. A tyrant. He was very demanding — of everybody, not just me. He'd whack you with whatever he had in his hand. God forbid it was a knife or a cleaver. Then you ran like hell."

He paused to take a sip from his drink. "Anyway, Maria started working at the restaurant when she was just a kid, a teenager like me. Well, you know we're the same age. We were both born in 1911. We started going out together, after work."

A sad smile crossed his face.

"Those were wild times, Vito, like the '60s and '70s when you were growing up, only more fun and less angry. Even though it was prohibition, everybody had enough money to have fun. Life was exciting. Maybe it's only because we were young, but I don't think so. The 1920s were a special time. Maria and I went out after work, in the early hours of the morning, to clubs and speakeasies. We danced. There was great jazz then, during the '20s; music was everywhere. We both loved those crazy dances — the Black Bottom, the Shimmy, the Charleston, and the Lindy Hop."

My father related this in a raspy, dreamy voice, colored by his childish excitement. I'd never seen him so open and unguarded. Never. I felt as though I was back in the 1920s, watching the two teenagers together. I was surprised. I realized that my father — my parents — might have had more fun in their teen years than I had. I was experiencing my father differently than I ever had before. Here was a man, a sexual being, not just a stern disciplinarian; not just a father, but a person capable of falling in love, a person with a tangible, unique history. I had never really looked at him before, or listened.

"It sounds like both of you had a wonderful time."

"Yes. It was full of wonder and joy. Such good times. Your mother was very pretty, petite, with fine features and a nice figure. We were very much in love, maybe as only two young people can be. It takes a certain kind of, I don't know, innocence to be carried away by the conviction that the love you're feeling is a once-in-a-lifetime experience. When you get older, you know better. You realize that passion isn't everything — and certainly not unique to you. And despite the euphoria, it is crazy making. We were in love that way — blinded by passion and lust. It was as if we found a home inside of each other's hearts. It's always been like that with us."

My father put down his glass and pulled a handkerchief out of his pocket. I'd never seen my father shed a tear before. My eyes started to fill, but I was in too much shock to allow myself to fully experience the moment.

"I don't think I ever appreciated how much you loved her," I said.

"Well," he said, wiping his nose and putting away his handkerchief, "we weren't raised to show our feelings in front of others — especially our children. Besides, as you know from your own experience, that youthful kind of crazy love doesn't last forever. It quiets down. Right?"

I had to agree. It was true — not only with Lydia, but also with every other woman I'd been with, even Carol. The novelty or excitement or whatever it is wears off and is replaced with something else. If it's boredom or annoyance, you move on. Sometimes, I guess, like with my parents, it can transform into something else, something positive and meaningful.

"What was that like for you and Mama, when the passion faded?"

He thought for a few moments and reached for his drink to take another swallow.

"As I said, it was like being home. It felt natural, the way it was supposed to be. We cared about each other. We were best friends and confidants. The passions die a slow death. You'll find out as you get older. But it's OK. Sex isn't the most important thing anymore, like it is when you're young. It was comfortable. It was home. We belonged to each other."

"What happened when the Depression hit?"

Pop got up and went to the table where the leftovers were still spread out. The housekeeper would clean up in the morning. He filled a plate with half of a sandwich, a piece of cake, a few pieces of cheese, and a handful of grapes. He offered some to me, and I took a few grapes and a slice of cheese.

"So what happened when the crash came?" I nudged him gently.

He nodded as he munched.

"It took a while. A lot of the swells and upper crust who came to The Algonquin had lots of money, so it took a while before business decreased to the point where they had to let most of us go, including your grandfather. By the end of 1930, we were out of a job and nobody was hiring. Nobody. Maria and I were terrified of the possibility of losing each other, so in our panic we decided to get married right away — as if that would solve everything. Well, not everything, but the most important thing — staying together.

"We got married and she moved in with Giansalvatore and me. And with no other prospects, I decided to join the navy. I assumed I'd be stationed at the Brooklyn Navy Yard and I'd have an income and we'd be OK. And for a while, that's the way it was.

"Then Hitler was made chancellor in Germany and, because of my size, I was assigned to submarine duty. Already, I think, they knew there'd be war and sooner or later we'd be in it — even though nobody wanted to go to war again. It turned out that I was away from home more than I had been, a lot more. And then we were in it — the war, I mean. That's when this happened," he said, pointing to his leg.

"The way I remember your telling it, a torpedo fell on you."

"You've got a good memory. You were still a little boy, I think, when I told you. We were off the coast of France. A German destroyer was clinging to us like a dog with a bone. In those days, we were pretty limited on how deep we could dive, not like the subs they have now. So we were like a fish in a barrel. There was only so much we could do to try to escape. The fucking explosions kept going off one right after another all around us. We held on to whatever we could so as to not be knocked around. We were desperate and scared shitless. Some of the men cried and whimpered every time an explosion rocked us — and the air was filled with hissing steam and the stink of sweat and ozone. We heard the seams creaking as the hull contracted or expanded, the clanging and banging of pipes breaking, orders being yelled, and horrible screams of fear. Fortunately, none of the depth charges hit us directly and, eventually, after what seemed like hours, we were able to escape."

Pop shook his head as he recalled the scene.

"In the process of trying to evade the Nazi bastard, one of the explosions shook a torpedo loose from its casing. It rolled out of its berth and dropped into the space where I was holding on to the framework for dear life. The fucking thing landed on me and broke my leg and ankle. With all the shit that was going on, it was quite a while before my mates could hoist the torpedo off me. Christ, Vito, you can't imagine the pain. Excruciating. Someone shoved something in my mouth, a towel or a rag, to muffle my screams.

"We rendezvoused with a supply ship a couple of days later, and they took me back to the States. Not too long after that, the war ended and I was home, although it took a while before I could walk halfway decent again."

I went over the dates in my head. Mama and Pop were married at 19, and he was in the navy for 14 years. At 33 he was home from the war, unemployed, married, and on disability — 15 years younger than I was at the time he was telling me his story. Then I remembered my brother.

"I just remembered about Gianni."

"Christ, you had to remind me."

"Sorry. I spoke without thinking. I was just thinking about all you'd been through at such an early age, and then I remembered — you and Mama had to suffer through that too."

"Yes, it was devastating for both of us. I'd been shipped back to Brooklyn to the navy hospital at the end of 1944, but I was home for good soon after that. Home with my wife and my son, home with my family. And just about a year or so later, he dies. My son dies. He wasn't even 11 years old. You have to remember, when I shipped out in '41, Gianni was six, so I'd seen him grow up and start school. And because he was born only two years after our first boy, Alberto, died from scarlet fever, your mother and I had put all our hearts into Gianni. And he was such a sweet kid. Jesus, he was such a loving boy. Everybody loved him. You couldn't help yourself. So when Gianni died, it just about killed us. Maria was destroyed. We both were."

He took a deep breath and wiped his eyes. He stopped to blow his nose again. "I need a refill on this. Get me another drink, will you?"

I refilled his glass. All my life — well, it seemed that way to me — I'd heard this about Gianni, how everyone loved him. That was the point. Gianni was so loveable and he died.

And you, you miserable, ugly, rat-faced weasel —nobody likes you, and you live. Where is the justice?

Maybe that's why I was unlikable — so I *wouldn't* be like him. What was so great about being liked? What did it get Gianni? I looked at my father. Part of me felt sorry for him, losing my mother, his best friend, his girlfriend, his confidant. But this business about Gianni had stirred me up. The question spilled out of my mouth before I could stop myself.

"How come you never liked me, Pop?"

He frowned at me. "What are you talking about?"

"You never liked me. You've never talked about me the way you talk about Giancarlo. I could never please you. Nothing I did was ever worthwhile in your eyes."

59

He was silent for a long time. He sipped his drink and picked absent-mindedly at his food. I began to think he'd forgotten the question or decided not to answer it. I was about to tell him that I was going home when he started talking again.

"What you ask me, Vito, is complicated. I want to answer it, but it's difficult."

When our gaze met, I saw pleading in his eyes. Or was he just tired? No, I have to be honest with this because I knew he was trying hard and it was difficult for him.

"When Maria got pregnant with you, we were 40 years old. It had been about seven years since Giancarlo died. After losing two sons, we couldn't go through that again. Well, you can imagine how you would feel if anything happened to Marie or Cathy. Neither one of us could endure that again. So we were totally surprised when she got pregnant after so many years. We even talked about the possibility of abortion, but it wasn't legal or safe then and, because of our religion, Maria was against the idea. So despite our fears, we had you.

"It was a difficult birth. Your umbilical cord was wrapped around you and, after a long labor, they finally decided to do a caesarian.

"You were such a tiny thing, just under six pounds, as I recall. Bald and puny and crying all the time. You were a pain-in-the-ass baby, Vito. Unless your mother was holding you, you'd start wailing. If I tried to hold you, you squirmed and arched your back and wouldn't stop screaming. Our whole life was turned upside down. We couldn't sleep or eat, nothing. You completely consumed your mother. And she devoted herself to you. No way was Maria going to let anything happen to you.

"The truth is, I didn't want another child. I didn't want to risk loving and then losing another son. Maybe if you had been a girl, I might have felt different. So you entered our lives uninvited, so to speak. I didn't welcome you. I looked for reasons to reject you: your size, your temperament, your moodiness, your withholding nature. You have to admit, Vito, you aren't a very lovable person. You never were — except in Maria's eyes.

"Still, in spite of that, you were my son and I felt protective of you. Remember that time with the priest?"

"I remember," I said. "I remember feeling so proud of you then. I wanted to be just like you — tough, physical, dominating."

"Really? I never knew that." He smiled and nodded his head for emphasis. "That's great," he said. "But it's only one example of how much I was on your side. Nobody could say anything bad about you to me. I wanted only the best for you. That's why I pushed you and pointed out your errors, so you could be successful."

He paused. "But I never felt close to you. Maybe it was all the shit that surrounded your birth. Maybe I was protecting myself because of Giancarlo and Alberto. Maybe I'm to blame for all of it. But I have to tell you, Vito, you never made it easy. You were always so remote, so tightly bound up within yourself, so inaccessible. I never felt that you loved me, or even respected me. The truth is, sometimes I felt as though you and your mother shut me out. The two of you were a closed system, like the earth and the moon. There was no room for me. And I guess I resented that. It's true. I resented both of you.

"But in spite of all of that, I still took great satisfaction in every one of your successes, like when you graduated from college and law school. Remember when I helped get you the job in the mayor's office? I thought I felt happy then, but when Mr. Savona got you the job with the state attorney general, I thought that was something. I told everybody about you. And when you won the state for President Clinton and got made an assistant U.S. attorney — I couldn't have been prouder. Maria and I both had tears in our eyes, we were so happy for you. We were so proud to be your parents, to live to see your accomplishments. Not bad for the son of two people who never finished high school.

"I'm very proud of you and I admire you. I'd put my life on the line for you any day of the week. I've always been there for you. And, of course, your mother felt the same way. She lived for you. You know that. You were her moon and stars, her everything. She never felt one iota of negativity toward you, ever. Not ever. God, she loved you so much.

"But unlike your mother, I saw your faults. I saw your unfaithfulness, your dishonesty, your coldness — the way you manipulate and bully people. I saw all that, but you're my son. You're mine, part of me, and I would defend you to anyone."

Tears streamed from his eyes and his lips trembled. As he reached for his handkerchief, I put my arm around his shoulder and he broke into sobs. Tears welled up in my eyes, too, and we stood that way, my arm around his strong shoulder, holding his heaving body close to me for the first time in my life.

61

7

In July, I received another major shock. Tony had come up from DC on the Acela Express, and we met for lunch in Center City.

"I'm going to resign from the Office of Legal Counsel," he confided.

"What? No kidding," I said. I wondered what he might be moving up to. Attorney general? Supreme Court?

"Are congratulations in order?" I asked.

"Not exactly."

I waited. Tony had a flair for the dramatic. He knew how to milk a moment — I remembered how he'd informed me of my job with the U.S. attorney's office. So I sipped my drink, expecting some big news, something to lift my spirits.

"Actually, Vito, I don't really have anything lined up."

"Don't bullshit me, Tony. What is it? The Supremes? Tell me."

"No, Vito. I'm serious. The truth is, they suggested that I resign. Well, I say suggested. That's just the polite way of putting it."

"Who? Who asked you to resign? The attorney general?"

"Of course. But that's not where it originated. The attorney general doesn't make these decisions in a vacuum."

"Clinton?"

Tony nodded.

"Why? Christ, you've been there for seven years. Why does he want you out now? I don't understand. Is he letting you go so you can do something more lucrative after the election? I mean, no matter who wins, Gore or Bush, come February, you're out of a job."

"Who knows? I think I might have stepped on some toes, maybe taken an unpopular position on something. I'll never know."

Wow. If the guillotine could fall so suddenly on Anthony Savona, the most powerful individual I knew, then it could happen to anyone.

63

My next thought was that I'd just lost the protection of my mentor and could no longer assume I had the protection of those higher up. I wondered if this move would strip him of all of his power.

"What does this mean for you? Does this make you persona non grata, or will your friends still stick by you?"

"An excellent question, Vito. We'll just have to wait. I'll be handing in my letter of resignation next week, and then we'll see what happens — who will offer me a job and who will run for the hills."

Tony and I also discussed my position. I was still furious about Arnie getting the promotion that I deserved. I'd thought about getting out of the U.S. attorney's office all together.

"I don't know what to tell you, Vito. If something opens up in a big firm, I wouldn't advise against it. But you could do worse than stay where you are. I can't picture Arnie White being there for too much longer, or Mulligan, or Garrett, or Chaudhary for that matter. The powers that be know you were screwed and they owe you one. Your turn will come, I'm sure. Although if Gore loses and the Republicans get in, all bets are off."

He paused for a moment, then added, "Meanwhile, you've still got your little side deals to keep you going."

That sounded like decent advice, and it confirmed that my thoughts on my future were reasonable, so I decided to stick it out.

Bush and Cheney did get elected in November of 2000 and, as soon as they took office, my life was immediately impacted: Janet Reno was out, and John Ashcroft was appointed as the new attorney general. I wondered what would happen in our office. As it turned out, Lucky Chaudhary, who had taken over as the first assistant U.S. attorney, essentially as Matt Garrett's chief of staff, not only had a history as a fervent supporter of Clinton — even more than I had been — but had found other ways to piss off the Republicans. Maybe it was a racial thing, I don't know. At any rate, they found a way to get rid of him.

The unexpected result was that I was promoted to take Chaudhary's place. But he wasn't the only one to go. Garrett was persuaded to resign and someone entirely new, an important Republican supporter named George Jones, was appointed by Bush to be our new U.S. attorney for Eastern Pennsylvania. Jones didn't know much about what the job entailed. Actually, he didn't know anything about it. Maybe that's why I had been made the first assistant U.S. attorney, to guide him through the day-to-day demands and hold his hand.

It was perfect. Jones had no intention of learning his job. He was interested only in the title and the ability to carry out whatever hatchet jobs got passed down from Ashcroft. In effect, I was the U.S. attorney, a position I now realized I'd never be appointed to. To his detriment, Jones came from Missouri, a different culture, and he never fit in. Nobody went to him; everyone came to me, and that's just the way Jones wanted it. Who was I to complain?

I immediately began to think about how to change things. It was obvious to me that the position of first assistant U.S. attorney was inherently powerful, but up to now the men who had occupied it hadn't appreciated that. I began to use my new post to influence who was placed in important positions: chiefs and deputy chiefs, team leaders, senior investigators, even favored paralegals. I wanted people who would be more cooperative about my decisions. As Carmine Belloni had predicted, I aimed to be The Man. My newfound power and influence allowed me to do favors for people and, in the process, earn their loyalty. Consequently, I could do whatever I wanted. I made bigger and bigger deals, influencing any major case I wanted to, and the rewards poured in. I began to get seriously rich.

My father died of a heart attack that year. The housekeeper found him one morning in his bed. She had thought he was sleeping peacefully.

I was disappointed that I hadn't had a chance to say good-bye, but I don't actually know what I would have said to him. I could have told him that I loved him, but I don't know if that's true. Maybe I did without knowing it. I'm not sure if I've ever really loved anyone. I've cared about people — my parents, my children, Carol — but have I really loved them? I do know that he was very proud when I was made first assistant U.S. attorney, and that made me feel good. I'll remember him fondly, but no, I can't say I loved him. I respected him. He did all right with his life. But he never did anything for me. I've gotten more from Tony than I ever got from my father. Tony's been there for me. He's helped me get jobs, put in a good word for me, given me sage advice, encouraged me. Tony's been more of a father to me than Pop ever was.

We had a service at the same church where we held Mama's funeral, not that he would have cared. All religious rituals were just so much bullshit to him. But Lydia insisted, and I knew how it would look if I didn't have a funeral for my own father. At the gathering back at our house, it was mostly my family, Anthony Savona, and some people from my office. I think my daughters were the saddest of anyone there. Lydia had been close to my mother, but never really felt close to Pop. Well, not many people did. I think he and I were much more alike than he realized. He, who accused me of being a cold fish, ha! This apple didn't fall very far from that tree.

Tony and I spent some time together after the funeral. He stayed in town for a couple of days and we went out to lunch. Tony had been totally consumed since Clinton's impeachment, so this was the first opportunity in a very long time for us to spend some time together. He was in a solemn mood even though he had been out of the Office of Legal Counsel — and Washington — for a few months. At first, I attributed his somberness to my father's death — maybe it had triggered a memory from some earlier event in his life, like the death of his wife. But I was wrong.

"So how do you like your new job?" he asked me.

"I love it. I'm right at the center of everything. Nothing goes on in that office that I don't know about. It's even better than I'd dreamed it could be. It's almost like being the attorney general. I feel like I'm the boss. Everything runs through me."

He nodded and smiled in approval. "I'm happy for you. Your mama would have bust a gut with pride if she had lived to see it."

"I know," I said. "But Pop lived to see it. He was really proud. It made me feel really good, you know?"

"Of course I know. A parent's approval, especially a father's approval, is very important."

There was something in the way he said it, the tone of his voice, that made me think he knew how I felt about him, that I regarded him as a father figure.

"All the time I was growing up," I said, "I felt as though I never existed for him. But after my mother died, he seemed to change. He paid more attention."

We sat in silence for a while, eating, drinking our wine, but Anthony seemed distracted. I asked him what he'd been doing since he left Washington.

"I kept my office at my old firm and I work from there. I'm still on a few boards, of course, but that doesn't take up much time. And I'm doing some traveling. I went to Europe for a while, Italy, saw some old friends and relatives." He paused and put down his fork, leaning closer to me. "And I'm consulting with some old friends of ours."

I looked at him quizzically. Who was he talking about? Was I supposed to know?

"You remember the heavyset guy you met at my place when Clinton won in '92? The big guy who got annoyed with you."

I nodded. I assumed he was talking about Carmine Belloni.

"He's been doing some work for friends of ours, and from time to time I give them some legal advice." At that, he raised his eyebrows.

I recalled that Belloni had been doing work for the Romano family, and I assumed that's who Tony was referring to. I nodded.

"It's good, but sometimes it's difficult to get up-to-date information, you know? Otherwise, I'm doing OK." He took a few bites of his lunch.

I had never known Tony to be so cautious. Obviously, he was concerned about being overheard. We both knew that the government, whether FBI or another branch, could eavesdrop almost anywhere they wanted. If Tony was concerned about being bugged, it meant that I should be much more careful than I had been. Up until then, I'd been making deals, nudging cases one way or another in return for monetary advantages. It was worth a lot of money to people to have their case postponed or dismissed. Now I realized that I might have been careless. From now on, I'd have to be more circumspect. I waited until he looked up at me, and immediately switched the subject to my daughters, now 17 and 15.

We kept the conversation away from business for the rest of the meal. While we were having coffee, Tony scribbled something on a paper napkin and slid it across the table. The note suggested we run into each other at Rittenhouse Square that night. I nodded, making the usual banter as we separated.

———————————

That night I went out for a walk and casually strolled in to Rittenhouse Square. I spotted Tony across the park and slowly made my way in his direction. When we were close enough, he hollered out in greeting, and we acted surprised to run into each other. As we shook hands, he slipped a folded paper into my palm. I took out a handkerchief to blow my nose and put both the paper and handkerchief into my pocket. We kibitzed for a couple of minutes. I asked him to come for a drink, but he declined and we said good-bye. Back home, I went to my study to read his note.

Tony suspected he was being investigated and warned me to be vigilant about my own financial dealings. I was sitting on millions at this point and, if I were investigated, I would likely spend many years in prison. Up to now I had felt completely safe. Tony had been very careful in setting up shell corporations, trusts, and numbered accounts so I'd be protected, but nothing is foolproof. Tony described a way for us to communicate without being monitored. He thought it wise for us to avoid direct contact until things blew over. He would communicate from time to time through this new channel to arrange some deals and exchange information regarding Belloni and the Romano family, but that would be our only contact. He urged me to be cautious in all matters.

I made myself a drink. Reviewing our conversation, I decided that unless a deal was foolproof or came directly from Tony, my days of deal-making were over. I had more than enough money, and my investments would grow on their own. I could afford to go straight.

8

I sometimes find myself daydreaming about one lazy afternoon in the fall of 2002. I had begun seeing Lena and we often got together in her apartment. I remember her lifting up her head to kiss me one last time before getting out of bed to shower. I watched her as she crossed the room, her amazing firm ass swiveling just so. I heard her singing in the shower, her voice strong and clear and beautiful, just like the rest of her. I was struck by how lucky I was to have such a beautiful woman in my life. Her petite, athletic body matched her intense and uninhibited sexual appetite. The song she was singing was infectious and I found myself humming along for a moment — but I stopped, suddenly feeling self-conscious.

I contemplated my own body lying under her sheets, which smelled of her perfume and sex. Not bad for 50. I still worked out, still boxed and practiced my judo. Once again I was thankful for the thin, wiry body build I'd inherited, and proud that I was still attractive to someone so much younger, and that I could still satisfy her sexually. She called me her stallion.

I was sitting on the edge of the bed when Lena returned with a towel wrapped turban-style around her head. I admired her naked body, grateful once again for her beauty and sexuality. And I also enjoyed feeling flattered by her admiration of the power I can wield. But despite my ecstasy, I felt a nagging indignation at her lack of appreciation for the realities of my position as a federal prosecutor. She's too simplistic: In her pretty little head, I'm important and powerful and know influential people, and so I can do anything. I'm absolutely invulnerable. She had no idea of the difficulties I'd face if I were investigated. She was an incurable optimist — which was ironic, considering her cynicism about government.

I suddenly had the urge to slap her face.

"Are you going to take a shower?" she asked.

"Yes. I was just admiring you. You're so beautiful."

Lena smiled and leaned over me, sticking her tongue into my mouth. I cupped her young breasts in my hands as I returned her kiss.

"You're going to get me started again," I told her.

"No, I'm not. I'm famished and ready for dinner. Go take your shower."

Dinner. Yes, now that she mentioned it, I was ravenous, too.

Drying myself after the shower, I caught the reflection of my face in the mirror. At first I was surprised by my serious expression — I thought I felt relaxed after our afternoon escapades. But studying my image, I saw the embodiment of my father's determination and capacity for violence. I was proud of my physical prowess, the capacity to physically dominate. Pursing my lips, I nodded slightly to my reflected self. I was pleased with what I saw, with who I was.

Of course Lydia gave me flak about seeing Lena. She tried to suck me in to arguments with her, but I denied there was anything to fight about and she'd relent for a while. Once she showed me copies of some emails my daughters had exchanged. I kept them.

Email from Marie to Cathy:
April 28, 2003
Cathy, I just read in the Inquirer *(thank you for the subscription — it's fun keeping up with what's happening at home) that Daddy is running around Philly with his girlfriend! I don't understand it! He's still living with Mommy and she's putting up with it! What's wrong with her? I hate him! I don't know who I hate more — him for being such a bastard or her for being so totally stupid. I wish I didn't have anything to do with either of them. I don't know how you can stand living in the same house with them while they're being such jerks.*

Email from Cathy to Marie:
April 28, 2003
It's not as bad here as you think. Nobody talks about "her." You'd think nothing was going on. Once I brought it up with him and he denied everything,

said it was gossip planted by his enemies and that there was no truth to the rumor that he's dating someone. He said he met Lena at a party and, as a favor to a friend, he promised to help get her a job. He said it's preposterous to think he'd be dating someone almost the same age as me. He denies everything and Mommy acts like she totally believes him. It's all so unreal! I can't wait until I graduate next June and can get away to college. You're so lucky to already be there in Vermont and away from this asylum.

BTW, Happy Birthday! I have something for you and will give it to you when you come home at the end of your semester.

Email from Marie to Cathy:
April 28, 2003
Thanks for remembering my BD. I haven't heard anything about it from either of them so far; I think they've forgotten. Shows how wrapped up in themselves they are.

I just Googled "her" online and there are stories on various blogs that say Dad was also seen in Washington restaurants with her. Did you know she's an Olympic gymnast?

Email from Cathy to Marie:
April 28, 2003
Yeah, I read online that she competed for Kazakhstan, where her father is from. Can you believe it? She's just two fucking years older than you — and only four older than I am! Dad should be so ashamed of himself. He's so disgusting; it makes me want to vomit. Yuk!!

Of course, Lydia showed these to me to punish me. And it did hurt to know that my daughters felt this way about me. Lydia did a damned good job of turning them against me. And even though most of the time she kept silent, she let me know how much she hated my guts. She heard that I'd fathered a child (well, there's really only one that I know about). She said she wondered how many little Vitos were running around and that the sewers of Washington must be teeming with little Rat Faces. I will never forgive her for that remark.

71

She told me once that she'd get even with me, but she knew she had to be careful. I reminded her that I knew a lot of powerful people and she couldn't just walk out on me or have me served with divorce papers, as if I were some schmuck attorney handling wills and chasing ambulances.

Other times, Lydia took a more conciliatory position, one that reflected her sense of helplessness on one hand and irrational hope on the other. The reality was that she was powerless, but part of her inertia stemmed from the fact that she didn't want to lose me. Maybe she already had, she told me once, but she remained hopeful that my desire for girlfriends was a phase I'd grow out of. After all, I was no longer a young stud — and even if I were, I wouldn't stay one forever. Hopefully sooner rather than later, I'd appreciate what a loyal and loving wife she'd been.

I remember her telling me, "We have so much together. This magnificent house, our two beautiful daughters, a whole history together — and investments, property in both of our names, savings, brokerage accounts. You can't turn your back on all of it. You're too pragmatic for that. And I know you still love me. We still make love together. We still go out together. We still dance together beautifully. We entertain. You still bring me to your political and business functions. I'm still your wife."

But Lydia knew that the tension, the subterfuge, the strain of keeping silent wasn't sustainable. At some level deep within, she knew. And in spite of her fantasy that I'd once again become the loving husband she wanted, she could not deny her smoldering anger, and her hope for the delicious, sadistic pleasure she would derive from punishing me for the pain I had caused her. In Lydia's mind, all I cared about (besides younger women) was my position — power, prestige, and money. That's where she would have to strike when the time came. I did what I could to protect myself; only a small portion of my assets was jointly held.

9

Lena and I were seated at a table at La Croix. I was carefully slicing my filet mignon, savoring each delicious mouthful. The meal, as usual, was superb and I was enjoying a moment of sensuous luxury even though I'd dined here many times — with Lena and with others. I realized that Lena was talking to me and, with some reluctance, I turned my attention from my excellent meal to her.

"This October the European gymnastic championships are being held in Rome. I'd love it if we could go. Imagine — Rome, together. Wouldn't it be fantastic?"

"It's not possible."

"But, Honey, we wouldn't have to stay for the whole time."

I put down my knife and fork and leaned back.

"Vito," she continued, "it's not until October. You'd have plenty of time to make plans …"

"Did you hear what I said?"

"Yes. Of course I heard you."

I looked at her and raised my eyebrows. Then I picked up my utensils and resumed eating.

"Wouldn't you enjoy being in Rome with me? It would be so romantic: the Tiber, the Colosseum, the food."

"Lena! Why are you persisting in this? You know better than to be stubborn with me. Do you think I have a regular nine-to-five job? My position requires me to be available 24-7. Don't you know that?"

"Vito, even the president gets a vacation. You have a phone — and it's not like Italy is in another solar system."

"Lena, I am not going to Rome to see fucking gymnastics. If I want to look at a tight little ass, I've got you. I don't need to watch 14-year-olds posing and prancing around."

She started to say something, but I put up my hand to stop her. "I understand that these competitions mean something to you, but they mean nothing to me. Nothing. If you want to go, then fucking go. I'm not going."

"But why?"

"Lena, you're ruining my dinner. Just shut up, OK?"

As we ate in silence, I knew she was furious but it would be self-defeating for her to show it. I assumed she felt like walking out and leaving me sitting at the table by myself, an object of derision to the other diners and staff. But she knew if she did, she'd never see me again. She'd lose her apartment and everything else that came with being my mistress.

"I'm sorry," she said finally. "I guess I was so excited by the idea of spending time with you in Rome that I didn't think it through. Of course I appreciate how much responsibility you have. I guess I got carried away with my romantic fantasies. I'm sorry if I upset you."

I looked up at her from under my brow. Again I placed my knife and fork on my plate. I leaned forward, with my elbows on the table, and stared at her.

"Lena, what am I going to do with you? On one hand, you drive me so fucking crazy with passion that I can't even begin to imagine life without you. Then, in the very next moment, you enrage me with your selfish lack of consideration for the demands on my life. Then I can't bear having you in my life for one more minute. You're very frustrating."

"I'm sorry. It's only that I love you so much. I can't get enough of you. I always want more of you. And you're right, I do know better. I'm very well aware of the demands of your position. I get carried away, but I know that's no excuse. I'm sorry I cause you so much grief."

"OK. Enough. I understand. Let's forget it and get on with our meal."

"Of course," she said and returned to picking at her lobster tail.

I have these encounters all day long. People think they can manipulate me. It's bad enough at work; I don't need that bullshit in my personal life, too.

People may wonder why a man like me, successful and powerful, would get involved with a girl 30 years my junior. I've seen the look in enough people's eyes to realize what everyone thinks — that it's all about sex and

74

power, the domination of a younger (albeit beautiful) woman. I have to admit there's a lot of truth in that.

I first met Lena at the Olympic games in Atlanta in 1996. The people I was with were taking us around and introducing us to some of the athletes. The gymnastics team from Kazakhstan happened to be at one of the social gatherings and we were introduced. She was only 14 — and she looked even more childlike because the way these girls train inhibits their physical development.

But there was something about her face — her large, dark eyes, her Asian features — and her vivacious personality that captured my attention and made her stand out. She had been born and raised here in the States and so had no foreign accent. She was a delightful child, warm and effervescent. There was something about her that portended an intense sensuality in spite of her physical immaturity.

In 2002, when the Olympics were in Salt Lake City, I met up with her again. At 20, she was a mature young woman. It was obvious that her rigid training could not completely suppress her physical development. She was wonderfully attractive, a wild animal when it came to sex, and intensely responsive to everything I did.

About a year or so after we started seeing each other, after I'd been made the first assistant U.S. attorney, Lena overheard me on the phone. Right away she realized what was going on and, when I got off the phone, she circled her arms around my neck.

"I didn't know you were such a strongman," she said.

"What are you talking about?"

"I heard you on the phone just now, making some big-shot lawyer agree to pay you a lot of money to postpone his case. I didn't realize you were capable of doing that."

For a moment, I was afraid she was accusing me of corruption and might tell someone. "What are you saying?"

"I'm saying that I'm proud of you. Where my father comes from, everyone in government takes advantage of his position to make more money for his family. It's the honorable thing to do. But you always seemed so straight, so rigid; I didn't realize you could bend the rules too. I'm proud of you."

She kissed me and pressed herself against me. Realizing that my deal-making was a turn-on for Lena was an unexpected surprise, like a jolt of adrenalin. We ended up fucking each other right there on the spot.

After that, Lena showed a real interest in my work. Often she'd encourage me to ask for more money, to be more subtle or more demanding. She was totally involved and I felt like I had a true partner, someone who fully embraced who I was and what I did. It was extraordinarily exciting for me.

And yet, I can't say I'm in love with Lena. Maybe it's only that I hesitate to admit it. I enjoy her. I care about her and value her opinions — and, most importantly, I trust her. I want her to be happy and I enjoy doing things for her. But I know I could dismiss her from my life fairly easily if I chose to.

After the Olympics were over, Lena settled in Philadelphia. She started a gymnastics school with a little financial help from me, and has done surprisingly well for herself. She's a shrewd and resourceful businesswoman. The truth is, now that I think about it, she could have dumped me any time she chose and still have done all right for herself.

10

Lydia sued me for divorce in 2004.

One Saturday night we had gone out to dinner with friends and it was early Sunday morning by the time we got home. While I was paying the cabbie, she bolted toward the house and, as I was about to follow her in, she slammed the door in my face. When I got inside, I went for her.

"What the hell was that all about?"

She ignored me, tossing her coat onto a chair and heading up the stairs.

"Wait a fucking minute," I yelled. "What's wrong with you?"

She spun around and almost lost her balance. She was drunk.

"What's wrong with me? What's wrong with you! You can't even keep your eyes in your head when we're out with friends. You have to humiliate me like that?"

"What're you talking about?"

"I'm talking about the brunette at the table across from ours. You couldn't keep your eyes off of her all night. Jesus, Vito, you're disgusting."

"What brunette?" Truthfully, how was I supposed to not notice her — those dark, elongated eyes, the plunging neckline revealing enough rounded breast to capture any man's attention?

"You just can't stop, can you? How many women do you have to have in your harem, Vito? That child gym rat isn't enough? You have to constantly be on the lookout for more?"

"You're crazy, Lydia. You have no idea what you're talking about."

"Oh, you're so full of shit, it's coming out of your ears. You lie so often you don't even know when you're doing it. It's in the papers for crying out loud. You ought to be ashamed. She's hardly older than your daughters, for Christ's sake."

"The papers are full of stories, Lydia. Gossip. That's all it is. Rumors intended to ruin my reputation and destroy my credibility. I've told you that before. There's nothing to it. It's all bullshit. I'm surprised you pay any attention to it."

"Vito! How can I not pay attention to it? Do you deny that you go out to dinner with her? To La Croix? The Four Seasons?"

"I go out to dinner with lots of people. It's business, that's all. You've got some bug up your ass. You're getting paranoid — and besides, you're drunk. I'm not discussing this crap with you anymore. It's nonsense."

I started up the steps, heading to bed. There was nothing to be gained by arguing anymore. I was halfway up the stairs when she shouted, "I want a divorce!"

I turned and stared at her.

"You're drunk and you're nuts. You don't know what you want." I continued up the stairs as she ranted on. "I may be a little drunk, Sweetheart, but I'm not nuts and I'm not paranoid. I'm going to file for divorce, and I'm going to take all your fucking money. You hear me, Vittorio? The properties, this house, the stocks, the offshore account, I'm taking it all. You'll be a sorry son-of-a-bitch when I'm through with you."

How did she know about an offshore account? Was she guessing? Did she know about all of them, or just one or two? Of course she knew of those assets that were in both our names, mostly properties, a checking account, and a brokerage account. But I was sure she had no idea of the shell companies or the trusts. Still, if she were serious, it would mean she'd end up with a shitload of my money. At first I was angry and thought about ways of stopping her. But then I reasoned, what the hell? When she dies, whatever she gets will go to the girls, which is where I'd leave most of it anyway. Besides, if she only knew about one of the offshore accounts, and nothing of the shell companies and trusts, or the properties that didn't have her name on them, then there'd be plenty left for me. And if I were free of her, life would be a lot easier, a lot calmer.

Maybe she has a good idea for once in her life. Let's see where it goes.

One night, before the divorce was finalized and before I moved out, Tony and I were talking business in my office at home. Lydia opened the door and just walked in.

"What do you want?" I said. I was annoyed that she thought she could just barge in to my sanctuary whenever she felt like it.

She looked briefly at Tony and mumbled hello to him. Then, with hate simmering in her narrowed eyes, she demanded, "I want to know when you're going to move out. It's very unpleasant having you here."

"It's my house, Lydia. I'm staying here for as long as I want to." I glanced at Tony and saw that he'd lowered his eyes. I understood that this was embarrassing him, so I tried to mollify her.

"Look, Lydia, it's not as easy as you think. I'm trying to stay out of your way. I'm not bothering you or expecting you to do anything for me, am I? So hold your horses. Just be patient, all right? I'm looking for a place and, as soon as I find one, I'll move out. OK?"

"No, Vito, it's not OK."

She turned to Tony. "I'm sorry to put you in the middle here, Tony, but your protégé and I are getting divorced, if he hasn't told you, and he promised to move out."

Then she leered at me. "And you're still here, Vito. I don't want you here. You shouldn't still be living here. Go live with your child whore or with your bastard son."

"Jesus, Lydia, are you fucking drunk again? Get out of here. Get the hell out of my office. You have no right to be in here anyway."

"I can come in here any damned time I want to, Vito. This is my house. What, are you afraid I'll see some more of your fucking secrets? Find out where you hide all your money? You fucking crook."

Was she implying that she had gone through my desk, my computer, my files? Glancing back at my desk as though I could see some apparition of her in the act, I caught a look of fear or apprehension on Tony's face. He was looking at Lydia and suddenly I realized what had happened.

"Tony, did *you* give Lydia the information regarding the offshore account?"

He was caught totally off guard and I saw immediately that I was right. He must have seen the shock of comprehension on my face. His posture went slack and he lowered his head. He didn't even bother to deny it.

"Jesus, Tony, how could you?"

I was devastated. The bottom of my stomach dropped away and my skin suddenly felt clammy. Tony, my mentor, my friend, my confidant, my lawyer. Tony, who I had trusted with everything, who knew everything — this man had given me up? To her? What? Was he fucking her? Were they going to split the money?

"I'm sorry, Vito. Lydia came to me. She was frightened that you would leave her without enough for her and the girls. You know how much I care about Catherine and Marie. I felt I had to do something to help her. She was desperate, so I gave her the number of the account."

Although his voice was full of contrition, the look in Tony's eyes caught my attention. And then I realized what he was silently conveying to me: He had deliberately told her about the newest and least funded account. And that's all she knew about.

As I stared at him a smile of recognition came to my lips, but I quickly suppressed it. I knew Tony had seen it. I turned to Lydia. "You selfish bitch. You go to this man who's been like a father to me and ask him to betray me? How fucking low can you go? What were you prepared to do to get him to sacrifice his relationship with me? Were you willing to blow him? Fuck him? And for what, Lydia? For a few lousy bucks? For that you'd come between Tony and me and take everything I have? Everything I earned with my own blood and sweat? Did you really think I wouldn't take care of you and the girls? Or is it just that you hate me that fucking much?"

Lydia was speechless. I think she was terrified at what I might do — to her and to Tony. Tony spoke up, continuing the charade.

"I'm sorry, Vito. I didn't mean any harm, really."

"Oh, Christ, Tony. I don't know what to say. You of all people. Do you know how this makes me feel? Do you have any fucking idea what you've done to me?"

Lydia interrupted. "Vito, listen to me. You can't do anything. I know this is stolen money. I know you didn't pay taxes on it. There's nothing you can do about it now. If you make a fuss, you'll only get yourself in trouble. I only did it to make sure the girls and I would get our fair share, that you weren't holding out on us."

"Fair share? Jesus, Lydia, you've got well over 50 percent of everything, including this house and everything in it. You can have it all, everything. Fair? Fuck you. You want this room? You haven't got enough? I'll give you the fucking room. Take it, goddamnit. I'll be out by the end of the week. Now get the fuck out of my office before I physically do something I don't want to do."

Lydia shot me a look that was a mix of hatred and fear. Before she left the room I hissed at Tony, "And that goes for you, too. Get out. I never want to see you here again." I winked as I said it.

Tony winked back as he muttered dismally, "I'm sorry, Vito. I hope someday you can forgive me."

By the following week I had moved out of Delancey Street. Shortly afterward, Tony and I had dinner at his condo and he explained his rationale: If he didn't give Lydia something, she'd have turned over every stone. He was afraid of what a forensic auditor might find. Now she thought she had it all, when it was really only a small portion of what was truly hidden.

––––––––––––––

Nothing is ever as easy as anyone hopes it'll be. The divorce dragged on for almost two years. Lydia brought in forensic accountants and specialist attorneys just to make sure she was squeezing every goddamned nickel out of me. I agreed to most of her demands, but it was clear she wanted a fight. If I gave in on something, it only seemed to infuriate her and make her demand more. The good news was that Tony had done his job well and most of the hidden assets went undiscovered. That was a relief on a number of fronts: If her legal team didn't discover these assets, then in all probability neither would the IRS or the FBI. Of course, I still had to be careful not to live too far above my means — which explains why I'm here still here in Philly instead of in a condo in paradise.

11

I was sitting at my computer this past Sunday and Lena was busy making arrangements for a dinner she's putting together for my 63rd birthday next Saturday. It was a peaceful day until her asshole brother, Rudy, dropped in, unannounced like always. I can't stand him. He's an ignorant loser and jealous of my success. Before I knew it, the jerk was insulting me — in my own house! No way was I going to let him get away with it. I screamed at him, "Who the hell do you think you are, talking to me like that? You're nothing, and you come into my house and fucking insult me?"

Lena tried to intervene. "Calm down, Vito. He didn't mean anything."

"Shut up, Lena. Your brother is a piece of shit. You know that, don't you, Rudy? You're shit."

"And you know what, Vito? You're an asshole. I'm done apologizing. You take offense at everything I say. So go to hell."

"Rudy, don't talk that way to him."

"Bullshit, Lena," he grunted. "I've had it with him."

"What do you mean, you've had it with me? You think you can come into my home and insult me? Really?"

"Vito, don't take him so seriously. You know Rudy just likes to hear himself talk."

"Jesus, Lena. You're taking his side? Fine. Then you can get the hell out of here with your asshole brother. Both of you get out. Go on. Get the fuck out of my house."

"Come on, Rudy, I'll walk you to the car."

I watched through the window as Lena walked him to his macho pickup truck. I know I put her in the middle, but no more than her asshole brother does. I watched her kiss him on the cheek and he climbed into his truck and pulled away. When she returned to the house, I was back in front of my laptop.

"You cold?" she asked me.

I didn't respond, my attention focused on the screen where I'd been writing. She looked at me and I noticed the expression on her face; she was probably thinking that my once-handsome face, with its chiseled features, was now fleshy and wrinkled, my fine, blond hair now reduced to thin wisps. I'm about to turn 63, for Christ's sake. I know how she sees me. She's told me often enough that my facial expression could have been cast in stone: pursed lips and cold, unexpressive eyes. She used to brag about how intimidating I was. Now she sees an old man, defeated maybe, but still determined.

"You look cold. You want a sweater?"

I lifted the glass from the table next to my computer.

"I can use more soda."

Lena went to the kitchen and brought back a two-liter bottle of soda.

"I'm out of ice," I said without taking my eyes from the screen.

Can't she see that? Can't she figure that out for herself?

She returned with a glass full of ice cubes and refilled my soda.

"Here," she said. "Anything else?"

"Your brother is a worthless piece of shit."

"Rudy didn't mean to insult you. He was just saying that you aren't what you used to be. That's all. No big deal. We're all getting older, Vito — you, me, even Rudy. And he wouldn't deny it. It's no crime, getting old. It's OK. He wasn't saying anything bad."

I heard what she said. It wasn't even worth responding to. I know she loves her brother, but he's still an asshole. He never amounted to anything. He's ignorant. Not like her. Lena is shrewd. She knows how the world works.

And her asshole brother knew exactly what he was saying — he said I was losing it. Fuck him. I've got 25 years on him and I could still take him. I could drop him like a stone if I wanted to. Losing it! He'll never be half of what I was. Not a tenth. I was somebody. Look at this house! I built this fucking house. Sure, it was here, but I had it totally gutted and remodeled. Everything in it is the latest and the best: granite, marble, gold plate, state of the art. And look at the dump he lives in. Lena knows. She doesn't talk about it because she doesn't want her stupid brother to feel bad, but she knows what I accomplished. She knows who I am, what I can do if I want to.

I leaned back from my computer and looked through the doorway to where Lena stood in the kitchen. I admired her trim athletic figure and her perfect little round ass. I watched as she cleared the sink, then went outside and sat on the back steps, probably to call Rudy's wife. She is so predictable.

Watching out the window, I saw Lena strolling slowly around the back yard of our home in Girard Estates, one of the nicer sections of South Philadelphia. Neither of us does any gardening anymore. We pay a lawn service to come in once a week to mow the grass and do whatever else is necessary to keep the landscaping fresh. But we often enjoy sitting out there and looking at the lawn and flowering bushes — azaleas and rhododendrons and a magnificent old dogwood. A fence separates our property from the neighbors, who never go outside anyway, so it always feels peaceful and private. I felt myself breathing more slowly just watching Lena absorbing the tranquility of our yard. I guess we both needed to calm down.

Maybe I should have gone outside and joined her. But observing her was enough. I was eager to get back to writing my memoirs, or whatever you want to call it. Lena complains that I spend most of my time moping in front of the TV or staying up half the night writing. Won't she be surprised when I turn it into a tell-all blockbuster book — maybe even a movie!

She says that either I'm withdrawn or irritable about anything and everything, that ever since I stopped working I've become so thin-skinned and touchy that living with me is increasingly difficult. Of course I'm irritable! You think I enjoyed being forced out of my job and caged up in this house with nothing to do?

Lena poked her head into the living room.

"You OK, Hon? You want anything?"

I barely shook my head. I feel bad about it sometimes, getting annoyed so easily. I know she means well, but constantly being interrupted pisses me off.

"OK, then. Holler if you need me. I'll be in the den."

When I was a young man, nobody messed with me. For the most part, that's still the case. Sometimes an asshole like Rudy will try to get away

85

with some shit, but I don't let anybody get away with anything. They know better than to mess with Vittorio Putino. Rudy's a joke. He's a peanut. When I was working in the U.S. attorney's office, I dealt with assholes like him all the time, and I put them away where they belonged. Those were the days. What a time that was.

"Right, Lena?" I asked, as if she could read my thoughts. I had joined her on the back deck. "Wasn't that a fucking time?"

"What?"

"The gang wars. The trials. When we put away all the mobsters. You remember."

"That was before my time, Hon. I wasn't with you then."

"You weren't?"

"No. We didn't start seeing each other until 2003. I don't remember anything about any gang wars."

What was she talking about? Of course she was there. I remember. She came almost every day to watch me and once she even brought the girls.

"I remember seeing you at the trials."

"No, Vito, that was Lydia. You were married to Lydia then, not me."

I'd have sworn it was Lena. But, of course, if the girls were there, it had to have been Lydia. Funny, I hardly remember what Lydia looks like; it's as if there's only been Lena. The trials, that's when I made my name as a federal prosecutor. I was a prosecuting attorney in some of the biggest mob trials ever held in this country, and I was an essential part of them.

"I played an important part in sending those assholes to prison. I received commendations, I did such a good job. 'Outstanding,' they said."

"Vito, I know how important you were. And you still are, Honey. You're still important — to me and to your daughters."

"And to Philadelphia. They don't forget me down at City Hall and the Federal Building."

"I know, Hon. I know. You want some more soda?"

12

It was really sweet of Lena to have arranged my birthday party. I know she's worried about me and is trying to cheer me up. It's true, since I left the federal prosecutor's office I haven't exactly been my usual cheery self. That was a blow. It was so out of the blue. Last June, in 2014, Olzewski, our newly appointed U.S. attorney in charge of the office, and for whom I served as the first assistant U.S. attorney, called me in to her office.

"Sit down, Putino."

I sat. Olzewski was a fire-eater. She had a long history as a DA and a reputation as an aggressive, no-holds-barred prosecutor. In her late 50s with short grey hair, she looked like a tank commander — and she relished being in charge. The bitch thought it was her office. She'd find out soon enough who really ran the show.

"What can I do for you?" I asked.

She looked at me for a moment and rocked back in her chair.

"To be brutally frank with you, you can hand me your resignation."

I smiled at the joke.

"I'm not kidding. I want you to write a letter of resignation effective immediately. You can use whatever excuse you want: your heart attack, other medical or personal reasons, whatever you're comfortable with. I want it on my desk by close of business today."

"Why? What's this about?"

She sighed.

"It's about an ongoing investigation into corruption in this office. You are deeply implicated — in fact *you* are at the center of it — and if you don't resign immediately, you *will* be arrested. You will be found guilty. You will be heavily fined and *you* will spend many years in a federal prison. If you resign now, all of that can go away. I'm sure you know how this works."

I was shocked. She wasn't asking any questions. She wasn't moralizing. She was set in her conviction. There was no wiggle room, no opportunity to plead my case. It was obvious she believed I was guilty as charged. Clearly she held all the cards, or believed she did. She wouldn't have taken this aggressive position unless she had seen enough evidence to be absolutely convinced of the validity of the charges. Without knowing what the charges were, I imagined the worst.

"You can't be serious. Corruption? That's insane. How am I supposed to be involved? You can at least tell me that."

"No, I can't. I have no patience for this sort of thing, Putino, and I'm absolutely furious that I have to be a party to any of this. If it were solely up to me, I'd have you arrested right this minute. I think you're a disgusting piece of shit, using this office to enrich yourself. But fortunately for you, some people think that the Department of Justice will be better off if you simply resign. You have until 4:30 this afternoon, after that the deal is gone and you *will* be arrested. Is that clear? One way or another, you will be out of here by day's end."

I was sick to my stomach. I briefly, very briefly, tried to think of a plausible way to kill her and actually get away with it. Maintaining my poker face, I thought of bluffing, threatening her with a lawsuit or something.

"You're making a big mistake. You can't really be serious." Even as I said it, I realized how weak it sounded.

She rattled off four or five cases that I'd interfered with. Shit!

"That's just for starters. We have lots more."

Stone-faced, I tried to project calm, confident control. Inwardly, I was a whirlwind of confusion. My vision blurred and my limbs trembled. I folded my hands in my lap to control them. I needed to urinate.

"In case you're wondering, Putino, nobody in the office will be sorry to see you gone. I've never met anyone who is despised by as many people as you are."

Who cares? Did she think I was running for class president?

"So everybody in the office knew about this investigation except me? I find that difficult to believe."

"That's the way we wanted it. Nobody alerted you because everybody wants you out."

In the end, I agreed to resign. I didn't know how much they knew, but it was obvious they had more than enough to indict and convict.

"Fine," I said. "If that's the way you want it. It makes no difference to me. It'll be your loss, you'll see." I knew I sounded pathetic.

An hour later I handed in a letter of resignation and cleaned out my desk. Nobody said anything to me. No tearful good-byes, no warm handshakes, no farewell dinner. I don't know if it was my imagination, but I thought I saw some worried faces, heard a few suppressed giggles. Well, the hell with them.

I told everybody that I'd gotten into an argument with Olzewski and couldn't put up with the bureaucratic bullshit anymore, so I'd resigned. That sounded believable to people who knew me. It was OK, really. I would still get my pension, still had my medical insurance, and still had my buried treasure. I'd be more than comfortable and I'd have time to write my story. What the hell, it wasn't that bad.

Of course I told Lena the truth. She was my partner in crime, so to speak. Her first words, when I finished telling her about my sit-down with Olzewski, were calm and reassuring. "Relax, Vittorio. Everything will work out for you."

She knew exactly what to say to make me feel better. I knew right then that she really loved me. A strange thing happened: My eyes filled up with tears. I don't know where the hell they came from. I mean, I don't cry. I never cry. But right then, my chest heaved and I held back a sob. Lena hugged me then and I let myself go. Even though Lena's much smaller than I am, she felt larger. I felt protected and safe.

The worst part is knowing that, somewhere in the bowels of the Department of Justice, there's a file with my name on it — and in it is enough shit to send me to prison for the rest of my life. I get nauseous every time I think of it. Sure, Olzewski gave me a deal, but how do I know if, sometime down the road, someone might decide to come after me? What if some whistleblower releases my file and shows John Q. Public just how corrupt the Department of Justice is? I'd be screwed. For the time being, I have to sit on my money. I can't risk giving the IRS — which is not part of Olzewski's deal — any excuses to come after me.

It's at times like this that I wonder what it was all for. Just so no one would call me Rat Face anymore? Is that what it comes down to? For all I know, that's exactly what that bitch Olzewski is calling me right now. And the others in the office who I manipulated with favors and threats — what are they calling me now, with their jobs and reputations, maybe prison time, on the line?

But does it even matter? Who cares what they call me? I never cared what anybody thought, as long as I got to do my thing. Power, that's all that matters. Power is everything. And now? I'm freer than I've ever been. I do what I want and I go where I want. I've got money, I've got Lena, and at 63, I still control my life. I've still got that power. I still win. So fuck them all. And after I'm dead? Who cares what anyone will think or how I'll be remembered? I'd be dead, so who the fuck cares?

Anyway, Lena is trying to cheer me up with this party. Good old Lena. She turned out to be more than just a pretty face. I think she's happy. She enjoys running her gymnastics school and we have a damned good life together. We travel a lot and we eat out often at expensive restaurants. We make trips to Vegas and the Bahamas a couple of times a year to gamble. She has more clothes and jewelry than she can wear. We have a nice home and two big cars. The house looks really good from the outside, but it's on the inside that I sunk all the money. Inside, everything is top of the line, but I can't be seen as living too high on the hog. I don't want to attract attention from the IRS. We have no financial worries. If anything should come up (like having to hire a lawyer), I know the money is there. So everything is good — although sometimes I miss the satisfaction of making the big deals, the intrigue, the mind games. I miss exercising power.

13

One day shortly after my premature ejection from the prosecutor's office, I was having dinner with Tony at the Saloon on Seventh Street. Describing my close call with Olzewski reawakened my anxiety over the possibility of having to go to trial.

"Yeah, I know what you mean," Tony admitted. "I spent a bundle you wouldn't believe getting out from under that FBI investigation a few years back."

"That seemed to drag on forever," I said.

Tony had never gone into the details of the FBI investigation into his activities before and during his time in the Office of Legal Counsel, and I knew better than to ask. Most of what I knew came from reading the papers. Basically, it boiled down to allegations of fraud, using his office for corrupt purposes, obstructing justice, bribery, insider trading, etc. In the end, he got off — except it cost him a fortune, not to mention the emotional stress. I hoped I would never have to go through that.

"In some ways, Vito, I feel like it's still not over. The feds weren't happy that I was never indicted and I think they still monitor every freaking move I make. I hear clicks on my phone line or see an SUV tailing me or parked across the street and it gives me agita, you know?"

"So you think they're still watching you?"

Tony shrugged. "Better safe than sorry, you know."

And right after he said that, who comes into the restaurant and over to our table but Carmine Belloni.

"Sorry I'm late," he says, shaking Tony's hand. And he sits down. I'm in shock. Tony is playing it safe? He thinks the feds are watching him and he's hanging out with Belloni?

I stared at Tony. "This is playing it safe?"

Tony and Carmine smiled like two kids sharing a secret.

"Vito, I told you I'm doing some consulting for the Romano Corporation. The feds know that. I'm on retainer as an attorney. It's legit. Carmine works for them, so in effect, he's my client. The feds know that, too. Our conversations are privileged. Besides, Carmine isn't a convicted felon."

"Ha! And neither are you," Carmine barked.

"So there's no law against us getting together for dinner. And you're retired now, Vito, so you're not under any restrictions. Relax. We're just old friends enjoying each other's company."

I sat back in my chair, dumbfounded. After more than 20 years of looking over my shoulder, being careful, being secretive, the idea of meeting out in the open like this was totally disorienting. And these two guys, both in their 70s, were still playing cops and robbers — and laughing about it.

"I don't know if I'll ever get used to this. It just doesn't feel right."

It was that evening that Tony filled me in on his long family history with Carmine. They'd been helping each other out for so long, they were closer than brothers.

i4

Note: *This last section was written by Vincent Putino, based upon personal observations and interviews with Vito's wife and daughters.*

Vito's birthday dinner was actually held three days late, on Saturday, Oct. 10, 2015. At 5 o'clock his daughter, Marie, and her husband, Louis, arrived at Vito's home in South Philly. Their BMW pulled in to the driveway and Vito heard Lena open the front door to greet them. At 30, Marie was beautiful. Vito and Lydia did make two stunning daughters. Louis, also bright and good-looking, was a good match for Marie. They made a handsome couple — both attractive, well-educated, successful attorneys.

Vito stood up to embrace his daughter and shake his son-in-law's hand. Vito had never been a complete social misfit and, besides, he liked them both.

"How about a drink," he said. "Let's give this celebration a little head start."

"Sure, Vito. I'll have a beer," Louis said.

Marie and Lena opted for wine. Vito decided to have another martini instead of his usual vodka and tonic. Actually, since he stopped working and no longer felt it necessary to keep a clear head, Vito had been indulging himself more. That day, he'd started early.

"This is my birthday and I'm 63 years old — although, if I'm honest, physically, I feel much older."

Like his mother, Vito had developed rheumatoid arthritis and moving around was often painful. And in the spring of 2014 — just three months before Olzewski lowered the guillotine — he'd suffered a heart attack.

"Inside, in my head, I'm still young," he went on. "I'm still Lena's stallion — but not physically. That heart attack slowed me down and scared the shit out of me. Did I say slowed me down? It stopped me in my fucking tracks!" He laughed excitedly at his self-deprecatory statements.

Louis broke the tension. "So, Vito, what are you doing with yourself these days?" he asked as he sat down on the sofa with his beer.

"Vito is writing his memoir," Lena volunteered.

"Is that so? Well, you've had an interesting life. How's it coming along?"

"It's nowhere near finished," Vito said. "Lena thinks it's a waste of time."

"No I don't," Lena objected. "It's just that you're spending so much time at it. He stays up half the night writing. He's not getting enough sleep," she confided.

"I get all I need," Vito protested.

"He has more energy than I do," she said. "I don't know how he does it. He doesn't even nap."

"That doesn't sound so good, Dad," Marie cautioned. "You're not 20 anymore, you know."

"Don't worry about me, Marie. This stallion isn't ready for pasture yet. You guys act as if once someone turns 60 they have one foot in the grave and the other on a banana peel. What do you want me to do? Sit around watching *National Geographic* on TV and twiddling my thumbs? The truth is I have more energy now than I ever had. I don't need a lot of rest and, like Lena said, some nights I don't sleep at all. I stay up all night thinking and remembering and writing. Writing gives me energy. It excites me. I feel driven. I keep remembering things and I have to write them down before I forget.

"If I'm really honest," he continued, getting more wound up, "I would like my daughters, or maybe someday my grandchildren, to read what I've written. It would make me feel good to know that someone in my family was actually interested in what I had to say and what I did. Even more importantly, it would be gratifying to know that all of you were interested in knowing me, who I am on the inside, my private thoughts."

He was quiet for a moment, seemingly lost in thought.

"But then again, I don't know if I'll ever let these pages see the light of day," he went on. "There are too many secrets that maybe shouldn't be told, too many big shot names. Boy, would there be hell to pay if some of those names got out. People could get killed. No, the truth is I'm probably writing it down just for myself, maybe to clarify my own thinking about who I am and what my life has really been about. I'd like to think my life had some significance — but really, are any of us any more significant than an ant?"

Vito spoke rapidly and gestured expansively. Marie and Louis looked at each other awkwardly. Lena attempted to interrupt him, but he kept running on.

"That was hard for me to admit. I certainly want to be more significant than a fucking ant. But am I? What have I been doing for 63 years? Who've I been? I need to accept the reality of my life story. I need to embrace who I've been and who I am. And so, in my writing, I'm trying to be as brutally honest with myself as I can. Sure, I've made a ton of money, but what good is it doing me?"

Suddenly, he turned silent and morose. Lena steered the conversation in another direction. Vito sat back and sipped his martini.

Catherine and her husband, Logan, arrived shortly afterward. Logan, between careers, filled his time by working in a restaurant. Cathy, an elementary school teacher, was as beautiful and bright as Marie, but more inhibited and shy. Vito said he thought she took to Logan because of his extroversion. They each gave Vito a hug, and Lena got a glass of wine for Cathy and a bottle of beer for Logan. Lively conversation filled the room, and Vito said he was surprised to be deriving so much enjoyment from the fact that they were all together.

"Imagine how my mother would have enjoyed this moment: her son and her granddaughters gathered together — a warm family scene." No one was sure if he was being sincere or sarcastic. He had a strange smile on his face.

"You know, you girls never mention your mother to me, and I appreciate that. I get annoyed when I have to think about Lydia. But I do wonder how often you get together with her. This is the first time in months that you've bothered to visit me. If you do come in to town to visit Lydia on Delancey Street — in that beautiful mansion she swindled me out of — then you're only a couple of miles from me. You'd think you'd want to visit your father, wouldn't you?"

Marie and Cathy exchanged a pained look then turned away. They stole glances at their husbands and at Lena. Logan and Louis were not sure whether to confront Vito and defend their wives. Lena shook her head to indicate they should let it go and she asked the girls to help her in the kitchen.

Logan asked how Vito was enjoying his retirement.

Vito glared at him. "Retirement? As if I wanted to stop working, as if I wanted to leave the office and turn it over to some asshole who doesn't know what the hell he's doing! Who has no concept of the power inherent in the position. As if I'd voluntarily give that up. How the hell do you think my *retirement* is going?"

Vito got up and made himself another martini. When he came back, he announced, "I didn't retire. They fucking pushed me out."

The silence, as they say, was deafening.

Lena hurried in from the kitchen and broke the spell by asking Logan how his restaurant was doing. Soon everyone was chatting again, and Vito withdrew into himself. It was if he weren't there; the whole family assiduously avoided looking at him. He seemed lost in thought, as if he were engaging in some internal dialogue about what he suspected was *really* being expressed and taking place before him — what people *really* meant.

The telephone rang and Lena answered it. A few moments later, she handed the phone to Vito.

"Is this Vittorio Putino?" asked a young voice.

"Who's this?"

"My name is Walter Reynolds."

A thousand thoughts must have gone through Vito's head.

Vito glanced around the room. Everyone was engaged in conversation. Lena snuck a peak at him, raising her eyebrows.

"Walter, yes, I know who you are. What a surprise."

"My mother suggested that I contact you."

"Oh, why did she do that?"

"She said that you were — are — my biological father."

"She told you that?"

"Yes. Actually, just a few days ago. It was after my father died, last week."

"Your father died?"

"Yes."

"I'm sorry to hear that. How is your mother?"

"She's OK. She's depressed, of course, about my father." He paused. "I was wondering if I could meet you," Walter said.

"Yes. That would be good. Perhaps we can get together for lunch sometime."

"Well, I'm here in Philly for just a short time, for a job interview. I was hoping I might be able to see you today."

"Today? I'm sorry, but today is impossible. When are you leaving Philadelphia?"

"Tomorrow morning. My flight leaves at 10 o'clock."

"That doesn't give us much time, I'm afraid. I assume you're going back to Washington."

"No, my mom and I are living out in California now."

"Oh. Well, I don't know what to say, Walter. Today is very complicated. Maybe, if you get that job you're interviewing for, we can make it another time."

There was silence on the other end.

"I knew I should have contacted you last week, Mr. Putino, but I was too nervous and kept putting it off. Yeah, I guess it will have to be another time."

"Write me," Vito said. "You have my address?"

"Yes."

"Good. We'll stay in touch."

"OK," he said. "I'll do that."

"Walter, I'm glad you called and I'm sorry we can't meet today. Really."

"I understand. Thanks. I'll be in touch."

"OK, then. Good-bye."

"Wait," Walter said. "I should have told you, I got your phone number from your cousin, Vincent Putino. He was the only V. Putino in the phone book, so I called, hoping it might be you. Anyway, he mentioned you're having dinner at a restaurant today. I wonder if it would be an imposition if I dropped by for a little bit."

Vito thought it over for a few moments.

"OK," he said. "You know where Dante and Luigi's is?"

"I'm sure I can find it easily enough."

"All right, then. Come for dinner." Vito told him what time. "I'll see you there."

When he put the phone down, Lena appeared at his side. "Who was that? You look so serious."

"The son of an old friend. Actually, *my* son by an old friend. He's in town and looked me up. Vinny gave him our number."

Lena raised an eyebrow.

"He's only in town today," Vito told her, "so I invited him for dinner."

"Ah, so this is the son that Lydia made all the fuss about?"

Vittorio nodded and sipped his drink.

Lena looked at Vito's daughters. "This should be interesting," she smiled.

Lena's brother, Rudy, and his wife, Lucy, came in and handed a stack of mail to Vito.

"The mailman was just delivering this and I thought we'd bring it in for you," she said as she kissed him on the cheek.

"Thanks," he said and walked to his desk in the next room. As he flipped through the envelopes, he noticed one was from the IRS.

"Shit," he murmured, tearing it open.

Vittorio couldn't believe his eyes. He was being called in for an audit regarding unreported income during the 20-year period he'd been employed in the prosecutor's office and in the Pennsylvania Attorney General's office. Including penalties and interests, they claimed he owed more than $10 million! His knees went weak and his face turned ashen. Lena rushed to him.

"What's the matter? You look sick. Are you all right?"

He handed her the letter. She read it and leaned against the desk. Then she read it again.

"This is bullshit. Let Tony handle it for you. He's a lawyer, he'll know what to do."

"I'm a lawyer, too."

"This is his specialty. He set everything up for you. Let him handle it. Don't even think about it. There's no way, Vito, that the IRS expects to collect this much money from you. Let Tony deal with it and let it go."

"You're right," he said.

The limos arrived and everyone piled in and drove to the restaurant.

15

I was at the restaurant a little early, nursing a vermouth on the rocks at the small, intimate bar and waiting for my cousin, Vito, to arrive. I recognized Anthony Savona as he entered and I nodded in greeting. Tony was an example of local boy makes good. He'd not only been a successful lawyer here in the city, but had managed to become a national figure, a member of the president's legal team. There had always been rumors of a tangential link to some Philadelphia mob members and, in my mind, rumors of this type were generally assumed to be true, whether or not there was evidence to back them up.

I'd lived much of my life in South Philadelphia and it's impossible to avoid hearing gossip relating to the Philadelphia mob. Almost everyone knows a relative or neighbor who is alleged to have been connected somehow. In fact there was some history in this very restaurant: an assassination, one crime faction attempting to eradicate another. Then I recalled that Vittorio had participated in the trials that had followed in its wake.

Savona and I made small talk while we waited for Vito and his family. Tony ordered a Negroni. Although probably in his late 70s, he still wore a made-to-order suit with a European cut, tasteful tie, and pocket handkerchief; his still-thick, white hair was brushed straight back, and even his nails were manicured.

Vito arrived. I hadn't seen him since his wedding to Lena, and he looked older — a bit heavier but at the same time more frail. We gave each other a perfunctory hug and exchanged a few pleasantries. Tony and I both wished him a happy birthday. My first impression was that Vito appeared happy and uncharacteristically expansive. Soon a waiter led us into a private room, where a table was set for 10. Place cards indicated our assigned seating: Vito sat at the head of the table, with Lena to his right. Louis sat to Lena's right, then Marie, Rudy, and Lucy. To Vito's left were Cathy, Logan, me, then Tony.

Before we had a chance to sit down, Vito pulled Tony to the side.

"Tony, I got a fucking letter from the IRS today."

"They sent you a refund in honor of your birthday?" Tony quipped.

"I wish. Unreported income covering over 20 years, plus interest and penalties."

Tony looked heavenward. "How much?"

"They're asking for over $10 million."

Tony looked down and whistled. "OK," he whispered. "I'll take care of it. Call me Monday and we'll set up a time for you to come in to the office. We'll go over the letter and see exactly what they've got. This will probably turn into a long, drawn-out negotiation, so don't worry about it, Vito. Relax. I've got this. OK?"

Vito let out a big breath. "All right. I'll call you Monday morning."

"Good. Now just enjoy your party. There's nothing you have to do. I'll take care of everything."

I watched Vito's face and could tell what he was thinking: *Yeah, sure. Relax. Everything will turn out all right.* But I knew he wouldn't be able to relax. Vittorio was congenitally tight and tense. He didn't know how to relax.

Once we were seated, a waiter appeared and poured prosecco for each of us. Another waiter put two large platters of antipasto on the table, while another brought four baskets of Italian bread. I heard Cathy, who is usually shy and inhibited, speaking to her father.

"Dad, why don't you ever call me?"

"What do you mean, why don't I call you? Why don't you call me? I'm your father, for Christ's sake. *I'm* the father, Cathy, not you."

"I know that. I have called you, but you never call me back."

"Bullshit. I've called you plenty of times."

"Yeah, I had hoped so. But you never have."

"Cathy, I'm the parent. It's your place to call me. All the times you've come into Philly from Jersey to see your mother, never once have you stopped by my house to say hello."

"First of all, Dad, Mom invites us. You and Lena have never invited us. Second, going to see you after being with Mom would be too much stress. I couldn't handle that."

"I don't see why not. And besides, you're my daughter. You don't need an invitation from me to visit. How do you think that makes me feel, that you don't want to see me?"

100

"Dad! I didn't say we didn't want to see you. Why do you always do that?"

"What?"

"I asked why you don't call, and now we're talking about how neglected you feel."

"Well, I do feel neglected, by both you and Marie." He said this loudly enough that Marie easily heard him — well, we all did. My cousin's demeanor was completely out of character from what I'd remembered. He was more excitable, louder and more expansive, much less reserved than usual. It was unlike him to be so revealing of his feelings.

"But that's all right. I don't complain." Vito continued. "I recognize that you have your own lives — lives that I made possible — and I try not to interfere. I give you the gift of freedom. I don't try to control your lives."

Marie chimed in with her two cents. "Dad, there's a difference between not interfering and ignoring us. I'm not complaining either, but Cathy is right, you've always ignored us."

"Bullshit! How can you say that?"

Lena leaned toward Cathy. "Girls, it's your father's birthday. It's his day. We're all here to celebrate and have a good time. This isn't the time or place to start an argument with him."

Logan put his hand on his wife's shoulder. "Lena's right, Cathy. Let it go. Eat your antipasto."

Cathy turned to her husband. "Logan, there's no need for you to be uncomfortable. My father and I are just talking."

"Lena's right," Vito said. "Let's just have a good time. I'm glad you came, all of you. I'm glad you're here. God knows how many more birthdays I'll have, so let's enjoy ourselves."

He picked up a bottle of prosecco from an ice bucket. "Here, fill your glasses." It came across more as a belligerent order than a conciliatory invitation.

As I glanced around the table, I saw Rudy peeking at his wife and shaking his head. Vito also noticed Rudy's gesture and his face grew red. It was obvious there was no love lost between the two brothers-in-law. I glanced to my left and gathered that Tony was also taking in this display of familial love.

"What are you shaking your head at, Rudy?" Vito bellowed. "Families have discussions. Your family is so perfect?"

"I didn't say a word, Vito," Rudy retorted.

"You don't have to. Your hostility is written all over you."

"OK, Vito. Enough."

Lena was asserting herself, trying to not let the situation get out of control. I think Vittorio counted on her for that, indulging himself because he knew she'd rein him in if he said too much. While the other guests deliberately turned their attention away from my cousin, I focused on him, and I heard him whisper to Lena.

"You know why the girls don't want to see me? It's because I'm always accusing them of something. I'm always criticizing and finding fault, picking a fight with them like I do with your asshole brother. And you know what? I just realized — that's exactly what my father used to do to me. Am I that much like him? How the fuck did that happen?"

He seemed lost in thought. At first, I thought he was sharing those reflective thoughts with Lena, but then I wondered if he'd just been talking out loud to himself, engaging in a soliloquy as if he were alone with his thoughts.

"I'm going to say hello to my cousin," he said suddenly. Lena grasped his hand and squeezed it.

"I'll be back soon," he said.

Vito made his way around the table and leaned in between Tony and me.

"Vincenzo, have you met Tony yet?"

"Sure, we're old friends by now," I said.

"Vito, you never told me you had a cousin," Tony said.

"I don't think Vito talks much about his family," I said.

"No, I don't."

"How are you related?" Tony asked.

"It's complicated. Vito and I are really second cousins. Our grandfathers were brothers," I explained. "Vito's father and my father were cousins, but they never really got along, so our two families weren't close. The truth is, I never really liked Vito or his family when we were younger."

Vito appeared shocked by what I'd said, and I immediately wondered what had prompted me to be so impulsively honest. But then he nodded as though he realized I had spoken the truth — and he had felt the same way about me.

Before my father died, the two families used to visit occasionally. Because I'm five years older than Vito, much of the time I regarded him as too young to be a companion. But as a little kid, I'm sure Vito looked up to me. Maybe it was after the two families had drifted apart that we began to feel some resentment toward each other. Maybe he was just aping his father and painting everyone in my family with the same black brush, but I knew he didn't like me at the time.

"But we've gotten closer over the years, right?" Vito said.

I looked at him. Was he serious? Closer? But it was his birthday and he was springing for dinner, so I went along.

"Yeah. With your parents' funerals and your weddings and the girls' graduations and weddings, we've buried the hatchet," I said, and held up my glass to salute him — not so much in friendship or admiration, but in recognition that we'd both passed from one status to another. We were no longer active enemies or antagonists, but simply two tired old men who recognized that it required way too much energy to continue holding on to useless grudges.

"*Salute*," Vito said, and raised his glass in return.

The waiters started bringing the soup, *tortellini en brodo*, and Vito returned to his seat at the head of the table. I felt badly that I'd admitted to not liking him very much. I could tell from his frown and clenched jaw that he was still burning about it. Given how unexpectedly open and expressive he'd been, I suspected that, at some point, he'd make me pay for it. I wasn't sure if his surprising volubility was due to his having consumed too much alcohol or if something else was going on with him. Usually, Vito was sternly poker-faced and played everything tight to his vest, but not today.

I stole a glance at Lena. She was focused on Vito, as if keeping his attention on her would prevent further arguments with his guests. As I watched them, I heard him talking to her.

"I know I'm probably half drunk, but I'm really pissed at Vinny and the girls. Who did he think he was calling me a prick — and right in front of my friends, and at *my* birthday dinner! And Cathy, saying I never gave a shit about her or her sister. After all I've spent on them, the schools, the European skiing trips, vacations, clothes ... "

Cathy, who was sitting next to Vito, had her head lowered and appeared mesmerized by her soup. There was no way she could avoid hearing what he'd said to Lena. I glanced at Marie and caught her looking at her sister and then at Logan, which is when she noticed me watching her. She gave a slight shrug of her shoulders and rolled her eyes as if to say, "What can you expect?"

103

Vito turned from his wife and again confronted his daughter. "Cathy, why did you say I never gave a shit about you? That's something your mother would say, but I'm really offended hearing such crap come out of your mouth."

Cathy shook her head and sat back. Marie came to her rescue. "Dad," she pleaded, "no one said you didn't give a shit about us or that you never did anything for us. Look, we're glad to be here. We're really happy you and Lena invited us. We were only saying it would be great if we heard from you even more. We miss seeing you guys. So we're glad we're here for this celebration."

I smiled to myself in admiration of Marie's diplomacy. I'm sure she's a successful lawyer.

"That's what I've been saying," Vito persisted. "Wouldn't it be fantastic if you made an effort to come down more often? You don't need to be a stranger to your own father, do you?"

"No, Dad. And we don't feel like strangers to you and Lena. We'll call more often. I promise."

"Don't just call, damn it! Anybody can call. I want you to come. Both of you. I want you to make the effort to visit me before I die."

"You're not dying," Cathy said.

"How do you know? You're a doctor now? You got promoted from the third grade and now you're a fucking cardiologist? I had a heart attack, a serious heart attack."

"Your father is only joking," Lena interjected.

"I only meant to say that you look good," Cathy clarified. "You seem fit and healthy. I'm happy to see that."

Cathy searched their faces for some sign of reassurance that she would be forgiven.

"Right!" Vito said, putting his glass down forcefully on the table. "I was just teasing you."

"I love you, Dad," Cathy said, reaching over to kiss her father on his cheek.

"Well," he said, looking mollified at last, "you girls know I love you, too. You're everything to me."

Logan, who was sitting between his wife and me, pressed his knee against mine and I returned the undercover communication. Louis nodded at me from across the table, as if to say, "We all know what an asshole Vito is. Why the fuck are we even here? Why are we letting this asshole get away with this shit?" I wondered how much longer I'd be required to sit here and put up with his nonsense. Vito had been a mean, sneaky kid, a repulsive cockroach. Then he grew up and turned into a bully. The ensuing 50 years hadn't changed him.

I turned to my left and tried to insinuate myself into the conversation Tony was having with Lucy and Rudy. I needed to distance myself from Vito's pettiness. It made me feel unclean. Tony, who was recounting a story from his White House days, had Lucy and Rudy totally entranced. Before he was able to finish his story, a young man entered the room and I watched as he walked over to Vito.

"Mr. Putino? I'm Walter."

Vito looked up from his seat and cracked a brief smile. He stood up and, putting an arm around the young man, led him a few steps away from the table. As the waiter set a place for Walter at the end of the table, Vito addressed us. "Everybody, this young man is Walter Reynolds. He's the son of an old friend of mine, someone I used to work with in the U.S. attorney's office."

Then after a brief pause, he added, "He's also my son."

I was shocked. When Walter had spoken to me earlier, he had given no indication why he wanted to contact Vittorio. He'd sounded so disappointed at the possibility of not meeting Vito that I impulsively mentioned the dinner and gave him the number.

Looking at the embarrassed boy, I found myself searching for signs of a family resemblance. Walter was tall and big-boned, with thick, dark hair, and in all those ways bore no resemblance at all to Vittorio. But he had the bright blue eyes and thin straight nose of his father, and I realized he was, indeed, Vittorio's son.

Vito kept his eyes down and focused on his soup. Everyone else stared at Walter, waiting for some explanation for this unexpected and awkward situation. Marie and Louis sat across from me and I looked to them for a reaction.

Marie shook her head in disbelief. She glanced at her sister and then at her father, who was oblivious. She turned suddenly to Walter and said loudly, "Hello, Walter. I'm your sister — half-sister — Marie. And this is your other half-sister, Cathy." Her voice was icy cold.

Walter mumbled, "Glad to meet you," and sat down at the end of the table. Ever the diplomat, Tony turned to Walter, offering his hand. "I'm Anthony Savona."

Lucy and Rudy followed Tony's lead and introduced themselves. I was so fascinated by the turn of events that I didn't even think of introducing myself. And when I did think of it, I rationalized that I didn't want to barrage the boy with more names that he'd forget anyway. Instead, I observed. Neither Louis nor Logan said anything to Walter, nor did Lena or Cathy. The tension was palpable.

Finally, Marie spoke up. "Tell me, Dad, why you've chosen to create this awkward situation. After all these years of trying to keep him a secret, why today? Why now?"

All eyes went to Vittorio. He looked down the table and, with a barely concealed malicious grin, said, "Walter, tell them why you're here."

Put on the spot, Walter blushed and finished swallowing the food he had just put into his mouth.

"Yes, Walter, tell us why you're here today," Marie urged.

Walter looked at Marie and they locked eyes. He lowered his head for a few moments, obviously trying to come to some decision. I thought if I were in his predicament, I might choose this moment to leave and save myself further embarrassment. But, eventually, he looked up again and spoke.

"I apologize for intruding on a family event. I know I'm not a real member of this family. In fact, I only recently learned that Mr. Putino is my biological father. I happened to be in town for a couple of days and I hoped to meet him."

He then directed his attention to Vito, who was still doing his best to maintain some distance from the scene.

"Naturally, I had some curiosity, a lot of curiosity, about who you are. I felt I needed to meet you. I don't know what I expected, or if I even expected anything at all. I just wanted to see you. I didn't mean to intrude on a family dinner."

I was curious, too. I figured, what the hell.

"Excuse me, Walter, I'm Vincent Putino. We talked very briefly on the phone earlier today. Your news is quite unexpected — at least to some of us. I'd be obliged if you — or Vito — would fill us in. How did you come to learn that you're Vittorio's son?"

"Vincent," Lena said quickly, "I don't think this is the time to go into ancient history. It's enough that Vito has acknowledged the young man. It's awkward for all of us. I'm sure it's uncomfortable for you, Walter, as well as for your sisters. Please, can we just try to enjoy this celebration?"

106

Marie got up abruptly. "This is too much for me. I'm sorry, Dad. I can't do this." She turned to Louis. "Come on. I want to leave."

Louis rose from his chair. Turning to Vito and Lena, he said, "Inviting him was not a great idea." A master of understatement, I thought.

Marie looked across the table at Cathy and Logan. Cathy nodded. "I'm sorry, Dad. I'll talk to you soon."

As she stood up from her chair, Vito reached out and grabbed Cathy's wrist. "Sit down," he ordered.

He turned to Marie. "You too. Sit down, for Christ's sake. What do you think you're doing? Jesus, it's not like you didn't know about him. Why the hell do you think your mother and I got divorced? That's all she could talk about. Now sit down and stop making such a fuss. He's just a kid, for crying out loud. He didn't do anything to you. Jesus, give him a break, OK?"

Everybody froze. Finally, Marie sat back down. Her sister and their husbands followed suit.

"Look," Vito addressed the table, "the kid wanted to meet me and I wanted to meet him. Don't tell me you girls were never curious about who he was. So now he's here. We all get to meet each other. Even cousin Vinny gets to meet a new member of the family. So relax and let's enjoy ourselves."

"Jesus, I'm really sorry. I knew I shouldn't have come." Walter rose to go.

"Oh, sit down, Walter," Lena said. "There's nothing to be gained by your leaving now. Like Vito said, we're all curious, not just you. So now you're here. Relax. Eat. *Mangia.*"

The tension around the table subsided a bit and, as the pasta course was served, we all sought refuge in our ravioli. Lucy made an effort to normalize the situation and asked Walter to tell us a little about himself.

"I'm not sure what to say," he started. "Like Mr. Putino said, I'm only in town until tomorrow. I was here for a job interview and I'm leaving early tomorrow morning to go back to California."

"I'm curious about your mother," Marie stated.

"My mother lives in California. I live with her for now, since I finished college and until I get a job."

"Yes, but what's she like? What's her name?"

"Carol. Carol Reynolds. What's she like? I don't know. She's my mother. She's nice. She's a great person. She's a lawyer, or was; she's retired now."

Surprisingly, Vito entered the conversation. "Walter, how did your mother come to tell you that I'm your father?"

Walter scarfed down the last of his ravioli and wiped his mouth. "Well, my father died last week. He'd had cancer for a long time and was in hospice, so we knew he was dying. My mom and I were in the kitchen making supper one night. My father was upstairs in bed. And, I don't know, I just asked her why he never seemed to care that much about me. I mean, he was usually pretty nice, but he was always distant, as though I was some neighbor's kid who just happened to be in the house. He was polite to me, but never warm. And she just told me."

He paused and looked around the table, clearly reckoning with his own swirling emotions.

"She said he'd always doubted that I was his. And so I asked her if he was right, and she nodded. She said she'd always denied it to him, and asked me please not to tell him, to let him die without having to deal with that. After he died, she told me that when she'd been working in Philadelphia she'd had an affair and gotten pregnant. And she gave me your name."

Vito nodded. Everyone at the table was silent. Finally, Marie turned to her father.

"Are there anymore half-siblings out there we should know about? Mom always suspected there were lots of little Vitos running around."

Vito scoffed. "Why am I not surprised? Your mother has accused me of all sorts of things. In her eyes, I'm the monster of the western world, a fertile Godzilla, leaving dozens of reptilian replicas populating the world. No. To answer your insulting question, Marie — no. Walter is — as far as I know — the only child, other than you and your sister, I have fathered."

While Walter had been speaking, I couldn't help but observe the behavior of everyone else at the table. Lena and Vito were focused on him with rapt attention. Louis and Logan averted their eyes, as though the scene were too personal — like walking in on a couple having sex or a person sitting on a toilet. Tony watched the young man like a trained lawyer scrutinizing a witness, storing up information to be used whenever the opportunity might present itself.

The two girls were the most interesting. They studied their half-brother, hung on his every word, inspected every facial twitch; but then, as if they felt guilty for having any interest in someone they were supposed to hate — what their mother would have wished — they glanced furtively around the table before being drawn back to the intriguing intruder.

I also took stock of myself. I wondered what was going through Vito's mind as he listened to this young man — his son! — talk about his mother and the dying man who'd raised him. What was my cousin thinking?

I turned to Vittorio. "Pardon me for asking, but I can't help wondering what you were experiencing as you listened to Walter, your son, telling you this." Of course, I spoke for the whole table, and everyone waited for his response.

"You really want to know? All right, I'll tell you. I'm sitting here, 63 years old — not really that old, but this body's not what it used to be — and I'm remembering who I was 22 years ago when my son was conceived."

He turned to Lena. "You didn't know me then. You thought I was a bull when we started seeing each other. You should have seen me then. And you, young man, you should have seen your mother then. I know she's your mother, but she is also a woman — and 22 years ago she was a hot-blooded, passionate woman. So that's what I'm thinking, Vincent. Walter reminds me of my past, how full my life was. Exciting and dangerous. I was a fucking powerhouse then. Look at me now. Except for this woman here, my wife, Lena, everything has turned to shit. My own daughters don't respect me. The fucking IRS wants to steal everything from me. I can't fucking move without pain. Even my own heart is betraying me, giving up on me before its time. But here is young Walter, a part of me. Look at him: big, tall, handsome. He oozes vital youth, strength, and energy. You see those eyes? Look. He's got my eyes, and my nose, my father's nose, the Putino nose. Through him maybe part of me will go on."

Marie slammed her fist on the table. "Thanks a lot! You call us shit and then gaze lovingly at a person you've never even met before?"

"Who the hell do you think you're talking to?" Vito bellowed. "You have no regard for me. You accused me of treating you like shit. You've dismissed and discounted everything I've ever done for you. Nothing I ever did for you matters. You've never cared about me. You have no fucking idea who I am or what I've accomplished in my life."

"Jesus," Cathy muttered, "maybe Mom was right after all to ..."

Vito's head swiveled from Marie to Cathy. "What are you talking about?"

"Nothing," she said and searched reflexively for her sister.

Vito caught it and turned back to Marie. "What?" he demanded.

We all noticed Marie's brief headshake in Cathy's direction.

"What's going on? What? Tell me."

"It's nothing," Cathy said, attempting to rescue her sister.

Now it was Marie's turn to be protective. "Just what you mentioned before, about the IRS."

"What about it? What do you know about that?"

"Nothing," Marie said, looking down at the table. "Just what you said before."

"What's Lydia got to do with it?"

"Nothing. How should I know?"

Vito stared at Marie for a few moments longer, then turned to Cathy. He leaned back and stared at her, tapping a spoon on the table. Everyone at the table sat in stunned silence — except perhaps for me. I wasn't embarrassed by this family drama. This was the dysfunctional Putino family style I'd always remembered. To me it was entertainment, like watching a play. I was curious what would happen next.

Vito shifted his gaze along the table, past Logan and me to Tony.

"Tony, my dear friend and mentor. My teacher and godfather to my two daughters. By the way, Walter, I'm sorry I never got to pick a godfather for you. I probably would have selected the devoted Mr. Savona here. Anyway, Tony, might you know anything about this? Do you have any idea at all what my two lovely, innocent daughters are referring to?"

"Vito," Anthony began unctuously, greasing the way for what was to follow. If I could see bullshit coming, Vito had to see it, too. I noticed that all his antennae were up, all his senses primed, like a wild animal at its most dangerous. I could feel the room hum with electricity.

"How should I have any idea what's going on?" Tony asked. "If this is about the IRS, I knew nothing until you told me about it earlier. Besides, Vito, whatever's happening between you and my goddaughters, I don't think this is either the time or the place."

"Oh, but it is. It is. This is the *only* time and place I get to see my loving daughters. So don't try to distract me. Don't try to get me off track here. I just want to know, Tony, my friend, how you came to advise my ex-wife to fuck me this way. Tell me. Did she invite you over to Delancey Street? Did she drag you up to her bedroom? Load you up with wine? How did she get you to help her with this?"

"Vito, you're drunk." Tony pushed his chair back and slammed his napkin on the table.

"Don't fucking leave the table," Vito growled. "I swear, Tony, don't fucking leave. I am serious." His voice trembled with rage. Tony remained seated. Vito turned back to Cathy and put his hand on her arm.

"As you can see, Sweetheart, I am deadly serious about this and I will not stop until I get the answers I'm looking for. Now why don't you help put a stop to this nonsense and tell me about your mother's involvement?"

Cathy looked at her husband and then at her sister. "You're right," she admitted. "Mom did contact the IRS."

"When?"

"I don't know. Maybe six months ago, maybe longer."

"What else?"

"She said you'd made a lot of money illegally, and she was going to see that you got what you deserved."

"And what role did Tony play in this?"

"I don't know. Mom only mentioned that she'd talked to him about it one time when he was over for dinner."

"Dinner?"

Cathy nodded. "Uncle Tony goes to Mom's for dinner fairly often."

"Oh, is that so? Well good for Uncle Tony. He always did enjoy Lydia's cooking. Didn't you, Tony? So, my friend, what have you got to say for yourself?"

Tony shook his head and looked first at the two girls and then at Walter. I assumed he was weighing just how much to reveal and how much to attempt to conceal. I suddenly noticed there was something reptilian about the rustle of his silk suit.

"Vito, I wish we could have had this conversation elsewhere, under more private conditions, but I can see that you won't relent until you get some sense of resolution. First, let me say that yes, I have often gone to Delancey Street for dinner with Lydia and the girls. Why shouldn't I? I've always loved your daughters as if they were my own, and just because you and Lydia got divorced doesn't mean I had to terminate my friendship with her. Given your paranoid attitude, I wasn't going to advertise this to you because I knew you'd interpret it as a sign of betrayal."

"Which it is!"

"No," Tony sighed and took a breath. "But I'm not surprised you see it that way. Anyway, sometime earlier this year, Lydia confided that, before you moved out, she'd copied all your computer files and was planning to contact the FBI. I persuaded her not to. I told her that she'd be opening up too many people, some of them good friends, to irrevocable harm. Fortunately, I was able to convince her. But she's terribly angry with you and wanted to hurt you. She's never forgiven you."

"For Walter?"

"For everything, Vito. For all the affairs, for years of ignoring her. She feels like you tossed her aside as if she were nothing. Somehow she came up with the idea of the IRS and reporting your undeclared income. For a long time she hesitated, whether out of fear or what, I don't know. Now, for some reason, she felt ready to do it. I tried to dissuade her, Vito, but there was nothing I could do to change her mind."

"I'm sure you tried your best, your very persuasive best."

"I did. Honestly. But you know Lydia. She was obsessed. When her emotions are running away, there's no stopping her. Her mind was made up. She was determined to get back at you, to hurt you."

"And of course, you never thought to warn me."

"Vito, would you have believed that I had nothing to do with it? You'd have accused me then, just as you accuse me now. Besides, my opinion then — as it is now — was that this would be a long, drawn-out inconvenience, a nuisance suit. Between the people we know and the time elapsed, I wouldn't anticipate that the cost would amount to all that much, considering the numbers involved."

I had to admit, Tony was good. I believed him, but I gathered that Vito hadn't wavered one bit. I could see the rage rise in him like bile, like lava boiling and spewing to the surface. His face turned a purplish red and he sputtered as he tried to speak. Trying to rise from the table, his eyes bulged, then he collapsed back on to his chair, gagging and grabbing at his throat.

Lena rushed to him, but even from where I sat, halfway down the table, I could see his eyes rolling back in his head.

"Call a doctor," I shouted.

Tony sat, stunned.

Marie dialed 911. Lena loosened Vito's tie while Cathy unbuttoned his shirt. Although there had been some initial choking, no sounds were coming from Vito, and I wasn't sure if he was still breathing.

The ambulance came within minutes. We hovered around in various states of helplessness, not knowing what to do other than to hope he was all right. In contrast, the EMTs were an efficient choreography of professionalism: An oxygen mask was applied, an injection given, a stretcher unfolded, and my cousin was whisked away.

What happened during the next few minutes is recorded in my mind only as something of a blur. Lena would go to the hospital, but there was some discussion about who would join her. It was decided that I would take Lena and the girls to the hospital. Rudy, Logan, and Louis would cab back to Vittorio's house to pick up their vehicles. Walter must have decided that his presence was unnecessary. No one noticed him leaving; it was as if he simply disappeared — probably relieved to get as far away as possible from his newfound, volatile Italian relatives. Tony said some consoling words to Lena and urged her to keep him informed of Vito's condition, then hailed a taxi and left.

On the way to the hospital, the women were mostly silent. While driving, I was preoccupied with the events of the evening. It was as if all the negative energy that my cousin had generated during his lifetime had coalesced in that room, at that table, and had risen up in him like a demonic force, grabbing him in its fist and crushing him like a bug.

We waited in the visitor's lounge at the hospital for almost an hour or so before a doctor came to find Lena. Vito was dead. His heart had failed him. They'd done all they could, but they couldn't save him. Lena took the news stoically. The girls cried and consoled each other, but Lena didn't shed a tear. Pale and haggard, she suddenly looked older than her 33 years. She mentioned feeling overwhelmed. Seeing her in shock, I offered to help her deal with some of the details, like the funeral arrangements.

Louis, Logan, and Rudy showed up soon afterward and grimly absorbed the news, although it was clear that their focus was on being supportive to their wives. Rudy's attempt to be sympathetic to his sister consisted mainly of reminding her what an abusive bully Vito had been. Lucy pulled Lena away from her brother and, with her arm around the new widow, tried to provide more meaningful support. Logan and Louis suggested to their wives that there was nothing more to be done, and that they should leave. I think Lena might have made some dismissive gesture as they departed, as if to say, "Good riddance." Only then did I realize that the girls and Lena had not spoken directly to each other the entire evening.

Lucy and Rudy stayed at the hospital with Lena while she dealt with the paperwork. I promised to call her in the morning, and left to drive back to my own home in Haverford. Memories of Vito flowed into my head: childhood images of a shifty, skinny brat; the mean, sullen bully he became during his teen years; and the seemingly miraculous metamorphosis into an actual college graduate and then lawyer! I remembered his first wedding and his lovely young bride, Lydia. I pictured all of the family events to which — as the only relative he had other than his parents — I'd received a perfunctory invitation. Then I recalled that he'd had two brothers who'd died prior to his birth, and I wondered what role their deaths might have played in his developmental path.

But these mental snapshots of Vito's life provided only superficial milemarkers in his journey. They didn't reveal anything about who he was or the meaning of his life. Now that Vito is dead, all of his concerns about wealth and power are gone with him. The whole of our inner life, so precious to us while we're conscious, floats away into nothingness on our last breath, a myth of significance. At least Vittorio had two daughters and two wives who would remember him — even if with some bitterness — and when they die, memories of Vittorio will disappear with them; a life written in invisible ink.

During the few days prior to the funeral service, I went to Lena's home in South Philly to help with arrangements. As Vito's only blood relative other than his daughters, I felt an obligation to do what I could for Lena. I was there for her emotional support, as were her brother and sister-in-law. It was an intense time. At one point, Lena mentioned the writings that Vito had been obsessed with prior to his death. When I expressed curiosity, she was more than happy to give me not only the specific file, but also his laptop computer, as if she wanted to be rid of any reminders of him.

I drove Lena to the funeral home and to Tony Savona's law offices (I can't even begin to imagine the fees they must charge to justify the luxuriant views from their 30th-floor aerie with high-end furnishings and original art). Tony took care of all the legal aspects. His law firm was top notch, and he had at his command many underlings who were delighted to do whatever he asked in order to make things easier for Lena. Of course she didn't share any details of Vittorio's will with me; this was her private matter and, besides, I wasn't really interested. I know only that she received everything. Nothing went to either of his daughters or to the newly discovered son — and, of course, nothing was left to Lydia.

Although Lena said she was overwhelmed by all of the decisions she had to make, she did not appear to be devastated by grief. Rather, she remained strong-willed and determined. Taking care of her gymnastics studio was of great concern. In fact, she expressed annoyance that attending to the funeral arrangements and settling the estate took so much of her time and attention and required her absence from work.

The funeral was held on the Thursday after Vito's death — a small service at their church and a brief graveside ceremony. Other than the immediate family and me, no friends, neighbors, or former co-workers of Vito's were in attendance. Not even Tony showed up. A half-dozen of Lena's employees, gymnastic instructors and some administrative people, came out of respect for her. One young man, an instructor, seemed to linger a little too long while giving Lena a consoling kiss on the cheek, but perhaps it was only my imagination.

We can only guess at the millions of dollars Lena must have inherited. She still lives in her home in South Philly and operates her gymnastics studio. However, I know nothing else of her personal life. I never hear from her, or from Cathy or Marie.

The obituary in the paper made mention of the daughters and wife who survived him. It reported his stint in the Pennsylvania attorney general's office and his years as an assistant U.S. attorney, including a role in the mafia trials of the 1990s. The write-up was a mediocre attempt at praise. Vito would have been disappointed. The world, he would have concluded, remained ignorant of how awesome and impressive he had been.

Perhaps, though, Vittorio would have taken some perverse satisfaction from the fact that I, of all people — I, who never liked him! — ended up writing a book totally centered on The Man, himself.

IN THE WAKE OF

Love

IN THE WAKE OF

A NOVELLA

Gerard R. D'Alessio

1

A sudden gust of wind slammed into the sail and almost pulled the main-sheet from Manny's hand, tipping the boat precariously over to star-board. Startled, Elaine let out a scream as she lost her balance and slid off her narrow portside perch. Their cooler and the small duffel bag containing the lunch she had made skidded across the bottom of the boat. Manny had an instant sense of relief that they were wearing life vests; the one secret fear he had was of drowning.

Tugging hard on the line and pulling the tiller slightly toward him, Manny regained control of the boat, and they began a speedy run northwest toward the New York side of Lake Champlain, away from the marina on the Vermont shore. Elaine screamed with excitement. They laughed and whooped, relishing the pleasure of their little rented boat racing across the water, the sails taut, the boat tipping thrillingly. In all of their excursions on the lake, this was only the fourth or fifth time they had been lucky enough to catch such a spirited breeze.

"This is what it's all about," Manny shouted. Elaine responded by raising her eyebrows in mock fear and then laughing her musical laugh. It was joy. Pure joy.

The New York side of the lake was less crowded with speedboats and water skiers than the Vermont half, and they let the boat drift lazily under the clear September sky while they ate their sandwiches and drank diet sodas.

"This is perfect," Manny said. "It's too bad this will probably be the last time we go sailing this year."

"We're lucky to have such a beautiful day," Elaine mused. "There's not a cloud in the sky. Our weekends are going to be pretty busy for the rest of the year. If we hadn't made it today, we probably wouldn't have had another opportunity."

Manny looked at his wife, stretched out in the bottom of the boat in her shorts and T-shirt, her long, auburn hair framing her face. "You look gorgeous," he said. "I wish I had a camera with me to take your picture."

Elaine smiled demurely. "Why thank you, Sir. How perceptive of you to notice."

After they finished lunch, Elaine took control of the tiller and mainsail sheet, and they headed southeast toward the Vermont shore. The breeze that had sped them earlier had calmed, and it took an extra two hours to tack their way back to the marina.

When they arrived home, they let both dogs out to run for a while, then walked into town for dinner at the Irish pub. Manny ordered his favorite Reuben sandwich and Elaine chose her usual bowl of chili. They each enjoyed a mug of beer while discussing their work and their daughters. Laura, Elaine's daughter from her previous marriage, was three months pregnant, and they were looking forward to their first grandchild.

They walked hand-in-hand back to the house, where Elaine put coffee on and Manny retired to the living room to watch TV. Elaine let the dogs out again and watched as they sniffed around the yard. She joined her husband in the living room, sipping the warm coffee and snuggling on the leather sofa in front of the TV. Glancing at his beautiful wife, Manny thought, as he often did, how happy he was, how fortunate to have such a satisfying and rewarding life. It was a typically comfortable evening — the perfect complement to a perfect day.

Aroused from a deep sleep, Manny realized that Elaine was gently squeezing his shoulder, speaking softly, as if she didn't want to awaken anyone else.

"What?" he whispered cautiously. *Had she heard a sound? Was she frightened?*

"I have to talk to you," she said, her voice more normal now that he was awake.

"Now?" he asked. Without his glasses, it was difficult to make out the numbers on the digital clock.

"What time is it? Two o'clock?"

"Yes," Elaine confirmed. "I haven't been to sleep yet."

"What's the matter?"

"I have to tell you something," she said urgently.

"It can't wait until morning?"

Elaine shook her head. Leaning on one elbow, Manny half turned toward his wife. She was sitting upright in bed. He reached up to turn on the bedside lamp, but she touched his shoulder.

"No," she said, her voice surprisingly firm, no longer quiet and soft.

Keeping his annoyance to himself, Manny propped his pillow under him. Now he was half sitting up and facing her. "All right, I'm listening."

After a moment's hesitation, she said, "I've been seeing someone."

"You mean like seeing someone in therapy?" he asked. Elaine had a history of mild depression, and had been in and out of therapy many times during the past 15 years or so.

"No, that's not what I mean. I've been seeing someone ..."

"Sexually?" he asked, his voice full of disbelief. He didn't expect an affirmation — it was more an attempt at levity.

"Yes."

What? What am I hearing? My wife? My Elaine? Sexually involved with someone else? Am I hearing correctly?

"You've been seeing someone? Sexually?"

"Yes," she said again. "But I'm trying to break it off."

Manny was vaguely aware of experiencing a number of reactions simultaneously. He felt anger. Or maybe he thought he should feel anger — but he felt compelled to hold it in check, not immediately give it free rein. But perhaps he shouldn't feel anger —maybe surrendering to that emotion would be jumping the gun, judging her precipitously. After all, there must be some reasonable explanation.

He was also aware of wounded pride. What else to call it? She had been cheating — no, *still is cheating on him*. Elaine, who had always been so insecure, jealous of any attention he paid to another woman or attention that was paid to him. *She* was cheating on *him*? Elaine, who constantly told him that she loved him, who had to continuously be touching him, maintaining physical contact whenever possible. With her overdeveloped sense of right and wrong, she was cheating on *him*?

And he was curious, too — although that made him feel slightly guilty, as if wondering about the details of her sexual activities (without him!) was somehow intrusive. Did he really need to know the details?

But he wanted to know the details.

"OK," he said, trying to keep his voice even. "Tell me about it. Who are you involved with?"

"Frank Gambon. He was my supervisor when I worked at the Hampton School. You may have met him once or twice."

"I don't remember clearly. What does he look like?"

"He's taller than you are, thinner, dark hair."

Manny shook his head. He had pictured a short, pasty, pudgy, balding guy; that is, a shorter, pastier, pudgier, more balding guy than he was.

"I don't remember him. But, why?"

"I don't know. I'm not sure. Last year, after I was diagnosed with the melanoma, I was depressed. I felt like you weren't — I don't know, concerned enough. I felt like I needed something, needed to do something to feel more alive. I'm not sure myself."

"You felt that I wasn't concerned about your cancer? That's incredible. How can you say that?"

"I didn't feel as though I could talk to you about it," she persisted.

"What the hell are you talking about? I never discouraged you from talking about anything." He stared at her profile in the moonlight. "So you went looking for someone else to talk to?"

"Yes. I think so. And, like I said, I needed to do something to feel alive."

"So screwing around with somebody else made you feel — what?"

Manny suddenly recalled a letter he'd received from Elaine's first husband, Ken, shortly after he and Elaine started living together. Ken had warned that Elaine would cheat on him, too. At the time, he had dismissed it as evidence that Ken hadn't really known her at all. No wonder she had cheated on Ken — he was an insensitive, ignorant asshole so consumed by his own bullshit that he could never appreciate his wife or daughter.

But now that warning came back to him. Had Ken been right after all? Was there something more centrally deficient in Elaine's core that compelled her to cheat? He hated the idea that Ken might be right. He was aware of an unspoken competition with Elaine's ex-husband, and he didn't want to admit defeat. Even though Ken had disappeared after the divorce, he remained a shadowy presence in their lives.

124

Or was Elaine accurately, if inarticulately, expressing some universal truth when she implied that concern about her cancer had led to a temporary regression, one that she sincerely regretted? Hadn't she said she was breaking it off?

"OK," he said, reluctantly. "Go on. Tell me the whole thing."

"Last spring, when I was diagnosed with the melanoma and had the surgery to remove it ..."

"I remember," Manny interjected. "In fact, I was the one who noticed it on your back and suggested you see the doctor."

"I know. After it was removed I had to keep going back for checkups. I was scared to death that the melanoma had already metastasized and would turn up somewhere else in my body."

"I know. You talked about that, about being afraid."

"My father died of cancer."

"I know. Lung cancer spread to his brain."

"I don't want to die like that."

Manny tried to keep quiet. *Let her tell her story. Let it come out. Just listen.*

"One day last June I went over to the Hampton School late in the afternoon when classes were over. Frank was alone in his office. He came out from behind his desk and sat next to me. We only talked at first."

Manny took a deep breath. He tried to keep an impassive look on his face, but it didn't matter; the room was dark, and she was staring straight ahead, out the bedroom window. He waited for her to continue.

Her voice was cold, matter-of-fact. "We talked, nothing important, caught each other up. And then, after a while, we started to kiss."

This must be difficult for her, but I don't want to make it any easier.

He waited, hardly breathing. Part of him wanted to hear everything, have nothing left out. Another part was filled with dread.

"One thing led to another." Elaine paused.

"Right there in his office? Where somebody might come in?"

Manny remembered their first time together, nine years ago. During a fund-raising dinner they had both attended without their spouses, they spent time dancing and flirting. He had been 44, she had recently turned 40. Manny had suggested they go get something to eat, and Elaine had followed him in her car to a café. After coffee and dessert, they sat in his car — *and one thing had led to another!* He remembered things they had done during that first year and a half together, before she had separated from Ken — crazy, daring, risk-taking things.

125

"Go on," he said. He heard the edge in his voice.

"Are you sure you want to hear this? I'm sure you can imagine ..."

"No," he insisted. "I want to hear it."

"We met a couple of times, and then he was gone for the summer. This past school year, we saw each other a couple of times a month. I've wanted to break it off for a long time, but he'd call and I'd agree to see him."

Manny sat up and looked at her. "So for this whole past year, you've been meeting him, having sex with him, a couple of times a month?"

She nodded. Looking briefly at him, she quickly returned her gaze to the window.

Was that defiance in her eyes?

"My God, you've been lying to me for so long! For a year and a half you've been with this guy and lying to me."

Manny pictured her sucking the skinny turd's cock, pictured him fucking her, kissing her, her kissing him. He felt disgusted, as though he'd been contaminated by her. He wanted to wipe his mouth. Shattered, he turned and stared at her. *Who is this woman? Has everything I believed during this past year been make-believe?*

"Do you love him?"

She faced him again, but her look was different now. Her eyes glistened in the dim light.

"No," she said. "I don't love him. I love you. I didn't want to hurt you. This didn't have anything to do with you, or with us. It just felt like something I needed to do. I don't know why."

"Why do you think?"

Elaine shrugged her shoulders. "Maybe I was angry with you."

Manny was shocked. "Angry? Why would you be angry with me?"

She lowered her head in thought. "I don't know. Maybe because you didn't have cancer. Maybe because you have a doctorate and you're teaching at a college, and I only have a master's and I work at an elementary school."

She raised her eyes to meet his.

Manny was speechless. Her explanation sounded so absurd that he couldn't even articulate a question. He thought about what she had said and suddenly he thought he understood. "You've really harbored a lot of resentment toward me, haven't you?"

"No," she said quickly, furrowing her brows.

Now that his eyes had fully adjusted to the dark, he could see her face clearly. He noticed the way the pale light played across her naked breasts, her long hair falling, hiding half of her face. Here she was telling him how she had cheated on him for over a year, had sex with another man, lied to him — and he was noticing the shadowy curves of her breasts. Anger and arousal arose simultaneously.

"No? It sure as hell sounds like it. Nothing is any different now than it was when we met. We still have the same kinds of jobs. In fact, you've been going to school, accumulating credits toward your doctorate. I've supported you in that in every way. If you're angry with me for being happy in my job, or for having more education, well that's been the case since the beginning. It's not my fault that you had a child and weren't able to keep up with your schooling when you were younger."

"I always thought I could get my doctorate."

"And you still can. You are. I don't understand where this envy and resentment are coming from. Why are you blaming me?"

Her tone became harder again, more confrontational. "Because you don't really want me to be going to school."

"What?"

"It's true. You tolerate it. You go along with it, but you don't really like that I'm taking courses and paying tuition. You resent it."

"Where the hell did you get that idea? I've supported you all along. I've encouraged you. I've made dinner when you came home late, done the shopping, cleaned the house to make it easier for you."

"But you don't really want to do those things. You'd much prefer if I did those things."

"Of course I would. That's the whole point, for Christ's sake. It is a sacrifice, but it's a sacrifice that I was more than willing to make so you could fulfill your dream. I didn't resent it. I was happy to do it."

"Manny, you just said you'd prefer if I were the housewife who stayed home and did all of those things."

"Elaine! Don't go putting words into my mouth. I never expected you to be the dutiful little housewife. You've got me mixed up with Ken or your father or somebody."

"You leave my father out of this," she said sharply.

"I'm just saying that you are totally misrepresenting what I said and who

127

I am. Yes, of course I'd prefer that you do the food shopping and the cooking and the cleaning, but I was willing to do it because I thought it was helpful to you, that it made it easier for you to get your degree. And now I'm finding out, not only that you've been having an affair, not only that you've been lying to me for over a year, but that you've been harboring this secret grudge against me the whole damn time we've been together."

"That's not true."

"It's not? It sure sounds that way to me. You just said as much."

Manny glared at her. His rage was palpable. Everything felt like a lie — his whole life, their whole life together.

"Tell me when you started to resent me."

"I don't resent you. It's just that — why do you get to have everything you want and I can't have what I want?"

"Jesus Christ, Elaine, what don't you have that you want?"

"Well, I don't have a doctorate. I'm not teaching at the college level."

"Elaine, whose fault is that? Is that my fault?"

"I didn't say it was your fault."

"Then why the hell am I being punished for it? Why take your frustrations and disappointments out on me?"

Elaine got up out of bed and, as she crossed the room to take her robe off the hook behind the door, Manny saw her ass, ivory white in the moonlight.

"That's it?" He was incredulous. "End of discussion?"

"This isn't accomplishing anything. There's no use talking to you. I told you about Frank because I wanted your help."

"How am I supposed to help? Should I beat the shit out of him? Or join the two of you in a ménage-a-trois?"

Elaine glared at him. "Tell him that you know, that you don't want him to call here anymore, that I don't want him to call here anymore."

"Elaine, I'll be glad to tell the son of a bitch not to call here anymore. But why can't you do that? Why haven't you?"

Elaine sighed deeply. "You don't understand. I just need you to do this for me. Help me put an end to this."

"OK," he said. "I can do that."

Elaine hesitated for a moment and then approached him. Kneeling on the bed, she kissed him tentatively. Manny wasn't sure how to respond, but habit took over and he pulled her closer and kissed her forcefully. "I do love you," she reassured him. "I want to put this behind us. I don't ever want to have to talk about it again."

"I love you too, but we need to talk more about this. I need some time to think. It's quite a load you've just dumped on me. I can't just push it out of my mind as if it never happened."

Manny felt her nodding against his chest.

"I don't want to feel rushed," he said. "We should take as much time as we need to work this out."

She agreed. They would talk again after dinner that evening. Claiming to be too wound up to sleep, Elaine went downstairs to make a cup of tea. Manny lay down in bed, but images of his wife going down on Frank Gambon, kissing him, jerking him off, letting him into her, tortured his mind. When Elaine did come back to bed, he laid next to her silently and pretended to be asleep. After a while, he drifted into a fitful sleep.

After Elaine left for work, Manny poured himself a second cup of coffee and went out onto the deck. It was warm for early September, and the morning sun felt healing as he settled himself into one of the big Adirondack chairs. With no class to teach until 11 and office hours later in the afternoon, he had time to reflect on Elaine's confession — and her accusations. He realized quickly that he was more angry at Elaine than at her lover, Frank. She had sought him out. She had gone to him. Even if he had made the first move, she had responded; she had been an active participant. He hadn't forced her to do anything. She had made it clear that she went there to be with him. And, of course, she was attractive and desirable. Who wouldn't want her? No, Frank would have to be warned off, but Manny didn't blame him entirely.

But he was enraged at Elaine. As he sipped his coffee and gazed out over the remains of the cornfield that abutted their property, he was overwhelmed by her betrayal. He had trusted her completely. He had taken pride in the unconditional openness and deep intimacy they shared. Now, Manny was shocked to discover that Elaine had kept secrets from him, terrible secrets. She had harbored a bitter, jealous resentment toward him all along — and he hadn't known! She had made a fool of him. She had led him to believe there were no problems between them, that he knew her completely. And he had believed her lies. Now he wondered if he knew her at all. What else might she be concealing? What other resentments might she be harboring? His faith in his capacity to know reality was deeply shaken.

One of the dogs ambled over and plopped down, laying her chin over his shoe. It reminded him of the way he and Elaine sought each other out. That kind of physicality was anathema to his first wife, Rose. Whereas Elaine always strived to make him feel loved, and to be loved by him, he couldn't remember feeling that way with Rose. That struck him as odd — he had known Rose loved him. She had often said as much. But in hindsight, he had never felt it — which was why he had cheated on her so often. He had believed at the time that he was only looking for sex, but now he knew better. It was about feeling wanted, valued. Rose had believed that as long as she cooked and cleaned, she didn't have to provide anything else, other than occasionally allowing her body to be available for sex.

Elaine wasn't like that. She made him feel loved and wanted and valued. Was that just an act? If she was indeed who he thought she was, how could she do this? Why would she do this? Was it really about the cancer? Was it about her Ph.D.? Turning 50? Becoming a grandmother? Why hadn't she mentioned any of these things before? Why hadn't they talked about them?

And this Frank Gambon had been her supervisor at one time. Manny tried to recall what Elaine might have said about him in the past, but nothing came to mind. Had they been involved when they worked together? Elaine had been working at the Hampton School when she and Manny met, and she continued to work there until about three years ago, when she took a job in another district. He wondered if this had been the first time she'd been involved with him — or with anyone else since they'd been together.

Manny remembered one woman he had seen briefly during his first marriage. They'd just finished having sex and she complimented him on being a good lover. Even though Rose had never made him feel special in that way, he shrugged it off as an obligatory remark she felt compelled to make. She had been taken aback, but after a minute or so, she said, "Yeah, I can see why you might mistrust what a woman says. We can be devious sometimes."

Is that what Elaine was? Was she devious?

He couldn't even remember the woman's name — Martha or Margaret, something like that. Manny recalled the sexual excitement of that brief affair.

In all the time Elaine and I have been together, I have never even looked at another woman, never even thought about another woman. And her, with her jealous possessiveness, she's the one who has an affair!

Manny shook his head in bewilderment.

Of course she was upset about her cancer. We did talk about it. She did bring it up, how she was afraid it might have already metastasized. I was supportive. How could she say that I wasn't concerned, or that she didn't feel she could talk to me about it? Bullshit.

Manny lifted himself out of the chair and stepped off the deck. Both dogs trotted after him. As he strolled slowly down the hill through the pine trees toward the edge of the property, the dogs scared up a woodchuck and chased it to its hole. They never caught anything, and he wondered if they would know what to do if they did. The fun was in the chase, he thought, as he plodded back toward the house to get ready for work.

When he returned home that evening, he smelled dinner cooking. Elaine looked prettier than usual, but he didn't know what was different. She greeted him cheerfully with a kiss and chatted easily about her day. It was the beginning of the semester and there was much to talk about. Manny suggested wine with dinner and Elaine readily agreed. He fed the dogs while Elaine finished setting the table. They were in the process of cleaning up when the phone rang. Elaine looked at him and, after the second ring, asked if he would please get it. Manny picked up the receiver. "Hello?"

"Is Elaine there, please?"

"Who's calling?"

After a moment's pause, "Frank Gambon."

Manny's eyes flickered in Elaine's direction. "Mr. Gambon, Elaine has told me all about her relationship with you. She doesn't want to speak to you and I don't want you calling here anymore."

"But ..."

"It's over, Mr. Gambon. You understand? It's all over. She won't see you again. I hope I'm making myself clear." Manny hung up the telephone.

Elaine looked at him and said, "Thank you. I appreciate your doing that."

Suddenly, Manny had an image of leaves floating on water; autumn leaves, gold and red and orange brown, drifting on the surface of a stream, sunlight reflecting off its glittering surface. Panic gripped him as he felt himself falling face down into the water, and he tightened his grip on the telephone for support. An overwhelming sadness surged through him. He put the phone down and went to the back door, aware that Elaine was watching him.

"I've got to go outside," he managed to say, barely glancing in her direction.

One of the dogs squeezed through the door as he stumbled outside, and accompanied him as he crossed the lawn toward the cornfield. His eyes filled with tears.

When he reached the opposite side of the field, Manny stopped to look back at the house. Only the downstairs was lit up, but he could see the outline of the house, the barn and trees, clearly in the moonlight. It was a cloudless night. He remembered reading that on such a night the human eye is capable of seeing only about 10,000 stars, but tonight the sky looked filled with so many more. The sight of such a multitude of stars always filled him with a sublime sense of wonder at the vastness of the universe. Still, looking at his home of these past nine years, he felt suddenly empty. He had known such happiness here.

Talking with Frank Gambon, actually hearing the man's voice, had made everything powerfully real and tangible. Manny stepped carefully through the drying field of cornstalks while the dog ran ahead, back and forth, sniffing, returning frequently to touch base with him. Looking at his home, he felt heavy with sadness, adrift and disconnected. He glanced at the dog and was glad to have her company, but the dog wasn't enough to make him feel grounded. He felt alone, removed — from his whole life up until five minutes ago. Everything was gone. Nothing was real. The dog lay down nearby, her tongue hanging out of the side of her mouth, as though she were smiling at him, waiting for him to decide what to do.

"I don't know," he said out loud to her. "I don't know."

—2—

Standing in front of the sink after his shower, Manny studied himself in the mirror. More gray was showing up in his receding hair, but he still thought he looked younger than 58. Not that it made any difference. He was what he was. And right now, he wasn't looking to meet any new women. He was in the process of coming to terms with that whole area of his life: dating, female companionship. As he finished drying himself, he thought about his date with Bea later that evening. They had been together for almost six months, longer than he had dated anyone else during the past three years, since his divorce from Elaine. One thing he could say for Bea: The relationship with her felt safe and comfortable — exactly what he'd needed after Elaine.

Not that comfort was the only quality Bea offered. She was truly a good person and, perhaps surprisingly, their sex was more than adequate. Actually, that had been quite unexpected. Bea was chunky — *stocky* was the word she used. Initially, he would have been tempted to describe her as *fat*, but in fact she didn't have much fat on her at all. In spite of her girth, her body was solid, her breasts large and firm, her skin smooth and tight — not flabby. All of this had been a welcome surprise. He was very pleased to learn that an overweight woman in her 50s could make a good sex partner, and he felt a pride of discovery as if he were the only man to have ever enjoyed this knowledge.

Still, Manny admitted as he got dressed, there was no spark. He recalled previous relationships, affairs he'd had during his marriage to Rose. There was one woman, before he met Elaine, with whom he had fallen in love. It was magic! He often found himself thinking of her, wondering what she was doing, if she was available. He remembered how much in love they had been, and how awful it was when she broke it off. Neither of them had been ready to divorce their spouses and make the commitment that would allow their relationship to grow.

When he found himself falling in love with Elaine, he knew he couldn't go through the heartbreak of separation again. He didn't want a life of serial affairs and endlessly recycled hurt. It was time to leave Rose and finally put an end to that cycle. It was a logical decision and he was astonished he hadn't reached it before. Remaining with Rose would have been like serving a life sentence. It made him depressed to even think about it. But the prospect of repeatedly falling in love and then having to break up was insanity itself. Getting off of the merry-go-round of affairs was the only solution. Of course, Elaine had to separate from Ken as well. And it had been the right decision for both of them. They were wonderfully happy together — not only in the beginning, but right up to the end, until that horrible night.

At least, *he* had been happy.

Sometimes he wondered why Elaine had ever told him. Why hadn't she simply broken it off with Frank, as Manny had done with former lovers? Wouldn't it have been better if he had never known?

Manny finished getting dressed and considered walking the mile-and-a-half or so to the 30th Street Station, where he would be meeting Bea. When he emerged from the front door of his building, he discovered that it was drizzling, a rather pleasant soft, spring rain. He went back into his apartment and found an umbrella, then decided to take the bus instead.

The evening plans included dinner at an Indian restaurant near the university in West Philly, then a dance program at the Annenberg Center. When Manny had moved from Vermont to Philadelphia, he had expected to miss the ambiance of a New England university town. On the contrary, he loved the stimulation of city life. There was simply too much going on to keep up with it all, and he regretted having to miss any of the myriad cultural programs.

Manny knew that Bea enjoyed attending events with him, although she admitted that it sometimes made her feel naive. Manny took pleasure in her company, but he couldn't discuss his interests with her. He couldn't share himself. He didn't think of himself as a snob; it was just that Bea wasn't intellectually curious. She wasn't interested in literature, theater, art, music, or other cultural pursuits. She had a great head for business and computer technology, and a very quick, practical intelligence. Still, beyond their mutual affection, there was little overlap in areas of interest. At first it hadn't mattered, but the cumulative effect had become burdensome, and he found himself increasingly bored in her company. He realized it was time to move on.

When he'd met Bea, he believed he was no longer capable of falling in love. He didn't know if he'd lost the capacity naturally, perhaps due to aging, or if it had been irreparably broken by Elaine's actions. At any rate, after Elaine, he sought relationships with women simply for social companionship, as well as for sexual release. He wasn't interested in commitment. The idea of that kind of intimacy frightened him. Bea was perfect — she didn't make demands. She remained emotionally distant and removed. Neither of them had ever said the word *love* to each other. Neither was looking for romance or passion. They provided each other with a safe companion and a comfortable and adequate sexual partner.

But over time, Manny had gradually come to realize their arrangement wasn't sufficient. He was no longer willing to settle for *adequate*. He wasn't ready for passion, but he needed more involvement than he had with Bea. He'd rather have no one at all than settle for less. Imagining the possibility of going through the rest of his life without anyone, he decided that would be OK. He'd rather be alone than with someone boring, someone he merely tolerated. The problem was telling Bea; he was genuinely fond of her and didn't want to hurt her. Yet he realized that it was something he would soon have to do.

Manny was waiting on the platform when Bea's train arrived from the suburbs, and he experienced genuine pleasure at seeing her wide smile and twinkling eyes. Similarly, there was no doubting Bea's pleasure at seeing him. She had come prepared for the rain and was wearing a raincoat and floppy pink rain hat that framed her square face.

"You look really cute in that get-up," he said.

"Do you like it? I wasn't sure about the color, but I thought I needed something bright, considering the drab weather."

"Well, it suits you."

Bea took his arm. "Where are we going?" she asked.

"There's a good Indian restaurant only a couple of blocks from the

Annenberg. I thought we might go there for dinner, if that's OK with you." He looked at her questioningly.

"Sure. That'd be great. I like Indian food. On the other hand," she laughed her deep-throated laugh, "what kind of food don't I like?"

"A woman of large appetites," he said. "Just what I like."

They went outside to Market Street and caught a bus to University City. By the time they finished dinner, the drizzle had stopped and they walked the few blocks to the Annenberg. During the performance, a wonderful mixture of Southeast Asian dances, Manny glanced at Bea — her head slumped on to her chest, her mouth slack, in a light sleep. He grimaced slightly, then reminded himself that she had worked all day before catching the train to meet him.

The performance was a marvel of physical athleticism and discipline. He was always impressed that a troupe of dancers was able to remember an entire choreography, and he wasn't aware of ever seeing anyone make a misstep. When the performance was over, he saw that Bea was applauding along with everyone else.

"How did you like it?" he asked.

"Oh, I really enjoyed the dancing," she said. "I'm not sure I liked the music all that much, but the dancing was beautiful. Although I think I might have dozed off for a while."

"You did," he said.

"Oh, I hope I didn't snore."

"No," he reassured her. "I just noticed that you were asleep and figured you must be exhausted from work."

Bea smiled weakly and agreed it had been a difficult day.

At a bar between the Annenberg Center and Manny's apartment, they stopped to share a burger and fries. They sat across from each other in a worn wooden booth. An NBA game was on the muted TV and music played from somewhere in the bar. Manny sat back and sipped his beer, glancing at the TV to see who was playing, although he had no real interest in professional basketball.

Bea took a sip from her mug and then leaned forward. "I have something to tell you," she said.

"Oh? Your boss decided to give you that raise you wanted?"

Bea smiled her beautiful, wide smile. "No, although that would be nice."

"So what is it?"

"Ernie and I have been talking recently."

Ernie had left Bea for another woman a little over two years ago. Manny could never remember all the details. Unaware that Ernie was seeing someone else, Bea had been devastated. Ernie told her he was leaving because she was too fat and accused her of refusing to lose weight. She had defended herself, swearing that she had been fighting weight her whole life and didn't know what else to try. Nothing worked. Then she found out that Ernie's lover was even heavier than she was.

"What's going on with your ex?"

Bea looked at him. "He wants to come back."

Manny, whose attention had been straying in the direction of the TV, suddenly snapped into alert mode.

"Ernie wants to come back?"

He searched Bea's face for some clue that there was a punch line. Bea possessed a strange quality: When happy, her exuberant smile and bright eyes made her look like a beautiful, vital woman. But when unhappy or worried, her lips hung slightly parted and her watery eyes became frightened and confused, like a little girl. Her face melted into toneless fleshiness.

"My God, you're going to let him come back, aren't you?"

"I'm sorry," she said, "but I thought I should tell you in person. I didn't want to do it over the phone or in an email."

What!? Shocked, Manny searched her face for confirmation. "No, of course not," he muttered. "I appreciate your telling me face to face."

He shook his head, as if it would somehow help him understand what had just happened. This kind, intelligent, reasonable, attractive — albeit chunky — woman was leaving him to go back to a louse who had left her for another — and fatter — woman!

"Well," he gave a nervous laugh, "please explain this to me. What made you decide to do this?"

Ernie had started calling her a couple of months ago. Things between him and Margo were not working out as he had thought they would, and he realized he had made a mistake. He now appreciated how good it had really been with Bea. And he had made some compelling arguments. Their son and

137

his wife were going to have a baby. Wouldn't it be better for everyone if the family were intact? Wouldn't it be easier for her financially? So they decided to have a couple of dates, sort of a trial run, to see if any of their old feelings were still there. She hadn't wanted to say anything to Manny until she was sure, one way or the other. She didn't want to upset him needlessly, she said.

Manny didn't miss the irony. He realized that Bea was interpreting his look of shock as deep disappointment — and he actually intensified the furrow in his brow. He was determined not to reveal his relief at not having to break up with her.

"Wow. I don't know what to say."

"I'm really sorry," she said. "I hope you understand. It feels like the right thing to do. Ernie and I have all those years together, all of that history. I hope you can understand."

"Oh, yeah, Bea. Sure, I understand. I probably would do the same thing myself, if I were in your shoes."

An image of Elaine flashed in his mind — her standing in the kitchen while he spoke to Frank Gambon over the phone — and he knew that he was lying. He wouldn't do the same thing at all.

"It's just so unexpected," he said. After a moment, he added, "I'm devastated, of course, but I understand. I just never thought that you and Ernie ..."

"I know. Up until a month or so ago, I didn't think it could ever happen either."

Manny understood then that Bea had been juggling two men in her life — just as Elaine had.

Some color and tone had returned to Bea's face, and Manny felt a grudging admiration for her, despite her deception.

Yes, well I've been dishonest, too, haven't I?

"So what do you want to do — about tonight, I mean?" he asked.

Bea shrugged. "I can still come over to your place. I thought we might smooch, if you want to. But if you don't want to, I could take the train back home." She looked at him. "It's up to you," she said.

Manny looked across the table at her as if seeing her for the first time.

One last roll in the hay? One for the road?

It was tempting. It might be his last opportunity to get laid for quite a while.

"Well," he drawled, "I must admit I'm tempted. But under the circumstances, it might be better if we pass. I'll get you a cab back to 30th Street Station."

138

Bea looked disappointed, but he no longer had any faith in his interpretation of how she might be feeling. She might be secretly thrilled. Ernie might even be waiting for her back at her house.

They agreed he would mail the few things she kept at his house back to her. At the station, they kissed good-bye in the cab and, with a mixture of relief and emptiness, he watched her walk quickly into the station.

~ 3 ~

A couple of weeks later, Manny received an email from a woman he did not know. She wrote that a mutual friend had suggested they might hit it off, and wondered if he would like to get together for coffee or a drink. Her name was Rebecca Rahzi, and she was a 50-year-old commercial designer.

Manny didn't write back at once. The message unnerved him and he wasn't sure how to respond. Was this some sort of joke? Was it a scam? And if the message was legitimate, was he really interested in meeting someone new? He didn't trust the email and he didn't trust himself. He spent the next couple of hours avoiding it, finding other chores to occupy his thoughts.

But in the end, he responded. "Who is our mutual friend?"

Rebecca wrote back. "A colleague of yours at Penn, Ed Bergman, is married to Signe, my best friend's sister. My friend had a little get-together recently and the Bergmans and I were invited. There was a conversation about how difficult it is for single people to meet someone who is both normal and bright, and Ed mentioned that he thought you and I might hit it off. Ed knows me only slightly, although his wife, Signe, knows me very well. I expect you might want to talk to them before getting back to me, one way or the other — but they did make you out to be interesting."

Manny wondered what was so interesting about him — and he wasn't sure it was a compliment. And, other than describing herself as a 50-year-old commercial designer, Rebecca hadn't mentioned anything about herself. What did that say about her? Manny decided he would talk to Ed first and find out what this was all about.

The next day, he dropped into Ed's office, which was just down the hall from his own. It was equally cramped and crowded with cascades of pamphlets, papers, and journals pouring out of stuffed bookshelves and various outcroppings.

"Ed," he said, "I just got an email from a woman who said you suggested she contact me."

"Ah, that would be Rebecca Rahzi, a friend of Signe's."

Manny looked at his friend and cocked his head. "I'm listening."

"What can I say? She's single, bright, attractive, interesting, a good sense of humor, and she's my wife's friend. She doesn't do drugs — that I'm aware of — and she shows no obvious signs of AIDS. She's interested in the arts. I thought of you immediately. I hope you don't mind."

"No," said Manny, "I don't mind at all. Actually, I'm kind of flattered. I'm just curious why you didn't say anything to me, give me a head's up."

"Actually, I never thought she'd contact you. As far as I know, she's been divorced for years and hasn't been seriously involved with anyone. I didn't think she'd go through with it."

Manny left Ed's office perplexed. The good news was that it was a legitimate outreach from a woman, and not some kind of joke. On the other hand, if she'd been divorced for years without being seriously involved, what was wrong with her? Maybe nothing. Maybe she was only being selective. What had her email said? Normal and bright? His chest puffed out slightly and he decided that no harm would come from meeting her for a drink.

An exchange of emails led to their meeting for coffee. She'd informed him that he would recognize her by her red Phillies cap and red windbreaker. As he approached the café, he spotted her at one of the outside tables, the only red ball cap and jacket combination.

"Rebecca?" Manny asked as he approached her table, an iced latte in front of her.

"Manny?

"Nice to meet you," he said. Rebecca was a petite African American woman. Between the peak of her baseball cap and large, whimsical sunglasses, not much of her face was visible, but he liked what he could see.

"And I'm happy to meet you," Rebecca answered, a lovely smile on her face. She didn't get up.

"I'm going to go order something. May I get you something to go with that?"

She shook her head. "No, thanks. I'm good."

"Then save my place. I'll be right back."

As he walked up to the counter, he was shocked to find that he was partially aroused.

Jesus, shows what deprivation will do to a guy. I don't even have a good idea of what she looks like and already I'm getting a hard-on.

When he returned, Rebecca had removed her cap and her glasses. Her hair was closely cropped and her eyes large and alive. There was an exotic look about her and, although Manny had never dated an African American woman before, he had no reservations about doing so.

"So you're a commercial designer," he said, sitting down with his iced coffee and muffin. He placed the muffin between them, indicating that she was welcome to share it.

"Yes, I design for a living, but I also do photography. That's my real passion. How about you?"

"Me?"

"Yes. What's your passion?"

"Oh, I don't know. I'm kind of diffuse," Manny explained. "Literature, of course. That's what I teach. But all kinds of art, I suppose, including photography."

"I'm not surprised. Everybody's a photographer nowadays."

"Yes, I suppose that's true. It's a very accessible medium, isn't it? Still, there's a good side to that. I think it's a positive thing that so many people can find an outlet to explore their creativity. I think it generates an interest in art in general, beyond photography itself."

"I agree, but I think it's led to a dilution of standards," Rebecca said. "It's almost as if anything goes. I find that depressing."

"That's true for art in general, isn't it? I mean, look at music, or what passes for popular fiction."

"Oh, I couldn't agree more," she exclaimed.

The next hour or so passed quickly, discussing work and interests. They discovered a handful of friends in common.

"I'm getting hungry," Manny said. "Would you like to get something to eat?"

Rebecca, who had mentioned another commitment, responded enthusiastically and pulled out her cell phone to cancel her engagement. They ended up at a Japanese restaurant and were pleased to discover their mutual taste for sushi.

"I gather you're divorced," she said. "What happened?"

"You do have a directness about you," he noted, reclining back on his seat.

"I know," she admitted, smiling. "Not everyone appreciates it."

"Well, you go to the heart of the matter, don't you?"

"Is it a touchy subject for you?"

Manny pondered for a moment. "Yes, I think I'm a little taken aback to discover it still is. But that's all right. Elaine and I divorced three years ago. That was my second marriage. We were together for 10 years before we separated."

Rebecca cocked her head to one side and waited. Manny smiled self-consciously at his own discomfort.

"I'm surprised that I still have difficulty talking about it. For the longest time, I was aware of deliberately avoiding the subject out of some vague sense of chivalry or something, as though I had a duty to protect her honor. Maybe I still do," he admitted. "She had an affair and, even though I forgave her —" Manny hesitated, fumbling for the right words, "maybe I never really did forgive her. I don't know. The bottom line was I completely lost my ability to trust her. Suddenly, everything she did or didn't do, said or didn't say, became a question in my own mind. Actually, it wasn't just the affair. It was her capacity for keeping secrets. I ended up not knowing, not believing who she was, what she was really thinking or feeling, what she was really doing. After a year I decided I didn't want to live that way anymore, and I told her I was leaving. The divorce came through the next year."

Manny looked away for a few moments. "I told the kids I was going through some kind of mid-life crisis and needed to get away, you know, the usual nonsense about having to find myself. I couldn't bear to let them know she had fooled around. I didn't want them to think of her that way."

Studying him sympathetically, Rebecca reached out her hand to his. "Thank you," she said softly. "I can be a bit of a bull in a china shop sometimes. I didn't realize it would turn out to be such a painful matter for you. I appreciate your candidness."

Manny nodded in acknowledgment, and returned to his sushi. "How about you? What's your story?" he asked, relieved to shift the focus away from himself.

Rebecca laughed softly. "Less poignant and more melodramatic," she said. "Mohammed and I met when I was in my mid-20s. I was getting my career established and wasn't always giving my beaus the attention I should have. I was just recovering from one nasty break-up when I met Mohammed. He was a musician, a good one, too. I think he was the first man who was strong enough to handle me.

"What I didn't realize at the time was that he was a typical Egyptian man. They're used to ruling the roost. He'd fight me tooth and nail on everything and I respected that — at least in the beginning. After a while, it got tiresome. I mean, Mohammed had to win every argument and make every decision. His interests always had to come first. It stopped being cute pretty quickly. It wasn't too long before the power struggle became physical. We separated a couple of times but, because of our son, Abdul, we kept getting back together.

"When Abdul was in first grade, Mohammed went to Egypt to visit his family. That's when he started getting more seriously involved with his religion. He wrote to me that it was important — no, *necessary* — for me to convert to Islam. Until then, religion hadn't been important to either of us. I was nominally a Baptist, though I never went to church. But when Mohammed ordered me to convert, suddenly everything changed. Faith isn't something you can force onto people. I don't know if I could have been made to attend a Baptist church, never mind a mosque. But I was completely taken off guard by how adamantly I refused to give up my Christian identity. I don't think it was just obstinacy on my part. Even though I wasn't religious in a devotional sense, it was still part of my identity, my heritage, and I didn't want to give it up.

"Mohammed returned from Egypt and all hell broke loose. He tried physical intimidation. He threatened to take Abdul from me and go to Egypt. Oh, you wouldn't believe what he did to try to make me give in. Finally, I had to get a court order to keep him away from me. Even then, he still made an attempt to kidnap Abdul. Fortunately, the neighbors were home and they called the police. Mohammed literally went out the back door as the police came in the front. The next thing I knew, he was back in Egypt and joined something called the Brotherhood, an old-time-religion sect. They want the world to go back to the time of the Prophet. They're against everything, especially America and women, so I rank number one and number two on his shit list."

145

Manny recoiled at the history of violence she had endured. "It sounds like you were lucky to get out of that relationship alive. Do you still have any contact with him?"

Rebecca shook her head. At the recollection of these events, her mood had turned somber. "Not anymore. He used to write, trying to convince me to send Abdul to him, but I'd write on the envelope, 'No longer at this address.' After a while, the letters stopped. Then I was afraid he'd just show up one day and kidnap Abdul, so I moved and got an unlisted number. I'm still terrified that he'll seek me out someday."

"How about your son? Does he want to see his father?"

"Abdul is curious about his father and we talk about him. Mohammed isn't a taboo subject in our home. But it's not an important issue with him. Of course, one never knows what goes on inside the mind of an adolescent. Abdul is away at military school; he's in eighth grade. Once he graduates from college, if he wants to go visit his father, I won't object. But his education comes first."

Rebecca's face had lit up when she talked about her son. Now she looked at Manny. "Do you have children?"

Manny smiled broadly. "I have a daughter from my first marriage and a step-daughter from my second, and one granddaughter and one grandson."

"Do you see them often?"

"Actually, I don't get to see any of them all that much. They're up in Vermont, which is where I'm from originally. So, once or twice a year at most; but we keep in touch with email."

"May I ask you about your first marriage?"

Manny laughed. "Much less pain associated with that, except I'm embarrassed to admit that I'm twice divorced. When I was growing up, I only knew one kid whose parents were divorced. People didn't divorce then. And here I am, twice divorced. It makes me feel like I'm some kind of moral failure."

"What happened? Don't tell me your first wife cheated on you, too."

"No, it was the other way around. I'm not proud of it, but I cheated on her for 10 years before I finally left. That's when I moved in with Elaine."

Rebecca looked at him askance. "You ran around on your wife for 10 years?"

"Like I said, I'm not proud of it. I should have left much sooner."

Rebecca looked away and rolled her eyes. "I'm having trouble with that," she said finally.

146

"I have trouble with it, too," he agreed. "At the time, I thought that staying in the marriage was a good idea. You know, keeping the family together, staying for my daughter, all that. And maybe it was the best thing. I finally realized I couldn't stay in the marriage without seeing other women, and I didn't want to continue doing that. I should have come to that realization years earlier."

"Then it was your idea to leave?"

"Yeah."

"Your wife had no idea you were cheating on her?"

"No. She was shocked when I told her."

"You told her?"

"Well, yes. I was leaving her. I had to tell her why."

"And you told her that you'd been cheating on her for 10 years?"

Manny shrugged, as if to say, of course. Rebecca looked around the restaurant for a few moments and then brought her gaze back to him. "I wonder how she felt," she said directly, "finding out that the previous 10 years had all been a lie."

Manny saw Rebecca only a few times after that. He learned more about Egyptian men than he ever cared to know. He discovered he was only lukewarm about Middle Eastern food and music, and that the most highly regarded belly-dancing teachers were men. Although they had enjoyed attending a couple of programs together, there were definitely areas that did not overlap. Rebecca let Manny know very early on that she had not been with a man sexually since her parting with Mohammed. If that was meant to assure him of her lack of contamination with any of the STDs, it did. It also waved a big red flag at him.

"I don't understand," he said. "Why would you go all these years without having sex?"

Rebecca bristled slightly. "I decided I wasn't going to subject myself to a series of bad relationships just for sex. Either the relationship is full and reward-ing and sustainable or it's not. None of the relationships I've been in have risen to that level. I think of it as self-preservation."

Manny thought that made sense and it mirrored his own thinking — but it demonstrated a degree of mental and physical discipline that he doubted he possessed.

Over seven years! My God!

He doubted most priests could match that.

Everything conspired to dampen their attraction. Their kissing was tender, though more polite than romantic. When he first had occasion to embrace her, he didn't expect an impassioned response and he didn't get one. But he did anticipate a degree of feminine softness, a feline flexibility that would allow her body to relax into conformity with his. He wanted hugging her to feel good. Instead, Manny confronted a solid sheet of muscle across her back and shoulders, and tight, firm biceps. She felt like a man.

He immediately wondered if she were. The idea of sliding his hand between her legs was decidedly unnerving.

I've never seen any pictures of Mohammed or Abdul. Do they really exist? And, she has no breasts!

Just as quickly, he dismissed his reaction as nonsense, but the emotional shock remained. Like a floater in his field of vision, he caught glimpses of boxer Sugar Ray Leonard whenever he looked at her. They went out one more time and then drifted apart, each making polite excuses and promises to keep in touch, but knowing they never would.

4

"I gather you and Rebecca aren't dating anymore," Ed surmised.

Manny leaned back in the wooden swivel chair behind his desk. "It just didn't work out for us."

"No chemistry, huh?"

"I guess. But that's OK. Not everything has to work out."

Ed stepped into the office and leaned against a filing cabinet. "Signe has a lot of friends. You want me to ask her if she knows anyone who's looking?"

"I don't think so, Ed," Manny sighed. "This whole dating scene is more trouble than it's worth. Sometimes I think I'd be a lot better off with a friend I could do things with, have intelligent discussions, without the necessity of all of this male-female courtship business. It's too bad you're not available, Ed."

Ed made a face. "You know how it is, Manny. You've been married."

"I know. You've got each other. I'm only saying that with women I want a complete relationship or it just doesn't work. I've got to have all of the parts right: the physical attraction, the intellectual and cultural compatibility, the sexual compatibility. I'm not willing to settle for a female friend who isn't also a great sexual partner, and I'm not interested in a great sexual partner who isn't also a good friend. I just don't think I'm willing to go through that shopping-around process anymore. It takes too much out of me. I'm getting too old for it. Sometimes I think I'd rather be alone."

"You think it would be different just hanging out with a guy?" Ed asked.

"Totally, because it's only about friendship. That makes all the difference. Look at us — we don't expect perfection in our relationship, but we can still be friends and enjoy each other's company. We don't need compatibility in every area of our lives in order to enjoy talking or sharing a beer. I wish I could be satisfied with having a woman companion who's only a friend, but I'm not. I want more."

"Did you ever have it? The whole package?"

Manny reflected for a minute. "Yeah," he answered. "Maybe a couple of times. Mostly when I was younger. And then in my second marriage, I thought I had it."

"What happened?"

Manny flipped the pencil he'd been toying with up into the air. "Reality set in, what else?"

Ed was about to ask another question, but Manny cut him off. "I'm sorry, Ed, but I've got some work to do. I'll talk to you later."

"Sure," said Ed. "See ya,"

Manny tried to get back to work, but his mind drifted back to that September day, four years ago — the beginning of the end. He could still feel the thudding of the boat as it skidded across Lake Champlain, Elaine's musical laughter singing in his ears. And then that shadowy night of her confession, the sickening reality of Frank's telephone call, his own dark mourning in the cornfield.

At home that evening, Manny had to admit to himself that what he said to Ed was true. He would like to have a relationship with a woman, a complete and satisfying one. He'd known how good it could be, and his experience with Bea had taught him that he was bored with anything less. Having an adequate sex life was not sufficient. Sharing an interest in art and culture was not enough. The fiasco with Rebecca had only confirmed that truth. So Manny decided to give the Internet a try. He looked into online dating services and searched out the possibilities. What harm could come of that? Maybe the woman he was looking for lived in cyberspace.

The profiles of a few women intrigued him. Of the women he contacted, two evolved into something of a correspondence. Only one of them, Stephanie, lived in the city; the other was almost two hours away. Stephanie taught nursing, had her master's degree, and owned her own home. She had been happily married for 23 years and was widowed suddenly when her husband had a fatal heart attack. Her two grown sons lived in California. A longtime resident of Philadelphia, Stephanie had a lot of close friends but was looking for male companionship. She described herself as "happy-go-lucky" and "a few pounds heavier" than she should be. Her friends told her she was attractive, and the photo wasn't bad, although she acknowledged that it wasn't recent. They decided to meet and, in view of their email exchange, Manny felt he already knew her well enough to make it into a real date.

He was waiting expectantly in front of the theater when a cab pulled up. The door opened and a woman emerged on crutches. When the taxi pulled away, she looked around and, recognizing him by the description he'd given, lifted one hand from her crutch and waved. Manny was shocked. In addition to the unexpected crutches, she was quite a bit more than "a few pounds" overweight and looked much older than he'd expected. He approached her.

"Stephanie?"

"Yes. Manny? I'm so glad to finally meet you in person." Her smile seemed to hang there in space, expectantly, waiting for his affirmative response. But he was speechless.

Finally he managed, "How was traffic? Did you have any trouble getting here?"

"No, that's one of the benefits of city life. Take a taxi and let the driver deal with it. Have you been waiting long?"

He had thought they would have time for a drink before the performance, but she arrived 15 minutes late. Perhaps better just to go inside, maybe settle for a paper cup of coffee first, if the refreshments bar was open.

"Not too long," he said. "Why don't we go on in, maybe get a cup of coffee while we're waiting."

Manny felt obligated to overlook the discrepancy between his expectations and the reality of Stephanie's appearance. What kind of a man would he be to ignore the mutual attraction and compatibility he'd felt during their email exchanges? After all, weren't the engaging qualities she displayed on the computer screen more valuable and important than mere physical attributes?

No, goddamn it!

151

He was pissed. She had lied to him. Certainly, a lie of omission — she'd never said she *wasn't* handicapped — she just failed to mention that she was. Later that evening Stephanie confided that three years ago — not long after her husband had died — a car had run a red light and hit her. She broke both hips, both femurs, and both knees.

Still, she had misled him about her disability and about her weight. He never would have recognized her from that picture. Jesus — was it from her goddamned high school yearbook? You never knew what you might be getting. Like Rebecca — he hadn't even been sure she was a woman, for Christ's sake! What was it about women? All the fucking lies and deception.

After the play they went for a drink. Manny enjoyed talking about the performance with her and found her to be as intelligent and perceptive in person as she had been online. But his antennae were up and he detected a morose, pessimistic quality about her that he found depressing. Perhaps Stephanie had been attractive when she was younger — and lighter. Perhaps her friends and family thought she was charming. Manny wasn't impressed. When the date was over, he dropped her off at her house and made no attempt to kiss her goodnight.

The following Monday he sounded off to Ed.

"I've just about had it. I don't understand what's going on out there anymore. People lie, conceal, engage in false advertising, and it's supposed to be all right? And me — what the hell is the matter with me? I feel like I'm supposed to overlook everyone's dishonesty and lack of integrity. My wife leads me to believe she's happy as a clam and devoted to our marriage, and then tells me she's seduced her former boss. And I'm supposed to condone it because she was depressed? Having cancer excuses everything?

"And then Bea is heavier than she's led me to believe and I'm supposed to overlook that? It's not really her fault, it's genetic. And then she dumps me and goes back to her husband, who'd left her for another woman who was fatter than her! And I'm supposed to understand, because they've shared this long history together. And then there's Rebecca. Her ex-husband is in the Islamic Brotherhood, for Christ's sake. That's all I'd need. The guy had to flee the country because he tried to kidnap their son and whisk him away to Egypt. And she's built like a professional boxer — I actually wondered for a second if she's really

152

a man! Did you ever see the muscles on her, Ed? And she hasn't had sex for more than seven years! But I'm supposed to understand. I'm only pushing 60. I've got all the time in the world. Actually, forget it. Sex is no longer interesting to me. I'm already over the hill. I'm only interested in matters of the mind."

Ed stood there as Manny continued his rant. "And then, Saturday night, this woman I've been having a perfectly delightful email correspondence with, shows up on crutches. She's crippled for life, Ed. Hobbles around. And she's 75 pounds overweight and looks 10 years older than she is! Maybe it wouldn't have been so bad if I'd known beforehand, but she never told me. I understand that she was afraid to tell me, but does that make it OK? Am I crazy or something? Is it supposed to be all right for people to go around misrepresenting themselves? Am I really expected to accept all of this as if it's OK? Tell me."

"I gather your date didn't go well."

"Come on, Ed, don't make it into a joke. I'm serious. I don't know which is more outrageous — these women lying about themselves, or me feeling like I'm supposed to accept it."

Ed cleared off a chair next to the desk and sat down. "Are any of us as honest as we pretend to be?"

"Oh Christ, Ed, of course we all hold stuff back, maybe especially from ourselves. I don't think that's what I'm talking about. Nobody expects complete disclosure in the beginning of a relationship. But God, there are certain basics, aren't there?"

"I don't know, Manny. I haven't been on the singles scene in so long I forget what it was like. I know Signe and I hold stuff back from each other, and we've been married a long time."

"But suppose you've been married for years, 20 years, say, and you've got a couple of kids."

"Like we do."

"Right, like you do, with two sons on the verge of adulthood. And suppose one night, Signe wakes you up and says she has something to tell you. And you, all groggy and sleepy-eyed, prop yourself up and say, yes, Dear, what is it — and she says, I didn't tell you before, but I'm a lesbian and I can't go on living a lie. I have to be free to be me."

Ed guffawed. "Boy, that's one hell of an example."

"But suppose she did. How would you react? Would you feel an obligation to the woman you've loved for some 20-odd years to try to understand and

153

to forgive her for not telling you sooner? Or to understand and to forgive her for having finally told you? I mean, wouldn't there be part of you that would feel entitled to have known this right from the very beginning? Twenty years of making love to this woman and now you find out she's a lesbian? Wouldn't you be furious that she hadn't told you — and at the same time feel you owe her some understanding?"

At first Ed laughed, but as Manny continued he began to look more and more serious and Manny wondered if his example, plucked at random from the ether, had perhaps struck too close to home.

"Yes," Ed said. "I see what you mean. Of course I would experience that conflict. I'd be angry, but probably also feel bad about being angry."

"Exactly!" cried Manny.

"Well, if that's what it's like out there, then I'm glad I don't have to go through it." After a moment's reflection, he added, "But I would imagine that women are running into the same thing from men — married men portraying themselves as divorced, or out-of-work-alcoholics passing themselves off as independently wealthy CEOs."

"Well, we see it with our students, don't we? The bullshit excuses they give us for being late with papers."

"Or dropping out all together and never informing their parents."

"And, of course, our politicians."

"That goes without saying," said Ed, getting up. "Well, so much for the joys of the carefree single life. I thank you, Manny, for helping to put my stable married life in perspective."

"That's what I'm here for."

His pique having passed, Manny somehow felt more relaxed. It wasn't just the women. It wasn't aimed just at him. Deception was a part of everyday life and, as Rebecca had pointed out, he hadn't been exempt from engaging in it.

5

Elaine stared at the ceiling. The water stain in the corner made an amoeba-like design, then morphed into a waterfall cascading down the motel wall behind the dresser. She turned to look toward the open bathroom door, sunlight streaming in from the rusted jalousie window at the top of the wall. Frank hummed in the shower. Smiling, she heard the water turn off and realized only then how quiet it was without the shower on. Peaceful. Elaine stretched out, tempted by the promise of sleep, but there were things to do. Reluctantly, she pulled the sheet aside just as Frank emerged naked from the bathroom.

"Are you all done in there?" she asked.

Frank took in her nakedness. "Yeah. Watch out for the hot water. They still haven't fixed it."

He planted a kiss on her belly.

"I hate this place," she said.

Frank walked over to the chair where his clothes were strewn. "It's convenient, that's about all we can say for it."

"We shouldn't need to be concerned about convenience." There was a note of annoyance in her voice. "I thought we'd be married by now. Isn't that how it was supposed to be?"

"I know," he muttered.

"I've been living alone now for four years." She tried to keep the petulance out of her voice.

"I said I know. You don't have to keep at it, Lainie. It's not just my doing. You agreed that we'd wait until the time was right. Don't keep acting as if it were me alone." He maintained the boyish grin on his face, as if to communicate that they were not really having a serious disagreement.

"For four years? You keep coming up with excuses. She's sick. She's depressed. She's suicidal. The finances aren't right. That's not me, Frank, that's you."

Elaine rose up suddenly and disappeared into the bathroom. He heard the shower running. After dressing, he leaned toward the mirror over the dresser and combed his salt-and-pepper hair straight back. When the water stopped, he stood in the bathroom doorway and watched her dry herself.

"I thought you understood that I had to wait. I want us to be together as much as you do. You know that."

Elaine wrapped a towel around herself and started applying makeup to her face. "Do I?"

"Oh, Lainie, don't be like that. You know how much I love you. The woman is suicidally depressed. What am I supposed to do? I can't just leave her like that, the way Manny left you."

"So because I'm stronger, because I have my act together, I'm the one who gets punished and has to do without? Is this what's meant by 'the meek shall inherit the earth'?"

"You're not being punished, Elaine. I'm as frustrated as you are. How do you think it is for me? I've got to go home to Anita every day, sleep with her every night."

Elaine glared at him. "Jesus, Frank, don't come to me for sympathy. You've been dragging this on for way too long."

She stopped what she was doing and put her arms around his neck, pressing her body against his. "Frankie, you've been miserable with Anita ever since I've known you. You've been talking about leaving her for years — but there's always an excuse. These aren't reasons anymore, Hon, they're excuses. When Manny and I separated, you said we'd be together. I'm still waiting."

Elaine gestured at their surroundings, the rusty window frames, the mildewed shower, the cheap furniture and worn-out carpet. "Is this what you want for us? We're not kids anymore, Frank. I'm too old to put up with cheap motels and so are you. I don't want to do this anymore. I love you. I want to be with you, all the time. Not just like this."

"I know," he said, hugging her, one hand pressing her bottom in to him. "I feel the same way. I go through the same arguments myself. You're right. We shouldn't be held hostage by Anita's emotional state. It's not right. It's not fair."

Elaine pushed herself back so she could look into his face. "So?"

"I'll tell her. I'll tell her tonight."

"You're sure?"

"Yes," he said, nodding, his eyes fixed on her breasts. "I know I've been avoiding it, but it's something I have to do — I want to do." He bit his lip. "I'll do it tonight."

Elaine looked at him with a mixture of sympathy and hopefulness, but part of her knew better than to trust that he would actually go through with it. How many times had he promised he would leave Anita?

"I know how difficult it is for you, Honey, but she'll be better off, too. This hasn't been easy for her, either. You haven't exactly been a loving husband to her all these years."

"Yes, that's true. Maybe she'll be able to get on with her life in some way. She might even be less depressed." He laughed as if he'd made a joke.

"Frank, you've been married to her for over 30 years and you've never succeeded in making her a happy woman. It's not going to happen."

His shoulders sagged in resignation. "I'd better let you finish getting dressed. We have to be out of here soon."

"Right," she said. "I'll be ready in a couple of minutes."

They left the motel in his car and drove to the shopping mall where she had parked her car. After a quick kiss, she called out, "Lot's of luck tonight," as he drove away.

Elaine hoped the telephone would ring that night — that Frank would call her, breathless, to say he'd actually done it. But 11:30 came and went, and she knew he hadn't kept his promise. Disappointed, she turned out the light and tried to sleep. It was a day worth letting go of — another day of false hopes and broken promises, another day that forced her to face up to her addiction to Frank. She wondered why she kept hanging in there. Sometimes she thought it was sheer stubbornness on her part.

How many times had she broken it off, only to drift back to him even though nothing had changed? Years of promising to leave Anita, years of excuses why he couldn't leave his wife even though he wanted to be with Elaine. If she was addicted to him, maybe he was addicted to Anita. What was the hold

Anita had on him? What was the hold he had on Elaine? If Frank was genuinely unhappy in the marriage — and Anita was indeed a miserable, chronically sick, depressed woman — what kept them together?

In the car on her way to work the next morning, Elaine's cell phone rang. "Lainie, it's done. I did it."

"You what?" Nearly losing control of the car, Elaine immediately pulled onto the narrow shoulder of the road. "You told Anita?"

"Yes. Last night. Christ, it was horrible, much worse than I ever imagined. We were up all night. I think we both got drunk. It was mad, insane."

"Are you all right?"

"Yeah, I'm OK. I'm not going in to work today. I just came out to call you. I had no chance to call last night. It was impossible."

"I understand," she said. Her mood of bitter disappointment had evaporated. He had actually done it. They could be together. They would be married. Everything would work out the way she had dreamed. "Everything is going to be all right now. I'm so proud of you. You've made me very happy."

"I wanted to call you as soon as I could. I didn't get any sleep last night."

"Do you want to go to my house to rest?"

He paused. "I told Anita — I promised I'd stay here until the end of the week."

"Why? Why on earth would you do that?"

"You don't understand, Elaine. She was crazy, out of her mind. She begged me not to go, threatened suicide, all kinds of craziness. I told her it was over, that I was moving out. Promising to stay for a couple days was the only thing I could do to calm her down. I figured that maybe after the idea sunk in, she might even be glad to see me go. It's only another few days, Sweetheart. Don't worry, I'll be staying in Abby's old room. It'll be all right."

Elaine didn't know what to think. She knew what Anita was up to; she thought that if she could have a week to work on him, she'd be able to convince him to stay. Elaine's first impulse was to tell Frank how stupid he was.

My God, doesn't he see what Anita is doing?

She'd been sitting in stunned silence for some moments. Frank was talking. "Lainie, are you there?"

"I'm here. I heard you. I just can't believe you agreed to that. I can't believe I heard you correctly. Don't you realize you're giving her mixed messages? You tell her you're leaving and then you stay another week?"

"It's not a week, Honey, it's just a few days."

"Frank! Today is Tuesday. The end of the week is — when? Saturday? Sunday? We're talking about a whole goddamned week, Frank. But that's not the point, whether it's a few days or a week. You're staying, for crying out loud. You're staying! You told her you were leaving and now you're staying. Frank, what the hell do you think you're doing? Are you coming or going? Do you even know? Jesus Christ!"

"Hon, you've got to …"

"I've got to get to work. I'm late."

She hung up and turned her cell phone off. She didn't want to deal with this while she was working. Christ! Men could be so stupid. Sometimes she thought she'd be better off if she were a lesbian. Women were so much more dependable and trustworthy.

That afternoon, when Elaine returned home, Frank was parked in front of her house, his tall, slim body leaning against his car. She pulled into the driveway of the little bungalow, and he approached as she opened the door.

"I didn't think you'd be allowed out," she said icily. "Do you have to get right back or do you have time for a cup of coffee?"

"You don't have to be sarcastic. It's not like you to be so cold, Lainie."

Elaine stared at him.

"Yes, of course, coffee would be fine. A shot of something in it would make it even better."

Slamming the car door shut, Elaine realized that she was belaboring the point, unnecessarily indulging her anger. Frank followed her into the kitchen, where she put a pot of coffee on to brew.

"I told Anita I wouldn't be back until after dinner. She knows I'm here. I thought we might go out to eat, to celebrate."

Elaine felt her shoulders relax. He could be maddening, but he usually came through for her. Even when he disappointed her, he had a way of making her feel loved. She turned and smiled at him. "That would be nice," she said.

159

She got out mugs, sugar, and milk. "You were right, of course," he said, taking her hand and pulling her onto his lap. "Last night was just so crazy, I was probably acting out of desperation when I told her I'd stay. I wasn't thinking straight."

"No, you weren't," she chided him. "But I understand. You said you were both drunk."

"Well, not falling down drunk, but yes, I had way to much to drink." He shook his head. "It was unbelievable. I knew she'd be crazy, hysterical. Still, I wasn't prepared for the intensity of it, the viciousness. It was like — short of killing her or punching the shit out of her — there was nothing I could do to stop her, the screaming, the threats, the name calling." He lapsed into silence.

Elaine stroked the back of his neck and kissed his forehead. "It's over now," she whispered. "The worst of it is over."

"I hope so."

She kissed his eyes and he raised his mouth to hers. He kissed her hungrily. Elaine returned his kisses, conveying that she loved him, that she desired him. Frank rose, lifting her in his arms with every intention of carrying her into her bedroom, but she giggled and protested as she held on to him.

"Put me down, Frankie, you'll give yourself a heart attack." He let her legs slide down to the floor and she looked at him tenderly, kissing him on the mouth once more before leading him into her bedroom.

Later, lying in each other's arms, Frank said, "There's no way I can stay there until the end of the week. I must have been crazy to think I could do that."

Elaine looked at him. "So?"

"So tonight, when I go back, I'll tell Anita I'm going to move my things out tomorrow. This is the last night I'll be there."

Elaine sighed. "You're sure? Don't get my hopes up, Frank, and then let me down again."

He shook his head as if to dismiss her concerns. "No, there's no need for you to worry. My head is clear. It's the only sane thing to do. It would be insane for me to stay longer. Tonight will be nuts, I know, but if it gets too crazy, I'll just walk out. I can't go through that scene again. I won't."

Elaine hugged him. "I'll make some room in the closet and dresser. We'll make out all right until we get a place of our own. We'll be crowded here. There's only the two small closets and not enough space for another dresser."

Frank looked around the small bedroom. All the rooms were tiny, but it had a lot of charm and the house had been perfect for Elaine while she'd been alone. Now they'd have to look for a larger home where they could set up permanent housekeeping.

"You're right," he said. "That'll be a first order of business, finding ourselves a house."

Late the next afternoon, Frank pulled into the driveway and lifted two suitcases from the trunk of his car. Elaine arrived home from work shortly afterward and helped him bring an armful of clothes on hangers from the backseat of his car.

"This should be more than enough," she joked. "Did you take everything you owned?"

"Just about," he admitted. "I thought, my God, what if she cuts them all up or burns them? I wouldn't put it past her. I know we don't have that much room, but I didn't feel right leaving my good things there. I just left some old tokens, so she can't say I cleaned everything out."

"But you will clear everything out, right?"

Frank gave her his little boy smile. "You're still worried that I'm going to go back?"

Smiling at him, Elaine sighed and shrugged her shoulders. "Should I be?"

Frank pulled her to him and enveloped her in his arms. "Don't be silly," he said. "I'm out. It's over. Finished."

Elaine snuggled deeper into his embrace. "I want to believe you."

They spent some time finding room for Frank's clothes and then made dinner together. Later, they sat in the living room, drinking coffee and enjoying their first evening together.

"It's like a honeymoon," one of them said, and the other agreed. They made plans. They talked about where they would look for a house. Frank mentioned finding a lawyer to take him through the divorce, and Elaine gave him the names of the attorneys she and Manny had used. They made plans for when school would be out, only two more months. Perhaps they would take a vacation together. It was exciting to contemplate all of the firsts that awaited them. In the morning, they made breakfast together before leaving for work — Frank to the Hampton School, where he was the principal; and Elaine to the local elementary school, where she was the guidance counselor.

When Elaine arrived home that evening, Frank's car was already in the driveway. She found him sitting on the sofa, a drink in his hand.

"What's wrong, Hon? It's not like you to be sitting in the gloom all alone."

"Pull up a chair and have a drink, and I'll tell you the news of the day."

Elaine took off her jacket and sat down beside him. "I don't think I want a drink. At least, not yet. Tell me what happened."

"It's sweet Anita. She's gone and done it."

"Done what?"

"She's in the hospital. She tried to kill herself. The mailman noticed exhaust fumes coming from under the garage door. She was in the car with the motor running. Apparently, they found her just in time."

"Oh my God. How did you find out?"

"They called me from the hospital. I had to leave work. I've been there all day."

"This happened this morning?"

"Yeah, I called Abby and she came over as soon as she found a sitter for Todd. The two of us have been there all day. Of course, Abby had to know why her mother wanted to kill herself, and when I told her I'd left, she went ballistic. How could I do that? Leave her mother after 37 years of marriage. At the age of 61, what the hell do I think I'm doing, going off with another woman and leaving her mother?"

"Of course Abby is distraught, hearing that her mother tried to kill herself. It certainly wasn't the best way for her to find out that you've been miserable for those 37 years. No one would expect her to be sympathetic to you under those circumstances. Give Abby time, Honey. When Anita recovers and Abby is less hysterical, she'll be able to understand that you need to live your own life. Young people understand that."

162

Frank cocked his head slightly. "I don't know. I'm not so sure. Abby is very close to her mother. She was really furious with me."

"But she must have had some idea of what you've been going through all these years, what your marriage was really like."

"Maybe. I tried to keep that from her. I might have been too successful in putting up a good front. I think Abby believes Anita and I have the perfect marriage."

"Well, you're going to have to enlighten her."

Frank drew a deep breath. "I don't know. I just don't know."

"What don't you know? You don't know if you can tell Abby how unhappy you've been? That you're in love with me? That we're going to get married? What?"

Frank drained his glass and bit his lip.

"Tell me, for Christ's sake, Frank. What is it you're not telling me?"

"I don't know if I can go through with this."

Elaine was stunned. "That bitch! She knew damned well exactly what she was doing." Seething, she needed to move, to do something with her rage. She wanted a stiff drink. She poured herself a glass of whiskey and took a large swallow before taking her seat next to Frank on the sofa.

"Look, Frank, I understand that you feel responsible. I really do. But she planned that suicidal gesture. Thousands of people break up every day and they don't do anything so stupid and selfish. Anita wasn't thinking of Abby or her grandson when she was sitting in that garage with the motor running. You know what she was thinking, Frank?"

She waited for him to look at her. "She was thinking of you. Thinking, 'If I die, Frank will blame himself for the rest of his life and Abby will never forgive him and I'll get my revenge on the son of a bitch. And, if I don't die, he'll feel so guilty, he'll have to come back to me.' That's what she was thinking."

Frank put his head in his hands.

"Was she right? Are you going to let her get away with this? Are you going to take responsibility for what she did and sacrifice the next 20 years of your life the way you've sacrificed the past 37?"

Elaine forced herself to stop talking. She took a sip of her whiskey and tried to gain control of herself. She reached out her hand to his. "Think about it. Don't be so quick to make a decision you might regret later. Give yourself some time."

Frank nodded but said nothing. He met her eyes briefly, then got up to refill his drink.

Elaine asked about Anita's medical condition, and he said she had been unconscious when they found her, but had come around later in the day. They were keeping her overnight and, if all went well, she could be home tomorrow.

Elaine forced a weak smile. "Well, that's good," she said. "She'll see that this was a stupid thing to do and it accomplished nothing other than upsetting her daughter. You'll see. Abby will be pissed at her for doing this. Your daughter isn't going to put all the blame on you."

Frank took a swallow from his glass and pushed himself up from the sofa. "I'm sorry, I've got to take a walk or something. I've been cooped up with this madness all day. I've got to go clear my head." He put his jacket on and headed for the door.

"Of course, Hon. Take your time. I'll get supper ready while you're out. Do what you have to do."

He came over to embrace her and she hugged him back.

"I love you," she whispered.

"Me too," he said and turned for the door.

Elaine watched through the curtains as her lover trudged down the road toward an old bridge about a mile and a half away. She imagined him standing there, watching the water flow away, easing his guilt about Anita. Poor Frank. Anita had always manipulated him into taking responsibility for her well-being. He didn't have the freedom to do anything for himself — at least not openly. Whatever time he spent on himself, he stole from her. He was her prisoner.

She thought back to when she first met Frank. God, that was so long ago! They were so young. Frank was already married. Elaine had broken it off a number of times because she wanted more, but Frank steadfastly refused to divorce Anita. Elaine had married Ken out of frustration — which led to her getting involved with Manny. Of course, being married didn't erase her feelings for Frank, nor did it stop them from staying involved.

Well, that phase of her life was over now. Manny was out of her life, and her marriage to him was a big blank. She could hardly call up memories of their time together, as if it had never happened. It was like trying to remember a

164

dream. How was that possible? They had spent eight years living together, and she had no more than a handful of snapshot memories. But she could recall almost every moment she had ever spent with Frank — stolen moments, but they were all so vivid, so intense. Why was that?

When Frank returned about two hours later, the little cabin had a warm glow to it. Logs burned in the fireplace and candles created a soft and cozy atmosphere. The aroma of roasted chicken emanated from the kitchen, where Elaine sat at the kitchen table, reading and sipping wine. She sensed him standing in the doorway and looked up at the sheepish smile on his face.

"I'm sorry," he said. "It's just that the whole day was hell. I needed some time alone."

"I understand," she said, offering up her mouth to be kissed. She glanced quickly at the kitchen clock and said, "Your timing is perfect. Supper will be ready in about five minutes."

During dinner he filled her in on more gory details of his day with Abby and Anita. Later, they snuggled on the sofa in front of the TV. That night they made passionate, tender love, and Elaine fell asleep happy and content.

The next afternoon, she found a note on the kitchen table:

Dearest Elaine,

I'm so sorry. I can't do this. How can I be happy with you if I know that I'll be responsible for Anita killing herself? She's not a normal person; she's not fully in control of herself. She's like a child, weak and vulnerable — not only physically, but mentally and emotionally as well. Perhaps that's one of the reasons I married her in the first place, so I could feel responsible and important. That motivation may no longer apply, but the responsibility I took on 37 years ago is still mine. I know she'll make another attempt — and next time it might be successful — unless I go back. I don't want to! I love you. I want to be with you! I'm sick about this. I feel like such a shit. I'm damned no matter what I do, but I simply can't think only of myself and what I want. Please forgive me, even though I know I don't deserve it. You've been the best thing in my life. I don't know how I'll go on without you, but somehow I must find a way. I will always love you. I hope you know that. I'm sorry to do it this way, but I knew I could never say goodbye to you in person. Please forgive me.

Love always,

F

Elaine's hands shook as she read, and her vision blurred with tears.

He's ending it!

She went into the bedroom. His half of the closet was empty, his boxes of clothes and shoes, gone. The dresser drawers she had cleared to make room for his underwear and socks, empty.

He's gone. Not just for today, but forever. Gone.

Elaine crumpled onto her bed. They had broken up so many times before, and each time had felt like the end — the final ending — though it hadn't been. They had always gotten back together. But this time really did have that feeling of finality that had haunted their relationship from the very beginning.

She lay on the bed for a very long time, his note still absentmindedly dangling in her hand as the room grew dark. Finally, she turned on a light and went to the bathroom. She peed and washed her hands and face. Seeing her reflection in the mirror reminded her that she was still alive. She changed into jeans and a sweatshirt and found some leftover chicken for dinner.

Rereading the note reignited the overwhelming sense of loss. Everything felt pointless, empty, colorless. Frank had been the spark in her life. Now there was only darkness. Sadness, anger, and betrayal forged a visceral pain. An urge to destroy something welled up inside her. Outside in the cool night air, she grabbed an ax and began to split logs. It was something she had done since moving here after her divorce from Manny. She split logs for a long time, until her arms and shoulders ached and she could barely move.

Saturday morning, Elaine remained under the covers until the insistent ringing of the phone forced her out of bed. Part of her desperately wanted it to be Frank, and part of her decided she would refuse to talk to him.

It was her daughter, Laura. "Hi, Mom. How are you?"

"Shitty," she said. "I think I must have picked up a bug or something."

"You're sick?"

"Not exactly, just a headache and no energy. I'll take it easy over the weekend."

Elaine didn't feel up to socializing, faking good humor, smiling. At the same time, she knew that moping around the house alone was not a healthy idea.

"I'm sorry to hear that, Mom. I hope you feel better."

"Thanks. I'm sure I'll snap out of it eventually. How are you? How's my grandson?"

"We're fine. Kirk took Kyle to the supermarket with him. Kyle loves riding in the shopping cart and getting to pick out cereal and cookies." She paused for a moment. "The reason I called is that I was wondering if you wanted to come over tonight for dinner. Kirk and I were thinking of going to the movies, and maybe you could baby-sit Kyle? But if you're not up to it ..."

Elaine thought for a moment before responding. "I think that's a wonderful idea. It may be exactly what I need. I'm not contagious or anything, just feeling under the weather, you know. What time should I come?"

"You can come as early as you like. We'll be eating about 5:30 or so."

"Fine. I'll see you later on this afternoon."

Elaine sat on a kitchen chair and looked out the window. Spring had arrived, and the bushes were sprouting tender green leaves. It had been a couple of weeks since she had seen her daughter. She always enjoyed Laura and Kirk's company, even if Laura often had a bug up her ass. Elaine chalked it up to the typical competition between mother and daughter, and tried to make allowances. And Kyle was a sweetheart, so adorable and loveable. It would do her good to spend a few hours with them, soaking up some of their good energy. She felt so depleted now. Tears welled up unexpectedly and a sob erupted involuntarily. *That stupid fool. How could he be so naive? He's just a big, tenderhearted jerk, too generous for his own good.*

—ᴍ—**6**—ᴍ—

Preparing for the end of the semester kept Manny busy, and it was late May before he thought about summer plans. He decided to take a trip to Vermont to visit with his daughter, Emily, and perhaps his stepdaughter, Laura. Maybe he'd do a little camping, and drop in on his colleagues at his old job. He hadn't seen any of them in a year and he was looking forward to getting out of the city and into the woods and hills of New England. Right after the Memorial Day weekend, he stuffed his tent and camping gear into the trunk of his car and headed north. He left Philadelphia and drove leisurely across New Jersey and New York and into Massachusetts.

Though it was still early in the day, he decided to stop at a campground and set up his tent during daylight. His tasks completed, he settled back in his folding chair and dialed Emily's home from his cell phone. His son-in-law sounded surprised to hear from him.

"It was a spur-of-the-moment thing, Mark. I needed to get away from civilization for a while."

Manny asked about Mark's job with the Forestry Service and about their daughter, Rosemary. Mark, in his laconic way, said his job was fine and asked if Manny wanted to talk to Emily.

"Of course I do. You think I want to waste all my minutes talking to you? Put her on," he joked.

Manny's heart leapt at the sound of her voice. Emily was delighted to hear he was in the area and insisted he stay with them for a while. "You can always camp out later. I want you here in the house. I want Rosemary to experience who you are. You won't believe how much she's grown this past year. You'll be amazed at how big she is for two."

Relieved, Manny accepted her invitation, pleased that she was so insistent. Em was very close to her mother, who still lived in the area, and he had wondered if he would really be welcome. He didn't want Em to feel caught up in the tension between Rose and him.

"Great," he said. "I'll see you early in the afternoon."

He warmed a can of beef stew on his propane stove and relaxed with a can of beer from his cooler. Later, he strolled around the campground, relishing the feeling of walking among the trees. It brought back memories of his childhood, playing with his friends in the woods, hiking, hunting. It was his natural habitat and he hadn't realized how much he'd missed it.

Returning to Vermont was, however, like returning to the scene of a crime. In Vermont, Emily had accused him of running off with another woman, abandoning her and her mother. Even though it had been 12 years since he and Rose had divorced, Em still hadn't completely forgiven him. She hardly ever mentioned her mother to him, and Manny had no idea about Rose's current life. Recalling these events, he unexpectedly found himself feeling nervous.

Manny thought he had been close to Elaine's daughter, but when he and Elaine separated, Laura had all but cut off communication with him. He missed her and Kirk, and their little boy, Kyle, too. He had tried reaching out to them throughout the years, but his efforts had not been warmly received. Apparently, Elaine had never told them the real reason for the breakup.

The next morning, rested and relaxed, Manny made breakfast and packed his gear in a leisurely manner. During the drive, he took his time, reveling in the scenery as if he had never seen it before. After an unhurried lunch, he lingered over his coffee and took time to read a local paper. He felt deeply relaxed when he pulled up in front of Emily's house and blew the horn. The young family came out to welcome him, Mark carrying little Rosemary.

Manny was amazed at how much she had grown. Not shy at all, she was happy in Manny's arms until she started to feel too heavy and he gladly delegated the responsibility back to her father. They led him through the house and out to the back deck that Mark had built.

Emily handed him a cold beer. "So what brings you up to Vermont, Dad? All the recent hullabaloo?"

Manny looked at her quizzically. "What hullabaloo?"

Emily looked at Mark and then back to her father.

"About Elaine." She was met with a blank stare. "You haven't heard? Nobody told you?"

Manny looked at her vacantly and then at Mark for help. "I have no idea what you're talking about."

"She's in the hospital," said Mark. "At least she was. I'm not sure if she's still there."

Manny waited for more of an explanation.

"She was attacked a few days ago. Friday. Apparently she needed some surgery. I hear that her wounds were pretty bad. Disfiguring."

Manny looked back and forth between the two of them. "Obviously, there's something the two of you are reluctant to tell me. What happened?"

Mark turned to his wife and said, "Why don't I take the princess out to the swings for a while and you can tell your dad what happened?"

When Mark had taken Rosemary out back, Emily leaned forward. "The love of your life was having another affair with a married man."

All of her old bitterness was still there. Emily had never forgiven Elaine for taking him away from Rose. He'd never been able to make Emily understand that it wasn't Elaine's fault he had left Rose — he'd been cheating on Rose for years. But she insisted on blaming Elaine. Now she was taking delight in telling him that Elaine had been involved with another married man.

"Apparently the man, a principal or something from a private school over near Montpelier, left his wife and she killed herself."

Manny lowered his head. He knew, of course, that the man was Frank Gambon. Unless Elaine had some crazy compulsion to seek out and seduce all of the private school principals in Vermont, it had to be him. So Elaine had gone back to him after all, or perhaps had never stopped seeing him. And Frank's wife had killed herself. What a horrid shame.

Emily continued. "They had a daughter, this man and his wife, and the daughter attacked Elaine."

Emily paused.

"Did you ever feel like going after her? When I left your mother?"

Emily's gaze never wavered. "Yes," she said evenly. "You better believe it.

171

I thought about it a lot. If I thought I could have gotten away with it, I might have done something like this woman did."

Manny thought for a moment. "You were 18 when I left. I had stayed all those years. I waited until you graduated from high school."

She shook her head. "It didn't make any difference, Dad. I still lost my family. I was still weighed down with taking care of Mom. I felt like I had lost everything because of Elaine. God, how I hated that woman."

"You still do," he observed quietly.

"Yes. I still do. She got what she deserved."

Manny took her hands. "What hospital is she in?"

"The Fletcher Allen Center in Burlington," she said.

That made sense. It was the biggest hospital around. "Do you know how badly hurt she is?"

"All I know is that she got stabbed or slashed in the face, and that it was pretty disfiguring."

Manny grimaced, imagining the pain.

"It was in the papers, a real *cause celebre*. That's really all I know, but I assumed that Laura would have told you."

Manny shook his head. "No, I think she's kind of pissed at me."

"Well, I can't say I blame her. You did to her what Elaine did to us. You not only wrecked her parents' marriage, but then you went and left Elaine, too. Christ, Dad, you're a pretty destructive guy. You know that?"

Manny's first reaction was to be shocked.

What? Me, the bad guy?

He thought of defending himself. Instead, he merely shrugged.

"What can I say, Emily? We do the best we can. Sometimes what we do in the name of love turns out to be very destructive. It was never my intention to hurt anyone. Just the opposite, in fact. But ..." he shook his head in puzzlement, "it doesn't always turn out that way." He looked squarely at Emily. "I'm sorry for all the hurt I caused you and your mother. I really am. I'm sorry."

"Yeah, well ..." Emily drank some of her soda. "Things have worked out all right, at least for me. We're happy. We've got a good family."

"How about your mother? How's she doing?"

"She's doing all right now. She was a mess for a long time. She was so dependent on you. She had no idea who she was if she wasn't a wife. She tried a few times to become somebody else's wife, but nothing ever worked out.

172

Eventually she started taking some courses and now she's doing OK. She has a job in town working at the Inn, and she's very involved in gourmet cooking and quilting. She's going to be fine."

"I'm glad," he said.

"So why did you and Elaine really get divorced?"

Manny's antennae went up. Did Emily know something? Did it matter anymore? Could he tell her? After all, the marriage was over and it no longer served any purpose to protect Elaine's image.

"Do you have much contact with Laura?" Manny asked.

"Not really, no."

"What does 'not really' mean?" he pressed.

"We may run into each other in town, say hello, wave, you know. No, we don't talk, if that's what you're asking."

"I was just wondering."

"Dad, we're not close. We're not real sisters. We don't mean any more to each other than if we had gone to the same high school. Besides, what has that got to do with why you divorced Elaine?"

Manny looked out over the lawn. Mark was playing with Rosemary in a sandbox. "Remember the sandbox I built for you?"

"That the dogs and cats always peed in? Yeah, I remember. Mom wouldn't let me play in it and you had to take it apart." She laughed at the memory.

He gestured out toward Mark and Rosemary. "You don't have the same problem?"

"It's plastic like everything else in the world, and has a cover that folds over it so the animals and the rain can't get in it."

"Elaine was seeing that guy, Frank Gambon, while we were married."

Emily's eyebrows shot up. "I knew it!" she said. "How did you find out?"

"She told me."

Emily cocked her head. "Just like that? She just admitted it?"

"Yup."

He suddenly recalled that dreadful night with Elaine — the moonlight through the windows highlighting her breasts, the cold, matter-of-fact tone to her voice, the images of her with her lover.

"So that's why you guys got divorced?"

"Pretty much," he sighed.

How to describe his loss of trust? How to explain that he had believed totally in the perfection of their marriage, the openness and intimacy, only to discover that she had been harboring resentment toward him from the very beginning? That she had used her secret, hateful jealousy to justify seeking out another man?

"I just found myself questioning everything she said or did. I couldn't trust her anymore. It all went sour."

"You never told me."

"Does it matter?"

Emily looked at him curiously. "Have you been seeing anybody else?"

"Not really," he smiled, thinking of his dating fiascoes. "To tell you the truth, Em, I think I'm past all that. I'm not up for the singles scene anymore."

"You?" she laughed. "You aren't up for a woman in your life?"

Manny's attempt at a wan smile faded quickly. He shook his head. "I don't think I have the emotional capacity to fall in love again. What used to be very fertile ground," he said, touching his fist to his heart, "is now paved over with concrete. Even weeds can't grow there anymore."

He saw the look on her face; concern or disbelief, he couldn't tell.

"It's OK, Em, it really is. I'm fine. I'm enjoying my life. I'm totally free to do whatever I want, whenever I want, without having to take anybody else's wishes into account. If I put an empty beer glass or coffee mug on the floor next to my chair, it stays there until I pick it up. I like it that way."

Emily looked at him, a smile playing around the edges of her mouth, little micro-quivers of her lips. "So I shouldn't invite any of our widowed neighbors over to meet you?"

He laughed and waved a finger at her. "I'm still your father," he threatened. "You'll behave if you know what's good for you."

"Ha," she laughed, "as if you could ever punish me."

He smiled and suddenly his eyes moistened. "You're right," he admitted. "You always could wrap me around your finger." Reveling in memories of her childhood, he felt a kind of renewal. "It feels real good to be here, Em. Real good."

They spent the rest of the afternoon catching up. Mark filled Manny in on his projects with the Forest Service. Emily was taking an online course with the University of Vermont. Even though the campus was so close that she could have attended in person, the online venue allowed her to be home with Rosemary. When Ro got a little older, Emily was hoping to get back into teaching — and the more credits she had, the more money she would make.

As it got closer to dinnertime, Mark and Manny lit the barbecue while Emily took Rosemary inside. Voices and laughter emanated from the kitchen and, a few minutes later, a short, blonde, matronly woman emerged. It took Manny a few seconds to realize it was Rose. He stood up anxiously, unsure of what to expect. Rose marched directly toward him, and her warm smile served as permission for Manny to relax.

"Hi Rose," said Mark, taking a few steps toward her and greeting her with a kiss on the cheek.

She returned the kiss and immediately turned her attention to Manny.

"Hi stranger," she said.

"Hello Rose," he said, aware that he almost called her *Honey* out of old habit. "I didn't know you were coming over."

"Nobody did. I just stopped by on impulse to see Ro. I had no idea you were here."

"It's been a long time," he said.

"Yes," she agreed, drawing it out.

"You're looking great," he said. "Your hair ..."

"What about it?" she asked frowning.

Manny felt embarrassed. "I was just startled to see you blond. And it's shorter, isn't it?"

"It was either this or gray and I never heard of gray having more fun. And yes, I've been wearing it short now for quite a long time. It's just easier."

Mark said, "As long as you're here, why don't you stay? We've got plenty of food."

She looked from Mark to Manny.

"It would be fine with me," he offered, although inwardly he wasn't too sure. They hadn't spoken in years and, although he didn't have any animosity toward her, he suspected she might feel differently.

She studied him for a moment and then smiled.

"Thank you, but I really can't. I'm on my way to work. We've got some tax filing to do." She looked at Manny. "How long will you be staying?"

"I'm not sure. I just got here this afternoon. I thought I'd see the girls and

175

visit some old friends at the university. Maybe a week or so. I'm in no hurry."

"Why don't you come down to the Inn tomorrow and we'll have dinner? I can vouch for the food."

"Sure," he said, "that'd be great." He reached out to shake her hand and she offered her cheek to be kissed. It felt odd, touching his face to hers, feeling it's soft fleshiness, seeing her wrinkles up close, remembering her floral perfume. He felt like he had wandered into someone else's bedroom, a guilty intruder trespassing where he didn't belong.

They made plans to meet the next day and then she was off. Manny watched her climb onto the deck and disappear back into the house.

"That went rather well," Mark observed.

"Yes, better than I would have predicted."

"The two of you never kept in touch?"

Manny shook his head and took a drink from the bottle of beer he was holding. "A few times after I left, but not once since the divorce went through. And Emily has been pretty diligent about not talking to me about her mother. So I thought Rose would still be angry." He looked questioningly at Mark.

"She never mentions you," he said. "She never makes any reference to you at all."

"How about Emily?"

"Oh, Em talks about you all the time — when we're alone, not when Rose is here. She'll mention what she did with you and Rose or stuff, like camping, that she did just with you."

Manny recalled those trips. Rose always refused to go, but he and Em treasured the time together, camping, canoeing, fishing. He realized that the hostility between Rose and him made it impossible for Emily to talk with either of them about earlier family memories. He made a mental note to talk to Emily about it.

The next evening, Manny drove into town. He and Rose had lived nearby and very little had changed — the shops along Main and Stowe streets and, of course, the Inn. Manny strolled leisurely along the sidewalk, enjoying the feeling of familiarity, like being back in old shoes. He was mildly surprised to find himself feeling disappointed at not running into anyone he knew.

In the lobby of the Inn, Rose was engaged in conversation with a woman behind the reception desk. She spotted him as he approached.

"Hi, Manny," she said, greeting him. "Hazel, this is my ex." Turning to

Manny, she continued, "Hazel practically runs the Inn. I help her with the books and sometimes in the dining room."

Hazel sized him up. Manny produced a sufficiently charming smile so as not to embarrass Rose, and they proceeded into the dining room. Each of the wait staff made a point of coming to their table and greeting Rose. Manny felt like they were receiving the royal treatment.

"You've made a lot of friends here," he observed.

"It's something of a second home. Everyone is so friendly. And, of course, I've known a lot of these people for a long time."

Manny reflected on how he had spent most of his time at the university or at home, and hadn't developed relationships with people in town. Rose had been more active in creating a social network of neighbors and friends.

"So, you do bookkeeping here?"

"And sometimes I help out in the dining room, hostessing or working in the kitchen, helping the chef. I've contributed a couple of special items to their menu, I'm proud to say. You remember my buttermilk waffles?"

"Of course. Emily said you're doing great. Now I understand why. You're in your element here."

"Yes, I think so. I think I finally found myself."

"I'm glad to hear that," he said.

The waitress took their orders. Rose made some suggestions, including the wine, and Manny was content to follow her lead. When the waitress left, Rose continued.

"It took me a while, though, to discover who I was. I felt so lost for such a long time."

"I know," he said solemnly. "I'm sorry about that. I really am."

"Good," she said lightly. "You should be. But," she continued, sitting up straight in her chair, "all's well that ends well. Actually, you did me a big favor. If not for you, I never would have expanded and grown. I guess I should thank you and Elaine for that."

"I'm glad you feel that way about it."

"How about you? Has it worked out for you the way you thought it would?"

"Well, you probably heard it didn't. You're aware, of course, that Elaine and I got divorced three years ago."

"I heard. I was shocked. I thought the two of you were so much in love."

"Yes, well, nothing lasts forever."

"I hope you don't mind, Manny, but I have to ask — do you grow bored with a woman after a certain period of time, or what? What happens to you?"

He shrugged and glanced briefly around the room. "No, it's nothing like that." Then he remembered how he had felt with Rose. Part of his dissatisfaction had been boredom. He remembered feeling exasperated that the only things Rose ever talked about were kids and recipes.

"What was it then?" she persisted. "Was it sex?"

"Are you asking me why you and I got divorced?"

The waitress brought their wine and they clinked glasses perfunctorily.

"What I'm asking you ..." she paused and then continued, "and I'm not intending to start an argument. I'm really not. I'd just like to understand, from your perspective, why you left me. I've never really understood what happened."

"Jesus, Rose, that was ages ago. It's ancient history. Let it go."

"Was it ages ago? Sometimes it feels like it was only yesterday."

"I tried to tell you then. Maybe you weren't ready to hear it. I knew you loved me. Up here," he said, pointing to his head. He paused, wondering if he should continue. Rose was looking at him intently, so he went on.

"But I never felt it."

He raised his hands in supplication. How could he explain how he had felt without it sounding like an attack? "I don't know, Rose. Maybe there's something wrong with me that keeps me from being able to tell when I'm being loved."

"I don't know how you can say you didn't feel loved."

Aware of a growing irritation, Manny sighed in exasperation. "Well, let me ask you, did you feel loved by me? I mean, really loved?"

"Of course I did, until you left me and told me those lies about having run around for years with other women, just to take the blame off Elaine."

Manny recoiled in shock.

Lies? Is that what she thought?

"I knew better, Manny. We were married for 20 years. You don't live with someone for 20 years without knowing him inside out. There's no way in hell you could have been having affairs with other women for all those years without my noticing something. I'm not a fool, Manny. I'm not stupid. I'm an intelligent and perceptive woman. I knew what you were trying to do, but it didn't work. Now it looks like she finally got what was coming to her."

"I heard. Emily told me yesterday."

"Is that why you came up?"

"No," he said, shaking his head. "I didn't even know about it. I came up to see the kids, visit some old friends, and get out into the woods for a while."

"Is that what happened with her, too? You didn't feel loved?"

Oh, what the hell. The cat's out of the bag. It's been in the newspapers, for Christ's sake.

"She was seeing that guy — the same guy, during our marriage."

Rose's eyes grew big and round. "Ah," she sighed knowingly. "So that's what happened."

Manny smiled sheepishly. Rose watched him for a few moments and sipped her wine. His smile slowly disappeared as he got caught up in the memory of that night.

"I'm sorry," she said. "I'm sorry it didn't work out for you."

Manny nodded, accepting her sympathy. Rose sat up a bit in her chair. "Well, at least a part of me is sorry. I guess, if I'm honest with myself, there's also a part of me that is filled with glee, yelling *I told you so! I told you so!*"

"Yeah," Manny said, "I guess I can understand that."

"But part of me is sorry, really."

"Thanks."

"You never had to worry about that with me."

"No, I didn't." Manny reflected for a moment. "No, I felt very safe with you."

"You didn't feel safe with Elaine?"

Manny thought for a moment. "Not at the end."

The waitress brought their dinners and they sat quietly for a few minutes. After a while, Rose spoke again.

"I felt safe too, until the end, when you announced that you were leaving me for another woman. It was like the bottom of my world dropped out, like I no longer knew up from down, what was real, what wasn't. I couldn't trust my own thinking or my own judgment about anything. Before that, I had total confidence that my beliefs, my perceptions, were valid and rock-solid. I had felt totally safe in our relationship. Up to that dreadful day, I had been wholly happy and completely in love, even after 20 years." She took a sip of her wine and wiped her mouth with her napkin. "You took all of that away from me with just a couple of sentences."

Manny watched her for a few moments as she resumed eating.

"You have a right to be angry about that, Rose. I apologize for hurting you. But that was 12 years ago. It looks to me like you've done a whole lot more than just make the best of things. Like you said, you've grown. I'm glad it's worked out for you. You've turned into a successful person in your own right. I'm glad for you."

"You're right," she agreed. "It was a long time ago and, to tell you the truth, I haven't thought about our marriage — or you — for a very long time. It's just, with you here, it brings it all back."

"I know. It does for me, too."

Rose smiled. "When I think of it, I'm amazed at the difference between who I was when you left and who I am now. You wouldn't know, but I started to have a drinking problem."

"You?"

"Yes, me. Emily was the first to point it out to me. I was drinking too many cocktails before dinner, too much wine with dinner, and too much brandy after dinner. When I realized what I was doing to myself, I stopped cold turkey. Actually, I was afraid I wouldn't be able to stop. But I did. I didn't have a drop for years, afraid I'd turn into an alcoholic."

"And now?"

"Now," she took a deep breath and looked around the dining room, "now I feel like I own the world. I couldn't be happier. Especially now that I've had a chance to tell you how I felt then, about being dumped and thrown out with the garbage."

"Oh, Rose ..."

"Well, of course I felt that way. What would you expect?" Then she looked him straight in the eye. "How did you feel when you found out Elaine was cheating on you?"

She might be as happy as she claims, but she sure as hell is still angry with me.

Manny sat back on his chair and met her gaze. Her point was well taken. If he was honest, he'd felt the same way: discarded, unsuitable, undeserving — and untrusting.

"Look, I'm sorry I've hurt you," he said. "That was never my intent." He paused. He wasn't going to attack her for not having been intellectually or

180

sexually stimulating enough. And there was no need to batter her by once again parading out his years of infidelity. It would serve no purpose; she didn't want the truth — she just wanted to hurt him, to get justice.

"I've already apologized," he said, his voice softer now. "What else can I say, Rose? Isn't it time to let it go? We're beating a dead horse here."

"I'm sorry. I hadn't intended to bombard you with old feelings. Except, I guess I'm finding out they're not so old. To tell you the truth, I thought I was over it. Really, Manny," she said reaching out to touch his hand, "I wanted this to be a pleasant evening. I'm sorry for ambushing you like this."

He squeezed her hand and thought about what she had said. "It's OK. I guess I had it coming. But now that you've had your say, let's move on, all right?"

"That's what I want, too. I was hoping we could be friends again."

Manny thought about his hope that Emily could reminisce openly about her childhood with both of her parents, and it would be preferable if Rosemary could grow up unhindered by a cold war within the family.

"Sure, that's what I'm saying. It would be good for Emily if we could get along."

Rose suddenly looked sad. Maybe it was the way her eyes glistened. "Good," she said.

They spent the rest of the meal gossiping about old friends and sharing stories about their work and their lives. Manny alluded to occasional dating without going into any details, and Rose made no mention of dating at all. When they had finished their coffee, Rose asked, "Manny, if I can make just one more reference to the past before we leave?"

Manny felt his body tense, wondering what else was coming — one last artillery shell to be lobbed. "Sure. Go ahead."

"When you left, I thought I'd never recover. I guess I already told you that. But what I didn't say was that, what made it so hard for me, so heartbreaking, was that I was so much in love with you. That's why it's impossible for me to hear that you didn't feel loved. But what I want to say is, I've gotten over it. I mean, I've gotten over you. You're still a fine person, a good person, and I've enjoyed this evening. But I'm not in love with you anymore. I've been afraid all these years that if we met, I'd still feel the way I did before. But it's OK. I'm

OK." She laughed. "I feel like a recovered alcoholic."

Manny was unprepared for his own reaction. *What does she mean, she's no longer in love with me?* As if it were some hurtful insult. But he immediately recognized it was good for both of them, and for their family.

He reached across the table and took her hand. "It's better this way, to be beyond the passion. After all, Plato said it was the ideal state."

They parted in the lobby and, this time, Manny felt quite comfortable giving her a peck on the cheek.

In bed, back at Emily's, he thought about their conversation — her anger and his willingness to absorb it. He was amazed at their different perspectives on their marriage: She had really felt loved and was convinced he had never cheated on her until Elaine. How had he managed to convey that to her? He had always liked her well enough. She was a sweet and good person in many respects. But he couldn't remember actually being in love with her. Looking back, he was no longer sure why he had proposed to her. Perhaps it was nothing more than her big boobs and the fact that he was ready to settle down. With Elaine it had been so much more.

The next morning, he enjoyed breakfast with his daughter and granddaughter. He told Emily about his dinner with her mother.

"We've decided to bury the hatchet. Actually, she buried it in me." They both laughed. "Well, I had it coming, I guess."

He peeked at Emily, half hoping to note some protest, but he saw her nodding in agreement. "Anyway, we're going to try to be more friendly with each other — for our sake, and for yours. I want you to feel comfortable talking to me about things you experience with your mother. She's a big part of your life and you don't have to be afraid of referring to her when you're with me. I'm not going to be upset if you bring up her name. OK?"

Emily gave him a hug and said she was happy to hear they had finally begun to make peace with each other.

182

While Em was busy with household chores, Manny called Laura. He reached her at home and, to his surprise, she invited him over for dinner that night. He hadn't been to her home in four years, since he and Elaine had separated. He hadn't seen his grandson — that's how he thought of Kyle — since he was six months old. He had felt a connection the moment Kyle was born. He was also fond of Laura's husband, Kirk, and he was looking forward to seeing them again.

In the afternoon, Manny drove to the university to look up some of his old friends. During summer session, the campus was quiet and almost empty. The grounds, the buildings, even the hallways and classrooms felt deserted and lonely, containing only the echoes of his footsteps. The secretary was busy in the departmental office, but no one else was around. She gave him a warm welcome and filled him in on news around campus — intrigues over sabbaticals and budgets and chairmanships. He got some addresses and phone numbers from her, but learned that all of his friends were away for the summer.

Laura lived on an old farm a few miles outside of town. Manny pulled up their gravel driveway and parked next to a sedan and pickup truck. By the time he emerged from the car, Kirk and Kyle were coming down from the porch to greet him. Laura, tall and lanky, was just behind them, wiping her hands on a dishtowel. They greeted him warmly and invited him inside. Manny knew Kirk was a carpenter, but he was caught off guard by his renovation of the old farmhouse. Everything inside was updated, yet in keeping with an unassuming, country style. They sat on the front porch, where the air was comfortably cool. Laura offered lemonade or iced tea; Manny opted for lemonade.

"I hear your mom had some difficulty recently. How is she doing?"

"I'm not surprised you heard," she said. "That's all anybody talks about around here." She took a breath and put a big cheery smile on her face. "Well, that's Mom. What can I tell you? She's still in the hospital. The doctor said she might need more surgery later on."

"I'm still not sure what happened. All I know is that she was attacked and her face got cut up, something like that."

Laura cast a quick glance at Kyle and then turned back to him. "Maybe we can talk about that later?"

183

"Sure," he agreed.

The four of them sat around talking and getting reacquainted. When Laura went inside to put the finishing touches on supper, Kirk and Kyle volunteered to give Manny a quick tour. Manny was impressed that Kirk had put solar panels on the roofs of their house and barn, and had installed a small windmill as well.

"We're not completely off the grid," Kirk explained, "but we're doing what we can to be environmentally sound."

Manny was amused. Getting off the grid was not just about saving money or being environmentally conscious — it also reflected Kirk's desire to be as self-sufficient as possible. In many ways, Kirk fit Manny's stereotype of a Vermonter: hard working and independent. Kirk would never use two words if one would do. Manny enjoyed the view of the surrounding hills from their open pasture, where they kept two cows, a couple of goats, and some sheep. They even had chickens and a decent-sized garden.

"You and Laura have really taken to this lifestyle," he exclaimed, impressed with their commitment.

"We like it and it's good for Kyle."

At four and a half, Kyle was big and very well coordinated for his age. Obviously, he adored his father and the two of them had an easy and natural relationship that Manny admired. When Kyle went chasing after one of the sheep, Kirk turned to Manny.

"Kyle was real upset by what happened to his grandmother. He's had some nasty nightmares and any talk about it gets the him scared."

Manny imagined some wild possibilities of how Kyle might picture someone knifing his grandmother, and he easily empathized with the boy.

"Of course," Manny agreed. "I should have thought of that myself."

They started back to the house, where Laura was ready to put dinner on the table. After a very enjoyable meal, Manny was surprised at how relaxed he felt, given how cold Laura was after he and Elaine separated and then divorced. He was tempted to comment on it, but was afraid that even that kind of conversation might be upsetting to Kyle, so he decided to wait for a better time.

Manny helped Laura clean up in the kitchen while Kirk got Kyle ready for bed.

"I have to thank you, Laura, for inviting me over and making me feel so welcome here."

"Of course. You're family, after all."

"I'm glad to hear you say that. When your mother and I split up, I kind of felt that you were putting some distance between us."

"Yeah. I was angry with both of you. I didn't want anything to do with either of you."

"Why would you be upset with your mother? It was my decision to divorce."

Laura looked at him in astonishment. "Oh come on, Manny. I know how much you loved her. You never would have separated from her if she hadn't been up to her old tricks." She laughed, "No pun intended."

"What do you mean?" he asked, pausing as he wiped the dishes.

"Well, in light of what happened recently, I'd say it was obvious that she was having an affair with Frank Gambon. Isn't that why you split?"

Manny was taken aback. "Is that what she told you?"

"Ha! No, my mother would never talk to me about anything like that. But it's true, isn't it?"

Manny was not ready to concede the point. He still felt some old obligation to protect Laura from this knowledge. "What makes you say that? Why would you accuse your mother of that?"

Laura picked up a dishtowel and leaned her thin frame against the sink. "Are you kidding me, Manny? My mother always ran around. She's always cheated."

Manny was shocked — more than that — horrified at her accusation.

"Don't act so shocked, Manny. Did you think you were the first person she cheated with?"

Manny pulled a chair out from the kitchen table and dropped down heavily onto it. "Actually, Laura, I did."

"Well," she said, "you weren't. She was seeing Frank on and off during the whole time she and my father were married. And not only him," she added. "There were others, too."

Manny felt all the air go out of him. The horror of that awful night flooded through him again: shock, anger, disbelief, sadness.

"Are you sure?" he asked.

"Oh, I'm sure," she said sullenly. "Ever since I was little, maybe six or seven, I've known. My father always suspected, but I don't know how much he actually knew. They fought about it often."

Assuming Laura was right, Manny still couldn't believe Elaine had never told him. He had been so convinced there were no secrets between them. He had trusted her absolutely. It was as if Laura were telling him about an entirely different person, a stranger he hadn't known at all.

"How did you know?"

Laura gave him a mischievous look over the rim of her glass. "In a house of secrets, kids learn quickly how to be sneaky and devious. I listened in on her telephone conversations. I rifled through her purse and read notes and memorized telephone numbers. I made calls to check up on her whereabouts. You know, when you don't trust someone, everything they do is suspicious. I thought I was doing something that might ultimately protect my father." She lowered her head sadly. "Of course, I never told him anything. I couldn't bear to hurt him, even though he and I never got along all that great either."

After a prolonged silence, Manny exhaled. "I'm flabbergasted. I don't know what to say. I'm in shock."

Laura studied him. "I'm really surprised to hear you say that. I'd have sworn she would have told you or you would have found out sooner."

"Sooner?"

"That she was cheating on you, that she was seeing Mr. Gambon."

Manny suddenly remembered having wondered if Elaine had had a previous affair with Frank. Apparently she had, before he and Elaine had married. But was Laura implying something else?

"Are you saying Elaine was seeing Gambon, not only at the end of our marriage, but ..."

"Throughout your marriage. The whole time."

"Jesus," he mumbled.

"I'm sorry," she said.

"No, I'm glad you told me all this." After a moment, he looked up at her. "Does Kirk know? Have you told him?"

"No. I've never told anyone. This is the first time I've said it out loud." Her eyes began to water.

"So your mother doesn't know you knew all along?"

Laura shook her head and reached for a tissue to wipe her eyes. Manny suddenly realized how it must have been for her — aware of her mother's infidelities, guarding the secret, feeling complicit in the guilt. He looked at her with sympathy, understanding her burden.

"When did you find out that my mother had been cheating on you?" she asked, blowing her nose.

Manny told her about the night of Elaine's confession. He described how his mistrust had grown, cancer-like, over the ensuing year until he lost his passion for the marriage and for Elaine.

Laura recalled some incidents from her childhood that involved Frank. "I remember once, when I was about seven, my mother brought me to a park and we just happened to run into an old friend who was there with his little girl. She was a little older than I was. I thought there was something fishy about the way they urged this other girl and me to go off and play, while they sat real chummy on a bench together. I had suspected something for a long time, so I watched them. You know, if you're looking for something, you're more likely to see it — the way they spent way too much time together that day, the way she looked at him, the way she touched him. Later, I'd find notes from him in her purse. It wasn't the only time we 'just happened' to run into Mr. Gambon. God, I was so angry with her."

Laura lapsed into silence, then sighed, "I guess I found my own ways of getting even with her."

"I never knew," Manny said. "I never had any idea. So their relationship goes way back?"

"At least 28 years that I'm aware of."

"God!" he exclaimed, in awe that Elaine could maintain an affair through two marriages.

Kirk came back into the room. "Kyle's in bed. Out like a light."

Manny commented on what a fine boy he was and what a good job the two of them were doing with him. "He's seems to be very happy," he said.

Kirk noticed that Laura had been crying and looked from one to the other. Laura shook her head, dismissing his unspoken inquiry. Then she looked at Manny. "Tell me about your love life. Have you been seeing anyone?"

"To tell you the truth, Laura, my dating experiences have been pretty disastrous. At first, I wasn't really ready for another relationship. I wasn't sure I still had the capacity to love someone. So I've been settling for relationships that are pretty superficial." He shook his head. "I have to tell you both, it's hell out there. A jungle. Survival of the fittest. I don't know if I'm ready to go through all the crap involved in finding someone. I think I'd just as soon be a hermit as expose myself to that meat grinder again."

Laura laughed sympathetically. "I know what you're saying. I hear my single friends expressing the same thoughts." She cast a quick, warm smile at Kirk. "I know I'm so grateful to have someone and not have to be out there." Kirk reached for her hand and smiled. They looked happy together.

"Do you have any plans while you're up here?" Kirk asked him.

"Well, when I came up, I thought, in addition to visiting with you and Emily and Mark, I'd see a couple of my former colleagues and maybe go off and do some camping. But now with all this about Elaine ..." He turned to Laura. "Do you think it would be all right if I visited her?"

Laura's eyes widened. "You'd want to?"

"Sure," he said. "She's been through a rough ordeal. I'm sure she'd like to know that I wish her well, that I'm not dancing on her hospital bed."

"Well, she's not supposed to be discharged for another couple of days. I've called her every day, but I haven't made it down there yet to visit her."

Manny studied her for a moment, wondering why she hadn't yet been to see her mother. "How would you feel if I visited her? Would it be OK with you?"

"Why wouldn't it be?"

"I don't know. I just thought there was a chance you might be upset if I went to see her."

"That's up to you, Manny. If you can find it in your heart to forgive her, then that's up to you."

"Yeah, I think I'd like to do that."

Emily and Mark were watching TV when Manny returned that evening. He plopped down in a chair to join them and, when the program was over, Emily brought in three beers. "How did it go?" she asked.

Manny told them about how big Kyle had grown and what a wonderful job Kirk had done on the interior of the home. "He's made them pretty self-sufficient — solar panels on all of their buildings, a windmill, even a cow for milk and some chickens."

"Kirk's a neat guy," said Mark. "I've seen some of his work. He's more than a carpenter, he's a really skilled cabinet maker."

Manny took a deep breath. "Laura also told me some pretty interesting stuff that I'm having some trouble with."

"Like what?" asked Emily.

"About Elaine. She's pretty sure that Elaine was seeing this Gambon guy even before she and I got married — and maybe all through our marriage."

He was reluctant to add that Laura suspected Elaine had other affairs too, while she was married to Ken. He didn't want to think about it.

Emily and Mark were silent.

"That's really got to be very disturbing, to find out that kind of shit," Mark offered. "I guess the good news is that you're out of it now."

"Yeah, I suppose so." He took a swallow from his bottle of beer. "I'm going to visit her in the hospital tomorrow," he announced.

He got the expected reaction from his daughter and her husband. "You're going to go visit her? After all this? After finding out that maybe she was cheating on you the whole time you were together?"

"I've got my reasons. There are things I'd like to know. I can't let my history with her deteriorate into a list of insinuations, rumors, and accusations. I have all these questions. Did she do it or didn't she? And why? And where the hell was I while all of this was supposedly going on? How is it that I didn't know any of this? Am I that goddamned stupid?" He drained his bottle as a way of avoiding their eyes.

"One thing you're not, Daddy, is stupid. Blind, maybe, but not stupid."

Mark chimed in, "Love is blind."

"I guess," Manny said.

"Mom is another case in point," added Emily.

Manny looked up and met her gaze.

She's right. Rose did love me and is still blind to what I did, still can't believe I cheated on her for all of those years. And Emily was blind, too.

He saw Emily and Mark reach out their hands to touch. He could tell they felt lucky to be so in love, so trusting — and maybe even a little superior for having made good decisions. He wished them well. He hoped they would always feel so happy with each other.

Manny said, "I'm thinking back to when I was with your mother — how I deceived her and you. At the time, I thought I was doing the right thing —

covering up what I was doing — by keeping the family together, continuing to provide an intact family for you while you were in school. I gave myself credit for protecting you and your mother. Of course, I shouldn't have been running around in the first place, but I felt justified in doing that. I felt morally superior for making all of the little efforts, telling all the necessary lies, to keep my secret life from hurting either of you.

"I had a dream once that I was robbing a bank. It was like one of those old gangster films from the 1930s or '40s. I had this tommy gun under my right arm, my finger on the trigger, and I was carrying bags of money. As I backed out of the bank into a big intersection, people started moving toward me from every direction. I said, 'Stay away or I'll mow you all down,' just like James Cagney in the movies. I hoped that my warning, which was really a bluff, would keep them all at bay while I made my escape, because, of course, I didn't want to kill anybody.

"But they kept on coming, slowly surrounding me, drawing a circle around me, like a noose, tighter and tighter. And the closer they got, the more panicky I felt and the more I realized my dilemma: Either I would have to pull the damn trigger and kill all those innocent bystanders, or let them capture me and punish me for my crime. All my supposedly good intentions didn't count for anything — and then I realized there is no way to do a bad thing well."

"What happened?" Mark asked.

"In the dream? I woke up, of course. I didn't have to choose. In real life? I gave myself up. I confessed."

At that moment he realized that Elaine had done exactly the same thing — given herself up. But, he wondered, what had gone on in her mind? Had she convinced herself that she was doing a good thing, or doing a bad thing well by telling him about her affair? Maybe she hadn't even cared, hadn't even considered it.

—⚅— 7 —⚅—

The next morning after breakfast, Manny volunteered to watch Rosemary
while Emily ran some errands. A cuddly toddler, Rosemary snuggled
right into him, and it brought back memories of Emily at that age. How
innocent she had been. How would Rosemary grow up? Would she retain this
wonderful capacity for trust? Would the world break her heart?

When Emily returned home, Manny left for Burlington to visit Elaine. The
hospital was a huge, sprawling complex. He eventually found Elaine's room on
the second floor. As he walked past the nurse's station he saw various people
milling about — physicians, nurses, technicians, orderlies, housekeeping staff,
all clad in blue or green or paisley scrubs. A tall man, somewhat stoop-shouldered,
as if from fatigue or great sorrow, emerged from Elaine's room. On impulse,
Manny followed him to the end of the hall, where he watched the man buy a
can of soda from a machine and sink into a sofa overlooking the vast parking lot.

Manny approached him. "Pardon me, are you Frank Gambon?"

"Excuse me?" The man looked up warily. "Why do you ask?"

Manny thought he saw fear or guardedness. "My name is Manny. Manny
Randolph."

The man's eyes closed, as if in weariness. "Oh," he said, and indicated a
seat next to him on a sofa.

"Yes," he said. "I'm Frank Gambon. We've never actually met, have we?"

191

Manny took his jacket off and placed it on the sofa beside him.

"No. No, we haven't. But Elaine once described you to me and when I saw you coming out of her room, I took a wild guess."

Frank gave a crooked smile. "I assume you heard what happened?"

"Kind of. All I know is that she was attacked. Slashed?"

Frank leaned back into the sofa and drank from his soda. "Say, can I buy you a drink?" he asked, holding up his can.

"No thanks," said Manny. "I could use a real drink about now."

Manny assessed the man in front of him, his sad state of depletion. Even so, he saw that Gambon was a handsome man. "You look like shit," he said matter of factly, "like you've been run over."

Frank grinned. "I guess I haven't gotten much sleep these last few days. Between being here with Elaine or dealing with my daughter's legal issues."

"What the hell happened, for Christ's sake?"

Avoiding the question, Frank took a swig from his can. "You planning on going in to see her?"

"No, I came here to find you. Of course I'm going to see her."

Manny gathered his jacket and got up from his chair.

"Sit down," Frank said quietly. "They're doing some procedure in there and she won't be able to see anyone for another 10 minutes or so."

Manny eased back into his chair. "You going to tell me what happened?"

"Why did you come here?" Frank avoided the question.

"Why should I tell you?" Manny asked.

"I'm curious, that's all. I would have thought you'd be angry with her, and I wonder if you're here to gloat. She's been through enough without somebody gloating over her."

Manny stared at him incredulously. Who the hell did this guy think he was, with his proprietary attitude? "I didn't come here to gloat. Jesus, what's with you? You're not her knight in white armor. From what I understand, it's because of you that she's here in the first place. So where do you get off interrogating me like you're in charge of her?"

Frank gave another of his bemused smiles. "So you are still angry. I thought so."

"I wasn't angry until I started talking to you. What the hell did she see in you? You can't even give a straight answer to a simple question."

"It's not so simple. Look, I just want to make sure you're not here to cause

192

more trouble. We've been through enough. None of us needs anymore crap from anybody. That's all."

"For what it's worth, Gambon, I came here to visit Elaine because I heard she was attacked by your daughter and I wanted to pay my respects."

He realized, as soon as he'd said it, that it sounded like she'd been killed. He hurried to correct the impression. "I just wanted to visit her, see if there was anything I could do."

Frank was staring up the hallway.

"How is she doing?" Manny asked.

"Not too well. She lost an awful lot of blood. A lot of blood. She nearly bled to death."

Manny raised his eyebrows. *Almost died?*

Frank continued, "My daughter ..." he swallowed a couple of times before continuing, "she slashed Elaine across the face with a kitchen knife, a chef's knife, one of those big ones. She severed Elaine's right cheek, cut through the corners of her mouth, and sliced open her left cheek. The blade cut through muscles, nerves, blood vessels, everything. It even sliced her tongue."

His hands instinctively came up to his own face to demonstrate how Elaine's lower jaw had nearly detached from the rest of her face. His eyes were brimming with tears.

Manny pictured Elaine's hands flying up to protect her face, blood spurting through her fingers. He imagined his own mouth filling up with blood and, for a moment, he thought he might throw up. Bile rose in the back of his throat.

"My God," he managed to say.

Frank nodded, as if to say, yes, it was horrible, even more horrible than that. "I never saw so much blood. It was all over everything, everywhere." He put down his can of soda with a look of disgust, as if he too, could taste only blood. He ran his fingers through his hair and then studied them as if he expected them to be stained.

"When they brought her here, to the ER, they gave her blood. I forget how many units." He paused for a few moments. "They called in a plastic surgeon right away. The operation took hours," he added. He looked away and then got up and walked to the window as if something of great interest in the parking lot compelled him to look.

Manny sat there trying to piece together what had happened. Had Gambon been there? Had he intervened? Why had his daughter attacked Elaine?

What had provoked her? He was tempted to ask Gambon these questions, but seeing him framed in the window made him hesitate.

Another time.

"I'm sorry," he said simply. "I'm sorry for you and your daughter, and for Elaine."

Frank mumbled, "Thanks."

"I'd like to talk to you again, if that's all right."

Gambon turned to him. "When you go in, tell her I'll be back in an hour or so."

Manny nodded.

"Oh, and be prepared. She still looks like hell. Her face is all bandaged up. She can't eat any solid food yet."

"OK. Is there a number where I can call you? Maybe we can meet for a drink or something."

Frank gave him his number and walked toward the elevators. Manny watched as the doors closed behind him.

He knocked softly, then slowly pushed the door open. She turned her head toward the sound as he stepped into the room.

"Hi," he said, automatically adopting a cheery tone. He thought he saw panic in her eyes, and an impulse to turn away from him. He hesitated, scanning the room: bed, chair, bedside table, IV drip, a machine he recognized as a morphine pump.

"I met Frank in the hall. He said he'll be back in about an hour."

He hoped that making reference to Frank would reassure her in some way that he meant no harm. He thought he noticed her body relax. Her cheeks, covered with a cast to immobilize her jaw, left only her lips exposed. She looked like a war casualty. What he could see of her face was swollen and bruised. Her hair, grayer than he remembered, lay lifeless against the pillow.

"I came up here to Vermont to visit the girls. When I heard what happened, I thought I'd come and visit. I hope it's all right, my being here."

She briefly closed her eyes in what he thought might be resignation.

"I never expected to see you, again," she whispered. She spoke with a lisp, and he realized what an effort it must be for her to talk without being able to fully move her jaw or lips. He was reminded of a ventriloquist. The moving lips surrounded by the rigid white cast looked cartoonish and disembodied.

"Frank told me what happened."

Elaine closed her eyes and flinched at the memory.

"Are you OK?" He immediately realized the foolishness of the question. "I mean, Frank told me you lost a lot of blood. Are you stable now?"

"I'm getting stronger, but they're still evaluating my condition. They may change all this tomorrow," making a brief gesture with one hand to indicate her facial bandages. "I may go home in a couple of days. It's only a matter of healing at this point. Maybe speech therapy and some physical therapy."

Manny strained to decipher her labored and indistinct speech. He thought she smiled, but he couldn't be sure. He winced, imagining how painful a sliced tongue and mouth must be.

"Are you in much pain?"

She rolled her eyes toward the ceiling and then glanced briefly at the little red button pinned to her blanket.

"Frank told me they did plastic surgery."

Her eyes welled up and she fumbled at her side for the box of tissues.

"I'm sure they did a great job," Manny tried to sooth her. "You'll come out of this as beautiful as ever."

She slowly wagged a finger at him. "No, I'll have two grotesque permanent scars." She indicated lines radiating from her mouth across her cheeks. "Like a Cheshire Cat."

Manny wasn't sure what to say. She might very well be disfigured for life. The thought occurred to him that he was lucky to have been married to her during the prime of her life, and wouldn't be burdened by her physical and psychological wounds. An aftertaste of guilt lingered for a moment.

Sitting down in the chair next to the bed, he said, "I understand that Frank's daughter is in jail."

"Where she belongs."

"Do you know why she did this to you?" he asked.

Elaine's eyes closed briefly. "Frank's wife killed herself, slit her wrists. His daughter blames me." A look of pain engulfed her face, and Manny wasn't sure if it was physical or emotional — or both. Maybe it wasn't even appropriate for him to ask her about it.

He tried changing the subject. "I saw Laura yesterday. I had dinner at their house. It's the first time I've seen them in about four years. Kyle really has turned into one big boy. They're all very happy and healthy."

"I haven't seen Laura for a couple of weeks. It feels like so long ago. She hasn't been here." Manny saw her eyes flick away for a second, and he felt sorry for her.

Elaine continued. "I wondered if I'd ever see anyone again. I was so frightened. I don't think I've ever been so afraid in all my life. I was certain I would die. And I thought: Oh my God! I'll never see Laura or Kyle again, never look into those eyes again. It was so terrifying."

He tried to imagine enduring such an attack. He pictured himself bleeding to death, choking on his own blood, vulnerable and powerless. Does it take some kind of super-human strength to survive such an ordeal?

"Elaine, I know you're going through hell right now, but Laura told me something that I need to check out with you." He gave her a questioning look. She was already in so much pain. His glance took in the morphine pump and the thought jumped into his mind that maybe this was the ideal time to ask questions.

"She said you had been seeing Gambon for a very long time, even before we got married." He studied her, waiting for her response.

"I've known Frank for almost my whole life."

"When did you start seeing him?"

She looked at him sadly. "He was my first love."

"What do you mean, he was your first love?"

"My first lover." She saw that Manny was confused. "Ask Frank to tell you about us. Tell him I told you to."

"I will," he said.

Manny felt as if he was being dismissed. It was clear Elaine was in no condition to carry on a long or stressful conversation. He made some more small talk, telling her about his job in Philly and his visit with Emily, and then he wished her well.

Back in the hallway, he felt a palpable sense of relief. When he and Elaine had been married, being together felt more natural than being apart, as if he were complete only in her company. Now, he realized how uncomfortable he'd been in her presence. How completely everything had changed! Suddenly he knew that he was free of her spell.

How fragile a relationship is, to turn so completely on a single experience, a few words, a tone of voice, a look.

Outside, Manny reveled in the warmth of the sun. Deciding that some fresh air would be restorative, he drove to the marina on Lake Champlain. At a restaurant with a deck overlooking the water, he ordered a sandwich and beer, and sat contemplating the scenery. So Gambon had been Elaine's first lover. What a shocker that was. Laura had calculated that her mother had been seeing him since Laura was six or seven, but Elaine had probably known Gambon even before she married Ken. Manny shook his head in amazement.

He watched the boats entering and leaving the marina and thought of all the times he and Elaine had sailed together there. He imagined the wind flapping in the sails, the boat slapping against the water, Elaine's long, auburn hair blowing across her face, her bright smile, the sound of their laughter. Had she had ever gone sailing with Gambon? Or anyone else? Had Gambon's wife been aware of her husband's infidelity all along? Did she know Elaine? Mostly, Manny wondered how Elaine had managed to keep the secret from him for all of those years. He was shocked, once again, to realize how little he had known her — in contrast to his conviction that he had known her totally. But then, Rose had felt the same way about him, hadn't she?

—m— 8 —m—

When Frank entered Elaine's hospital room, an aide had just fed her some soup. She had been on a liquid diet, and they were supposed to start her on soft foods very soon. He saw a dish of pudding on her tray as he approached the bed.

"I'll do that if you want," he offered, and the aide relinquished her place and left the room.

"Where have you been?" Elaine asked.

"I had some things to take care of. I got back as quickly as I could," he said, picking up the task of feeding her.

Elaine looked up at the clock on the wall.

"You were gone over two hours. I was afraid something had happened to you."

He laughed, "What could happen to me?"

She stared at him as he spooned some pudding into her mouth.

"What could happen to you?" she finally managed to growl. "Where should I start?"

He sensed her outrage and the fear that it hid. With her jaw held shut, everything sounded angry, and he decided to ignore the accusation.

"Well, nothing happened, and I'm back, so all's right with the world."

"Yeah, right. Everything's hunky-dory."

"Elaine, calm down. You know what I mean. Relax."

"Were you at the jail?"

He lowered his eyes and concentrated on scraping up the last of the pudding with the spoon. He put it into her mouth and she swallowed before asking him again. "Were you?"

"I ran over for a little while, but I got hung up in that damn security process they have over there. It's like getting stuck behind a school bus or a garbage truck. Some lady kept setting off the alarm. She must have had to go through a dozen times, each time taking off one more thing. It was like watching a new version of strip poker."

He had hoped that the incident would amuse her, but her eyes bored in on him.

"I don't know why you do this to me, Frank. After what she did."

"Lainie, she's my daughter. I can't just abandon her. Besides, it was an accident."

"Accident? Frank, she tried to kill me."

"That's an exaggeration."

"Don't say that. *This* is no accident," she gestured toward her face.

"Elaine, she didn't mean it. She didn't plan to hurt you."

Elaine waved him away.

"You're blind when it comes to her," she finally mumbled.

It took him a few seconds to decipher what she had said. "I don't want to argue with you. You're wrong. I'm not blind to her. I know Abby very well. She blames you for Anita's suicide. She blames both of us. That's obvious. But that doesn't mean she'd try to kill you. It was just the heat of the moment, Lainie, an accident. She didn't intend for any of this to happen."

Elaine shook her head and looked at him contemptuously.

"Laura never attacked you or that precious wife of yours."

"What are you talking about? Laura never had any cause to attack anyone. Anita never did anything to her."

Elaine gave him a withering look and turned her head away.

"I never interfered with your relationship with Laura. Why are you trying to deny me a relationship with Abby?"

"She's got a husband to be there for her."

"She's got a father, too," he said firmly. "Lainie, be reasonable. My standing by her has nothing to do with my love for you. My love for you isn't diminished by my loving my daughter."

"Frank, you diminished your love for me by choosing to stay married to Anita for my whole life. Your commitment to me goes only so far, and no further."

200

"How can you say that? After what I've done?"

"What? What have you done? After all these years of being miserable, you finally had the balls to leave that pathetic, weak, suffocating bitch, and you want a medal? For what you should have done decades ago?"

"Elaine," he snapped. "What the hell's the matter with you? She killed herself, for Christ's sake. I've got her death on my hands."

"Did you kill her?"

"I might as well have."

"Jesus, Frank, are you going to continue, for the rest of your life, to take responsibility for everything Anita or Abby ever did? They're both adults. They're free agents. Make them take responsibility for their own actions. You didn't kill Anita, she killed herself."

"I'm just trying to accept my own responsibilities, that's all."

Elaine wearily turned her head from side to side. "Is that what you're doing? Is that why you're here, because I'm your responsibility?"

"Honey, don't make it into a bad thing that I love you and feel responsible for you. I'm trying to do what's right."

Elaine took a deep breath and looked at him with tears in her eyes. "Frank, for all these years, I've waited for you to do the right thing. For over 30 years, you were a prisoner of Anita and Abigail. And I was *your* prisoner. You finally did the right thing, and Anita chose to punish you by taking her own life. And your daughter, rather than rightfully being angry at her mother, took it out on me."

She paused and waited for him to make eye contact with her. "Now you've got to make a choice. I almost died because of her. For over 30 years, I let Anita live the life I should have had. Now her daughter, your daughter, tried to take it from me. I won't relive these past 30 years again. That's over. Either you're with me, really with me, or you're not. I can't live with leftovers anymore. I won't."

She shook her head and looked for the magic button on her morphine pump.

"Just go," she said. "I'm tired. I need to rest."

"Fine," he said, shoving his chair back and standing up. "I'll see you in the morning."

She turned her head away and closed her eyes. He watched her for a few moments and then left, closing the door softly behind him.

—⚒—9—⚒—

After walking around the marina for a while, Manny headed back to Emily's. He persuaded them to let him take them out to dinner, and they suggested a restaurant in Burlington. Seated at the table, Emily asked her father about his visit to the hospital.

"Interesting," he said after a moment's thought. "I ran into Frank Gambon, the fellow she's been seeing. I'm not sure who's in worse shape, her or him. He's devastated. I got the impression he was there when his daughter attacked Elaine." He briefly described her condition without giving too much gory detail in front of Rosemary.

"Apparently, it was pretty gruesome. I don't know if he could be more distraught if his daughter had actually killed Elaine. He must be racked with guilt at having caused all that horror."

"How did you feel, seeing Elaine again after all this time?"

"When I left her room, I realized I felt an immense surge of relief — that she's no longer my responsibility, and that I no longer have to wonder what she's really feeling or thinking or doing. I guess I was unprepared for how little I did feel. A wave of calm washed over me when I left the hospital. I'm just glad I'm not emotionally involved anymore."

He thought for a moment longer, recalling his last conversation with Rose. "Your mother told me the other night that she's over me. I was glad for her, but also," he gave an embarrassed chuckle, "I was a little hurt. You know, my ego got a little bruised. But when I left Elaine's room at the hospital, I realized I was truly over her, and that's a relief. It's like I'm on a riverbank and watching someone else in a small boat battling windy conditions and strong currents — and glad I'm not the one out there fighting to keep everything from going under."

Mark asked, "How did you feel about running into that Gambon guy?"

"Initially, I'm sure there was some competition going on between us, you know, two bulls, one cow. That was before I saw Elaine." For some reason he was reluctant to reveal that Gambon had been Elaine's first lover. "I can only imagine what he must be feeling about his daughter."

He looked at Emily. "Don't you ever do anything like that!"

Emily laughed and turned to Mark. "Only if this guy ever gives me good cause."

Mark raised his hands in self-defense. "Hey, I see what happens. I don't need a tree to fall on me."

"A tree falling on you would be merciful compared to what I'd do to you," she intoned in mock warning.

"Seriously," interjected her father. "I see what he's going through. He must be so conflicted."

"Don't worry, Manny, I know how to calm your daughter's spirits. Don't I, Babe?"

It was good to be able to joke about it, but Manny was serious. He was taken aback by the depth of his sympathy for Gambon. He still held a grudge against the man, but he also felt compassion for him. Instead of experiencing him as a competitor, it felt more like a brotherhood, with each of them having suffered because of Elaine.

When they got home from dinner, Emily put Rosemary to bed and Mark settled into an easy chair to watch his beloved Boston Red Sox. Manny wasn't a baseball fan, so he retreated to another room to do some reading. After a few minutes, he found himself recalling his encounters with Elaine and Gambon. He had so many unanswered questions. Finally, he got out his cell phone and called Gambon. They agreed to meet the following evening.

"Why don't you come over here?" Gambon suggested. "It'll be more private and we can talk. I'll cook up a couple of steaks if you bring the drinks." So it was settled.

Manny recognized that the idea of meeting Frank for dinner was potentially imprudent. It was awkward, unconventional, and downright weird, given their history. But he wanted answers. Besides, even when he had first found out about Elaine and Frank, his reaction to the betrayal was primarily directed at her, not him. And his pain, dulled by the passage of time, was no longer the issue. He had just learned that Elaine's involvement with Frank predated her marriage to both Ken and him. Yes, it might be strange for him to sit down with Frank, but he felt more sympathy for the man than anger or competitiveness — and he was grateful that it was now Frank who was responsible for Elaine.

Frank lived about 15 miles across town, in an area dotted with old farms. Manny turned into the long driveway that led past a modern garage up to an old farmhouse. Frank was sitting in a rocker on the front porch, beer in hand. Manny pulled up alongside an old pickup truck and climbed the slight rise to the front steps.

"You bring booze?"

"Some gin and beer," he said, half hoisting the two bags he was carrying.

"Sounds good," Frank said, lifting himself out of the rocker and opening the screen door. "Just bring it on inside. I'll fix us a drink."

Manny followed him into a dark vestibule that opened to a living room on the left, a stairway on the right, and a hallway that went straight to a modest kitchen. Manny placed the two bags on the worn Formica counter while Frank extracted a tray of ice-cubes from the freezer.

"I gather you like gin," Frank noted.

"That's why I brought it. I wasn't sure you'd have any."

"Oh, I've got a little bit of just about everything." Frank filled a couple of glasses with cubes, added a hefty amount of gin, then squeezed half a lime into each drink.

"Let's go on the porch," he suggested. Frank settled himself into his rocker and Manny took an old wicker chair that had seen better days.

"Cheers," he said, and lifted his glass toward Manny, who returned the salute.

"How do you like it out here? It's pretty far out of town, isn't it?"

"Oh, I don't know. I'm used to it, I guess. I've lived here since Anita and I got married. That was 37 years ago this month, on the 14th."

"You and your wife were married 37 years?"

"Would have been. Anita cut it short by three weeks."

205

Manny paused, then opted for blunt. "Why did she kill herself?"

Frank looked at him over his glass as he swallowed. "Well, therein lies a tale."

"We've got all night," said Manny.

Frank took another swallow and looked out over the front lawn. A semicircle of trees bordered the driveway and what Manny assumed was the edge of the property on the opposite side.

"I guess the bottom line is, I left her."

Manny waited as Frank grew quiet. They each took a drink from their glasses.

"How much do you know?" Gambon asked suddenly.

Manny contemplated his response. "Elaine told me you were her first lover. I know you saw her while she was married to Ken and to me, although she didn't confess that until toward the end. She told me just before that night you called the house, and I answered the phone."

Manny felt that familiar wave of sadness surge through him, and saw that same image of autumn leaves floating on water.

"Elaine gave me permission to ask anything."

"Why not? Did she tell you how we met?"

Manny shook his head. "No."

Frank smiled, drawing up one corner of his mouth. "I had just graduated from college, June 1957. I was 24. I spent two years in the navy, right out of high school. The first thing I did was marry my childhood sweetheart, Anita. We bought this farm that summer and I got my first job teaching high school in Montpelier.

"Anita and I had been together since she was a freshman in high school, about eight years. She was pregnant with Abby when we got married. Nowadays it wouldn't cause much of a stir, but in 1957 it was a very big deal.

"Anita was a shy girl, inhibited and introverted. I guess that appealed to me at the time. It fit in with my idea of femininity. Of course, she was beautiful. She really was. When we go inside, I'll show you her picture. Even as she got older, she was still beautiful, but in her 20s, she was stunning — her features were delicate, like porcelain. And her beauty matched her temperament — fragile. She was always very dependent on me.

"So even though I had been in the navy for two years, she was still the only girl I had slept with. And it goes without saying that when she died, Anita never knew what it was like to be with another man." Frank paused and looked into his glass. "Sexually speaking, her experience was very limited."

Manny found himself thinking of Rose, her narrow view of what *letting go* meant, her inability to experience orgasm, the relatively low priority she placed on sex. He knew what Frank was alluding to.

Frank drained his glass and got up. "Bottoms up," he said. "I'll get us refills."

Manny finished his drink and held out his glass. Gambon went into the house, the screen door creaking behind him. Scanning the property, Manny was aware of already feeling slightly buzzed. When Gambon handed him a fresh drink, Manny realized it was even stronger than the first. The idea of sitting on Gambon's porch and getting potted with him struck Manny as strange as hell — but also surprisingly comfortable, as if he and Frank were old buddies. No, not buddies, exactly — more like members of the same club: Victims Anonymous. Whatever anger he'd felt toward Frank had long since faded. He wasn't even nearly as pissed off at Elaine as he had been initially. At this point, he just felt glad to be out of it; glad that Frank — and not him — had to deal with Elaine. He simply wanted answers, to understand what had really happened.

"What did you teach?" Manny asked, curious to find out if they had English literature in common as well.

"History. American history. That's where I met Elaine. She was a junior in high school."

Manny did some quick calculations. "She must have been about 17?"

"Yeah." He thought for a few moments. "You should have seen her."

Manny was incredulous. "You and she ...?"

Gambon shrugged his shoulders. "What can I say? She was beautiful and sexy and I was young and stupid."

Manny thought of the Oscar Wilde line about being able to resist anything except temptation.

Frank continued. "Elaine was very seductive and I didn't know how to say no. She made me feel, for the first time, very desirable. You know how it is."

Manny did know how it was. Although he had drawn a line at getting involved with students, he had been tempted at times, and he knew of colleagues who did cross the line. It was very flattering to have a young, attractive woman come after you.

"You and Elaine started an affair while she was in high school? While you were her teacher?"

"Don't go all self-righteous on me. From what Elaine told me, you screwed around plenty in your first marriage. Besides, if you had been in my shoes, I doubt you would have acted any differently. Elaine was hard to resist. You know that."

Manny thought back to their very first night together, making out in the car. He wondered who had picked up who. And that night of her confession, when she had come back to bed and he had embraced her in spite of himself. He admitted there was truth to Gambon's assertion.

"But you were her teacher, for Christ's sake. And you were older than she was," Manny protested. "Seven years. You had seven years on her."

"That didn't make any difference. My being married didn't make any difference. I couldn't resist her. I didn't know how to say no."

"She told me that you were her first."

Frank gave a shrug. "I guess. Maybe I was, technically. But I think she'd had a lot more experience than I'd had."

"Christ." Manny shook his head in disbelief. "So what happened?"

Frank drank from his glass and stared out into the gathering shadows. "The school found out. Anita found out. Elaine quit school. I lost my job. Abby was just a few months old. The world came to an end. That's what happened."

Served the fucker right.

Frank got up and went inside, emerging a minute later with a couple of raw steaks. He ambled down off the porch and over to a portable gas grill that Manny hadn't noticed until now. He watched as Frank turned the grill on and climbed back on to the porch.

"What did your wife do when she heard?"

Gambon sighed deeply. "She got hysterical. She took an overdose. She was pretty much out of it for a while."

"And Elaine?"

"Her folks sent her off to a residential all-girl's school. They were divorced then and Elaine had been living with her mother in Montpelier. But after the scandal, her mother decided she couldn't handle her anymore. The father was remarried and his wife didn't want anything to do with Elaine either. So she was shipped off. But Elaine didn't want to be there, so she ran away from the school and married the guy she had been dating."

"Ken?"

"Yeah. She had been seeing him all along, even when we were together."

Manny ran his fingers through his hair. "I'm not sure I understand. Was she cheating on him or on you?"

"Jesus Christ — I was married, a new father, her teacher. I was in no position to demand fidelity. As far as I know, she had been dating Ken before we started seeing each other. She just kept up with that. It was good cover."

Manny thought back to the wife he had known for eight years, how he had idealized the intimacy he'd thought they'd shared. What a crock!

"I was able to find work in Burlington. I was there for a few years before I got back into teaching at the Hampton School. "

"You were able to get another job in teaching?"

"Things were different then. We're talking about the 1950s. Teachers and doctors could do no wrong, really. Everybody was ready to blame a slutty schoolgirl for causing a teacher to go bad — as if it wasn't really his fault. It's different now. Everybody's sensitive to sexual abuse and the idea of professionals abusing their power, like politicians and interns."

Once reminded, Manny realized that Frank was right. Times had changed. "So what happened then?"

"Things settled down here at home, kind of. But Anita was never right after that, and our relationship was never the same. I did what I could to try to make it up to her."

He looked steadily at Manny. His eyes were glassy and Manny wasn't sure if it was gin or sorrow.

"I did what I could, but it was like Humpty-Dumpty, you know? She just couldn't be put back together again. And it was all my fault. I don't think she ever forgave me."

"What about Elaine? You kept seeing her?"

"Her marriage to Ken was a big mistake. Did she tell you about him?"

"Kind of a redneck is my impression — ignorant, bigoted, abusive ..."

"Right, a controlling prick. It was trouble from the beginning. She had nowhere else to turn and he was a port in the storm for her. And when she had Laura right away, that just trapped her more."

"So you were each married and each had a kid."

"And we were young and in love — but not with our spouses."

"I thought you said you loved Anita."

209

Frank took a deep breath. "It was different. Anita was my fair young maiden. She was my wife, the mother of my daughter." He shook his head and drained his glass. "I loved her, but she was also my responsibility. It was my job to protect her. I owed her that. I don't think Elaine ever really understood how I felt about that."

He swirled the ice in his glass and took a swallow. "With Elaine, I felt alive. I had never known that kind of intensity with Anita. With Elaine, passion ruled. It took over. I lost my head, my senses, my bearings. I forgot about everything else when I was with her. It's still that way."

Frank's words were dim and dark from the gin, but Manny suddenly understood the passion, the intensity *he* had felt with Elaine — right up until that horrible night. It was exactly how he had felt with her. Gambon got up and walked down to examine the smoldering briquettes. He put the steaks on the grill.

Manny watched him. There was a lot about the man that he disapproved of: his taking advantage of a young high school student seven years his junior — not to mention having an affair with his former wife. But he also felt warmth and authenticity emanating from the man. Frank displayed a willingness to be open about himself that Manny found appealing. But maybe it was the booze that created a semblance of male bonding, of two guys, no longer really rivals, just getting drunk together.

"You want to take care of these while I finish up inside?"

Manny finished his drink and nearly stumbled down the stairs. Frank handed him a set of tongs.

"I like mine medium rare. Just bring them inside when they're done," he said and disappeared inside the house, leaving Manny swaying slightly in the twilight.

When Manny brought the steaks into the kitchen, the table was set with two plates and a large bowl of salad. Frank pulled two beers from the refrigerator before sitting down. He brought a framed picture to the table with him.

"This is Anita. It was taken that first summer we were married. She was 22."

Manny took his glasses out of his shirt pocket to examine the picture. He saw a petite, young woman with fine, delicate features. "She's beautiful," he said, handing the picture back to Gambon.

Frank studied it for a few moments before putting it aside. "I think I always saw her the way she was in that picture, a beautiful young girl, my virgin bride."

"You miss her?" Manny asked.

"We were together a long time. She was only 14 when we started dating." He popped open his can and took a long drink from it.

Manny piled some salad on his plate and was astonished to see that it contained apples, mandarin orange slices, and braised walnuts in addition to the expected lettuce and tomatoes.

"This looks like a gourmet salad. You do a lot of cooking?"

"It was sort of self-defense. Anita wasn't really much of a cook or housekeeper. Her heart wasn't in it."

Manny cut into his steak and began to eat.

"So, after you left the Montpelier school, and Elaine and Ken had Laura, how did the two of you start up again?"

"We found ways. It was as if we had some incurable disease. We couldn't go more than two or three weeks before having another relapse. She'd call me or I'd call her or we'd find a way to run into each other. We tried to end it so many times, I lost count. I finally gave up hope of ever being cured — or of wanting to be cured. Elaine would complain about Ken and beg me to leave Anita. When I was with her, it sounded like a good idea, but when I got back home I couldn't do it. I couldn't turn my back on my family. I couldn't abandon Anita. Part of it was that I really cared for her and I didn't want to hurt her. Part of it was that I knew she would make another suicide attempt."

Manny recalled what he knew of Elaine's marriage to Ken. They had been together for almost 24 years before they divorced. During that time, Elaine had gotten her GED, gone to night school for over 10 years to earn a bachelor's degree, then a master's degree. Manny had heard dozens of stories depicting Ken as a controlling and abusive bastard, with both Elaine and with Laura. When Manny told Elaine he was divorcing Rose and wanted to marry her, she finally left Ken.

"I understand Elaine had affairs with other men while she was married to Ken," Manny said.

"That's true. Sometimes I even encouraged her, hoping somebody would bring her happiness and maybe we could get off of our merry-go-round. But it was like taking methadone to try to get off heroin. It never worked. Not even with you. Oh, she was happy with you. I'll tell you straight up, Manny, you were the best thing that ever happened to her. You really were. You treated her well. You loved her. I heard all about it. I was even jealous of you, of all the time you got to spend with her, your nights in bed, your lazy weekend mornings. But in the end, it didn't make any difference. It was like we were bonded together. Nothing could break us apart. Not even you. Not even Anita."

Manny was confused. It was strange hearing Frank say he was the best thing that ever happened to Elaine. To get validation from this man, this rival, was irony beyond belief.

"So the two of you maintained this affair for ..."

"It was more than an affair! For Christ's sake, Manny, can't you see that? It's more than love, more than ... than a relationship or a marriage, more than an obsession, even. I don't know what word to call it. It encompasses everything, good and evil, right and wrong, heaven and hell, insanity. It's like life. It can't be stopped. It's energy." He paused. "Don't trivialize it by calling it an affair."

"I hear you. You're right, three decades is way too long to be called an affair."

Manny got up and retrieved two more beers from the fridge. "Tell me, how much of this did your wife know? She must have suspected something over such a long time."

Frank looked down and nodded his head. "I think she always suspected and, every once in a while, her suspicions would be confirmed and she'd confront me. Of course I'd promise to stop seeing Elaine, and I'd mean it. I meant it every time. I wanted nothing more than to justify Anita's love for me, to measure up to her vision of me. But as soon as I heard Elaine's voice or saw her, I lost my will. I could no more stop seeing Elaine than I could abandon Anita and Abby. I was stuck in a trap. I'm still stuck in a trap. I still can't choose."

"But your wife is dead."

"My daughter isn't. And she needs me. Now more than ever. She's in jail and facing prison time. And she's not helping herself."

"What do you mean?"

"Back in April, I finally managed to make the decision to leave Anita, but she made a suicide attempt and I ended up staying. I couldn't leave. Elaine was furious with me, of course. I had actually moved my things in to her bungalow, and the next day I left again. We almost broke up for good that time. She didn't call me and I didn't call her. For three weeks we went like that. That's about our limit. Finally, she showed up at my school, and that was that. It was like nothing had happened. We were back together again and that's all that mattered. She had been a wreck. I saw what a toll our separation had taken on her and I knew the hell I had gone through. You can't imagine it, my being with Anita, trying to console her, getting her back on her feet — and all the time not a minute goes by without me thinking about Elaine, wondering where she is, what she's doing. I was going crazy, starting to drink too much."

He emptied his can and got two more. "Then, a couple of weeks ago, on Saturday, May 21, I told Anita I couldn't do it anymore. I was like a dead person. My life was elsewhere. I had to go. I left that evening. I knew how she'd react. I knew it would be the end. When I walked out that door, I truly did not expect to see her alive again. I don't know if you can imagine how I felt. It's like trying to hold up a drowning person while you're running out of breath yourself. You want to save the person and you do everything you can, maybe even more than that, more than you ever knew you could. And then you reach a point where you have to let go. You hope and pray the other person can survive on their own, but there's nothing more you can do. That's how it was. I needed to breathe."

Manny leaned forward. "Go on."

"I went to Elaine's house that evening with some of my things. I'm not sure she was so glad to see me. I think I cried most of the night, knowing what was going to happen. I imagine she was afraid I'd vacillate and leave again, the way I had before. I don't blame her. I was afraid of that myself. The next morning the police arrived at Elaine's front door.

"It's hell, you know, being awakened by the police pounding on your door. I knew, of course. Anita had called Abby the night before and they'd agreed Abby would pick her up to go to church together the next morning. When Abby got there, she found her mother in the bathtub, her wrists slit, the tub full of blood."

Hearing the details of Anita's suicide was unexpectedly disturbing. "I'm sorry," Manny mumbled. "How awful for your daughter."

And how awful for you.

"The next few days were a jumble, coroner's inquest, the wake, and the funeral. Abby was a mess. She tends to be hysterical like her mother, so she was pretty heavily sedated for those first few days. By the end of the week, I thought things were calming down a little. Friday night, Elaine and I were getting ready for supper when Abby pulled up outside."

⁓——

"Look who just pulled up."

"Who?" Elaine was standing at the sink.

"Abby. I didn't think she knew where you live."

Frank went to the front door.

"I wonder if something's happened," he said, stepping outside.

"Hello," he called. "What a surprise. What brings you out here?"

Abby, wearing her perpetual pout, swung her car door shut and strode up to the house. "I had to come and see what was so wonderful over here that you had to leave us."

"What do you mean, leave you? I never left you, Abby."

"You left Mom. You left home. It's the same thing," she muttered, drawing near. "You broke up the family. Look what you did, what your girlfriend made you do."

"Abby, that was between your mother and me. It had nothing to do with you. You're married. You have your own home with Lenny and Todd."

"You don't understand, do you?"

"I know you're beside yourself with grief about Mom. We both are. Believe me."

Abby scrutinized the house and front yard. "It doesn't look like much. It's not nearly as nice as our house. It's tiny."

"Come inside," he said, ignoring her comment. Elaine dried her hands as Frank led Abby into the small living room that opened through an archway into the kitchen.

"Elaine, this is Abby." The two women briefly nodded at each other.

"I had to come see what was so wonderful that it caused my father to leave us and destroy our family."

Elaine looked at Frank, but he said nothing.

"I decided to come out and see for myself where you live." Abby looked contemptuously around the small cabin. "I expected more. I expected to see the Taj Mahal or something."

The three of them stood silently.

"I wish we could have met under better circumstances," Elaine began. "I'm sorry about your mother's death."

Abigail huffed and glared at Elaine. Frank tried to lighten the mood. "Abby, why don't you sit down? Can I get you something to drink?"

Abby remained standing. "No, I'm not staying. I didn't come to visit. I'm not sure why

214

I came. I just needed to see who this bitch was who stole you away from us and destroyed our family."

"Come on, Abby, show some respect ..."

"Respect? For this cunt? This whore?"

Frank recoiled in shock.

Elaine stared at him, enraged at his display of impotence in dealing with his daughter.

"Jesus Christ, Frank, are you just going to stand there? This is what you've done your whole freaking life, letting this spoiled brat and her mother bulldoze you and keep you from me. Look at her, Frank. Listen to her. She's accusing me of stealing you away from her. She's a jealous, vindictive bitch, Frank. Stand up for yourself, for once in your life. Stand up for me. For us."

Frank looked from one woman to the other.

"Jesus, Dad, how can you even stand to be with this horrible bitch?"

"That's enough!" Elaine shouted. "Look, I'm sorry that your mother killed herself, but nobody did that to her. She did it. Not me and not your father. It was her choice. She died by her own hand."

"If it weren't for you, she never would have done it. You were the cause of her death, and you were the cause of her unhappiness her whole life."

"Her whole life? You give me too much credit. Was I there when she was born? When she grew up? When she met your father and got pregnant and had to get married?"

"Now, Elaine, just wait ..." Frank was cut off by the two women.

"You drove her to suicide. You, trying your damnedest to steal my father away from us."

"Face up to it, Abby. Your father and I are in love with each other. We've always been in love with each other. We belong to each other."

"He belongs to us!" Abigail cried. "He was her husband. He's my father. He belongs to us, not to you. Who are you? Nobody! A whore."

"Abby, that's enough," Frank shouted.

"That's all right, Frank. She can't help it. She's her mother's daughter."

"What do you mean by that?"

Elaine laughed. "Don't deny that your mother was a depressed, hysterical neurotic." Elaine turned coolly to Frank. "I've had enough of this. If you want to visit with your daughter, I'd appreciate it if you took her outside. I don't want her in my house any longer." She turned and walked purposefully into the kitchen.

"Wait!" Abigail cried. "Do you think you can kill my mother and get off so easily?"

Frank grabbed for her arm, but she shook him loose and ran into the kitchen after Elaine. "You think you've won?" she screamed.

"What do you mean, won?" Elaine tried to look calm, arms folded across her chest.

215

"You finally got my father away from me and my mother. After all these years. She told me what was going on. I've known my whole life you were out there, like death, waiting for a chance to take him away from us."

"But I never did, did I? And what happened? Your mother, your poor weak mother finally gave him to me. Don't blame me for your mother's weakness."

Frank stood in the archway behind Abby. "Elaine, don't . . ."

"After all those years of being haunted by you, she gave in. How much can a person take? How long was she supposed to go on being hounded by you?"

"Oh grow up, Abigail. For crying out loud, you're an adult woman with a family of your own. You should know by now that we're responsible for our own happiness. Your father couldn't make your mother happy. She was responsible for her own life and her own death."

"No. Don't say that. I loved my mother. I saw how she suffered because of you."

"Did you ever notice how your father suffered? Did you ever once look at him and see his misery? Did you ever once consider how your mother's dependency was suffocating him?"

"He's a man!" Abby shouted back.

"So? He doesn't have feelings? They don't matter? You don't care about your father. You care only about yourself."

"Look who's talking. You call me selfish? Why couldn't you pick some other family to rob? Why couldn't you find a man of your own? Why did you have to pick my father?"

"Why don't you let your father choose for himself who he loves? Accept reality, Abigail. Your mother and father never loved each other the way he and I do. And your mother killed herself in a fit of self-indulgent jealousy because life wasn't the fairy tale she thought it should be."

"That's not true, you whore-bitch."

Abigail lunged forward and smacked Elaine hard across the face. Elaine retaliated with a swipe that knocked Abby into the kitchen table. She came up swinging, backhanding Elaine with her right arm outstretched. Elaine's knees buckled as her hands flew up to her face. Only then did Frank see the chef's knife flash in Abby's right hand, the blood pouring through Elaine's fingers as she held her jaw to her face.

"Oh my God!" he yelled. He stared for a hellish moment at Elaine, her eyes wide with terror. His daughter, frozen in front of him, clutched the bloody knife in her hand. He grabbed a kitchen towel and rushed to Elaine. Squatting down beside her, he pressed the towel to her cheek, the crimson blood oozing, the jaw hanging. He turned to look at Abby, her eyes dilated, a crazy smirk distorting her face. For a moment he was afraid she'd attack him, try to kill him. With one swift move, he twisted the knife from her hand.

"It'll be all right," he whispered to Elaine. "It's going to be OK. I'll take care of you."

216

Frank laid Elaine down on the floor, turning her head sideways so she wouldn't gag on her blood. He watched as her skin began to lose color. "What have you done, Abby?" he cried. "What in holy hell have you done?"

"When the ambulance arrived, I thought Elaine was dead," Frank sighed. "She had been unconscious for a while and I thought she had let go. My God! The two women in my life, Anita and Elaine — both dead! And my daughter, a murderer! It was incomprehensible.

"The ambulance crew was wonderful. They saved her life. When the police asked me what had happened, I wasn't sure. I hadn't actually seen it. I thought Abby had slapped her. It happened so fast. But the knife must have been lying on the table when Elaine knocked her back. She didn't even have to reach for it, it was just there in her hand and she came up with it. She couldn't have had even a second to think about what she was doing. There couldn't have been any intent. It was reflex, an accident really.

"But when the police asked Abby about it, she was out of her mind. She said things like, 'I wish she was dead. She deserves to be dead. I'm glad I did it.' And she's still making the same crazy kinds of statements now. Even her lawyer can't get her to shut up. I don't understand it. I don't know if she's suffering from some kind of breakdown or what."

Both of the men had finished another can of beer. Manny slouched back on his chair. "Jesus Christ," he said. "Jesus mother-fucking Christ. I had no idea."

He sat in shock for a few minutes, then asked to use the bathroom. As he walked down the dark hallway, he saw that the door to Frank's bedroom was open. Turning on the light, he noticed a picture of Abby with her husband and son. Manny studied the photograph. The girl was pretty, but not like her mother. Abigail had something of her father's features and, with a glum and glowering expression, Manny imagined her chronically unhappy and angry.

Manny felt his head spin as he retraced his steps down the hall. "I'm really smashed, Frank," he said. "I wonder if it's OK if I just camp out for a while until I sober up a little."

He plopped into an overstuffed easy chair. "I don't know what to say, Frank. You've been through hell. I guess you all have. Every one of you. I'm even thinking of your daughter's husband and her son. What's his name?"

"Todd. He's six."

"Yeah, even them. Everybody has suffered. Anita's dead. Your daughter's in jail. Is she going to be charged with attempted murder?"

"I don't know. Right now, it's assault with attempt to kill, but maybe that'll change to simple assault. I can testify that there was no intention there, in spite of what she says. On the other hand, they'd expect me to lie for her, so who knows. I've got her the best lawyer I can afford. He mentioned something about wanting to get some kind of psychiatric evaluation." Frank shook his head. "I may have to sell this house to pay for it all. And I may not have a job on top of everything."

"Why not?"

Gambon smiled his twisted, boyish smile. "I've got myself in the newspapers in a big messy scandal, complete with suicidal wife and a daughter who attempted to murder the principal's mistress. Juicy. Too messy for a private Vermont prep school. I have to meet with the board next week to see if my contract is going to be renewed. I'm not hopeful."

"My God, what will you do?"

Frank shrugged and swallowed from his can of beer. "I've got enough time in. I can retire and collect my pension. I won't need much."

"But what about you and Elaine? Will you have enough?"

"I don't know. I don't know if Elaine will go back to work. It's going to be hard for her."

Manny agreed. He thought about the emotional and physical scars, the publicity. "If you sell this place, where will you and Elaine live?"

"You're assuming we'll be together."

"After all this? Why wouldn't you be together?"

"I guess I didn't make it clear. I'm still between a rock and a hard place. Even with Anita dead, nothing has really changed. Elaine insists that I turn my back on my daughter and my daughter insists that I give up my 'whore mistress.'"

He smiled ironically and raised his beer can in a mock salute. "Here's to fate or destiny or karma, or whatever you want to call it."

"So Elaine won't stay with you unless you stand by her and give up your daughter?"

"By George, I think he's got it."

"What about your son-in-law? Can't he be there for her? Why does it have to be you?"

"'Because I'm her father. It's my job. I can't abandon my daughter.'"

"Come on, Frank, she's a grown woman. Sure, she needs support, but let her husband carry the load. That's his job, not yours."

"He won't carry it. The asshole is a real loser. He won't even try to scrape up bail money to get her out. They rent the dump where they live, so they don't even have a house to put up as collateral — not that he would if he could. Half the time he's out of work, the other half he's cutting firewood for a living. I can't count on him to do what's right by her."

"I still don't think it's all your responsibility."

"That's what Elaine says. I should be more selfish."

"You should be. Your whole goddamned life you dreamed of being with Elaine. Anita is dead, Frank. You're free now to live your life, to finally do what you say you've always wanted to do — and you're giving up now?"

"You aren't listening, Manny. I can't abandon Abby."

"I'm not talking about abandoning her, damn it. But why the hell are you insisting on sacrificing your life for her?"

"Because," he said, looking at Manny over the top of his beer, "because I've already turned my back on one daughter. I won't do it again."

"What do you mean?"

Frank stared at him. "Can't you guess?"

Manny looked at him quizzically.

"No one knows," Frank said.

"Laura?"

Frank let out a sigh and slumped back onto his chair, eyes fixed on the ceiling. Manny recalled the details of their earlier conversation. "So that was the scandal." Manny thought about it as the two men sat in silence. "Did your wife know?"

"No one ever knew for sure. Everybody wanted to believe Laura was Ken's. It was bad enough that they knew Elaine and I saw each other. Nobody wanted to believe I was the father of her child, although Ken always suspected. He would accuse her from time to time, but she always denied it and he never knew for sure. That's one reason Ken and Laura were never close. He never fully accepted her as his own."

"Then Laura must suspect, too. She must have heard Ken make these accusations. He wasn't the kind of guy who would have tried to shield her from his suspicions."

"I don't know. Maybe."

"What about now? Why not tell her now ..." he let his words trail off.

"I don't know. What good would it serve? It would just stir everything up. It wouldn't accomplish anything. Better to just let it lie."

"What if she's always wondered? What if she's always suspected? Don't you owe it to her? Doesn't she have a right to know who her biological father is?"

Frank looked at him, his eyelids half-lowered. "Do you really believe I have the right to interfere in her life after all these years?"

"Elaine then. Elaine should tell her. It might even make more sense coming from her."

Frank let his eyes blink closed and then open again. He smiled wearily as he turned his head from side to side. "Oh, nooo. Elaine would never go for that. Never in a million years, a zillion."

Manny tried to imagine Elaine telling Laura that Frank was her father. He had trouble visualizing it. Perhaps Frank was right.

"Well," he said, "I still think Laura has a right to know. She probably wouldn't be happy about it, but I think she'd be grateful, knowing for sure whether her suspicions or fears were valid or not."

Watching Gambon's eyes close, he thought, *I guess the conversation's over.* Manny adjusted his position and surrendered to the soft embrace of the stuffed chair.

Manny awoke with an urgent need to urinate. It was dark outside. The lights in the living room were still on, but Gambon was not there. As he trudged down the hall to the bathroom, he heard sounds from the kitchen.

Frank was pouring coffee when Manny returned. "Do you know what day this is?"

"Monday?"

"I meant the date."

Manny thought for a second or two. "June 6, I think." Then he realized its significance. "Elaine's birthday. She's 54 today."

"Some birthday present she'll be getting. She's being discharged today."

"How do you know?"

"She told me yesterday," Frank said. "She'll have to go back to the surgeon's to have her stitches removed and, after that, some speech therapy, I think, but she'll be home this morning."

"That sounds like good news. It all could have been so much more serious."

"Yes," Frank agreed.

"I assume you'll be going to get her," Manny wondered out loud.

"I still have to decide on that."

"Decide? What would stop you from bringing her home from the hospital?"

"Her," Frank answered. "I still have to make a decision — which I don't know if I can make."

Manny was confused. "What are you talking about?"

"When I saw Elaine yesterday, we argued again about my helping Abby with her defense. She said if I insist on helping someone who deliberately attacked her, then she doesn't see how we could be together. If I show up to take her home, it would mean I've washed my hands of Abby. And if I don't, then she never wants to see me again."

"What will you do?"

"That's my dilemma, Manny. I haven't decided." He looked at the clock on the wall. "It's 5:30 in the morning. She'll be discharged around 10 or so. I've got about four hours to decide the rest of my life."

"We talked about this last night," Manny recalled. "I remember — you said you can't abandon Abby because you've already forsaken another daughter."

"More or less."

"Frank, that doesn't make sense. One has nothing to do with the other, except in your own head. Whatever wrong you've done Laura, you've got to make right with her. Sacrificing yourself for Abby isn't going to help Laura or Elaine. If it were me, I'd let Abby's husband handle some of it."

Frank shook his head. "Lenny's useless. He hasn't even been down to the jail to see Abby. I don't think their marriage is going to survive this. I can't trust him. If I leave it to him, she'll get electrocuted."

"That bad?"

"Worse."

"Doesn't Elaine understand that?"

"Elaine doesn't care. In her mind, Abby set out to kill her, at least to maim

221

and disfigure her. This is the culmination of almost 40 years of dithering. If I had chosen, one way or the other, it never would have come to this. To Elaine — and I guess in reality, too — this is the ultimate shit-or-get-off-the-pot scenario: Abby or Elaine."

Manny sat back in his chair. "Gambon, you've lived your whole adult life in this pickle and I guess you're used to it. If it were me, I wouldn't be able to handle this purgatory that you've made your home. I'd have to put an end to it, one way or another."

Manny thought for a moment and recalled his decision to leave Elaine. "But it's your life and I won't tell you how you should live it. I'll just wish you luck and wisdom. I hope it works out for you."

Frank smiled his wry smile. "Thanks," he said.

It was light outside as Manny drove back to Emily's. When he arrived, Mark was leaving for work, and Em was in the kitchen feeding Rosemary.

"Wow," she said, "look what the cat dragged in."

"Yeah, I guess I need a shower and a shave. I slept in a chair in Gambon's living room."

"Sounds like you two hit it off."

"Yeah, strange to say, but we did. He's not a bad guy. He has trouble making decisions, but yeah, he's all right."

"You want some coffee or breakfast?"

"No, thanks, I'll just go up and shower, maybe take a nap."

Emily smiled and returned to feeding her daughter, who waved bye-bye as Manny went upstairs.

That evening, Manny offered to take Laura, Kirk, and Kyle out to dinner. He and Laura sat on the front porch before Kirk returned from work.

"You couldn't have picked a better day to take us out for dinner," she said, leaning back in a big, maple rocker. "I've been with Mom all day. It was exhausting."

Manny thought for a moment about his conversation with Frank Gambon. "You brought her home from the hospital?"

"Took her home, did some food shopping for her, blended up a bunch of stuff into mush because she still can't chew, and cleaned her kitchen. Ugh!" She shook her head violently in disgust. She looked at Manny and her voice was filled with anger.

"Do you believe nobody had cleaned up that mess from over a week ago? You wouldn't believe the amount of blood. It was terrifying. Was everybody just expecting her to come home from the hospital and clean it all by herself?"

Manny assumed that everybody meant Frank. Who else would she expect to clean up? "It must have been a shock for you to walk into that."

"Thank God I was with her. Can you imagine if she had come home alone to that? Seeing your own blood smeared all around your own house, fingerprints and footprints and pools of it. Oh, Manny, it was horrible."

"So you cleaned it all up?"

"I tried to. I did the best I could. I got most of it." Again, she shuddered at the recollection.

"Did you see Gambon?"

"No, he never showed up. I think she was hoping he would, but no, he never even called."

"Do you know why?"

"I think so he wouldn't have to clean up the mess his daughter made. That bitch. I hope she rots in hell for what she did."

"Did your mother tell you about that night?"

"Yeah. She said Abigail would have killed her for sure if Gambon hadn't forcibly taken the knife away from her. I can't imagine what it must be like to be viciously attacked in your own home, and be left horribly scarred like that." She shuddered again.

"Did you know I spent last night with Gambon?"

"You what? You spent the night with him?"

Manny was relieved to break the tension. "I don't mean I slept with him. I went over to his house. We got drunk together."

She looked at him unbelieving. "You can't be serious."

"I am. I wanted to talk to him. I needed to find out about his relationship with Elaine. I was married to your mother for eight years and, after what you told me the other day, I had to find out just how stupid and blind I had been."

Laura studied him curiously. "What did you find out? Tell me."

Manny silently cursed himself for opening his mouth. It was up to Elaine or Frank to tell her the truth, but he didn't want to lie to her, either.

"He told me how they met, how they fell in love, how they tried to cope with it. He said they tried to break it off time after time, but couldn't. Didn't. Neither one of them could let go. Your father and I," Manny paused involuntarily, remembering who her father really was, "both Ken and I were just substitutes for her. She used us to try to forget about Frank, but it never worked."

Laura continued to study him. "What's he like?" she finally asked.

"One thing I know for sure, he really loves your mother."

"If he loved her so much, where the hell was he today? She had to call me. You'd think that taking her home from the hospital would be more important than whatever he did today, if he loved her so damned much."

"I don't know for sure why he wasn't there, but I can guess. Did your mother say anything about it?"

"No, she just said she assumed he went to work, and that she had nobody else to help her, and could I do it."

"Hmmm."

"What's that mean?"

"I was just thinking about what he told me. I feel a little guilty, telling you what he told me. I wish your mother had told you more of this, Laura. I do know that he visited her every day in the hospital, which is more than you did."

"I couldn't go, I had Kyle to take care of. But I called her every day."

"I know. She told me. But she missed seeing you just the same. You know what she told me?"

Laura gave a quick shake of her head.

"She said that when Abigail sliced open her face, she had never been so frightened in her life. She was sure she was going to die and the first thing she thought of was that she'd never be able to look into your eyes again, or Kyle's."

Laura's eyes glistened and she turned her head down. "She said that?"

"Look at me," he said. "That's exactly what she said to me. She loves you very much, both you and Kyle."

Laura flashed him an embarrassed smile and looked out over her front lawn. "I know," she said. "I know I should have visited her. The truth is, I didn't want to run into Frank Gambon. Am I supposed to accept him as the new man in her life? After he broke up my family — twice? I don't think so."

Manny took off his sunglasses and rubbed his eyes. "He's not a bad guy, really. I guess I've got just as much right as you to hate him — well, maybe not quite as much — but there was something I liked about him."

"I don't know how you can say that, after what he did to you."

"I know. I used to feel that way. But I don't feel that way anymore. I don't feel like he's done something to me. I feel sorry for him, and for Elaine, trapped the way they were."

"They weren't trapped. They made choices. They married other people and had families. She married my dad and had me. She had no right to cheat on him. Or you. Frank Gambon wasn't entitled to cheat on his wife and drive her to suicide, and nearly drive his daughter to kill my mother. They weren't trapped. Don't give me that shit."

"No, they didn't have any special rights or entitlements. That's exactly the point. They built walls around themselves to keep away from each other and then they worked like crazy to climb over those walls, or burrow under them. Not because they're inherently bad people. Just the opposite. They're inherently good people trying to do the right thing. They just couldn't stop themselves. To tell you the truth, Laura, I'm impressed by the strength of their love for each other."

"Oh, come on, Manny. They weren't teenagers, like Romeo and Juliet. They're adults. Christ! I just remembered, today's Mom's birthday and I forgot all about it."

"Maybe you'd like to give her a call, maybe send some flowers?"

"Yeah, I better. She'll really be hurt if I don't do anything."

Laura left Manny on the porch. He was relieved to have gotten through the conversation with Laura without betraying Frank's confidence.

Kirk's pickup came up the driveway and pulled onto the grass. Almost at the same time, Kyle came running out of their barn, making a beeline for his father's truck. Kirk carried him up to the front porch. "Hey, Manny, good to see you back again. Laura inside making dinner?"

"Hey, how are you, Kirk? No, Laura's phoning her mother. She forgot it's Elaine's birthday today. You guys get washed up. I'm taking you out to dinner tonight."

Kyle's eyes opened wide. "Pizza?"

"Pizza it is!" Kirk said to his son. "Let's go get washed up."

The screen door swung closed and Manny returned to contemplating the front lawn. He guessed that Frank had decided he had to defend his daughter, and had respected Elaine's wishes to stay away. In spite of everything, he found himself feeling sorry for both of them.

At the restaurant, Kirk announced his big news of the day. "I had to go down to Burlington today to get some supplies, and I had lunch in town. Sheriff Mills was there, and he was talking about that woman who attacked your mom."

"Frank Gambon's daughter?"

"Yeah, Abigail something. The sheriff said her husband left her. This morning he filed for divorce and for custody of their child. I think they have a boy."

"Good," Laura exclaimed. "Serves her right."

Manny took a deep breath. He imagined what Gambon was going through. This would only add to his determination to stand by his daughter. At the same time, Manny could understand Laura's vengeful feelings. He steered the conversation in another direction.

"How's your mother making out at home on her first day?"

"She was sleeping when I called. She'll be mostly resting all week, I guess. She asked if I'd take her into Burlington on Friday to see the plastic surgeon. Her face and neck are still all swollen and black and blue. She looks horrible."

Manny tried to picture what Elaine would look like without the mummy mask covering her face.

While he was grateful for the opportunity to reestablish his relationship with Laura and get acquainted with her family, Manny decided during dinner that he needed to get away. The intense emotions of the past few days — the anger, resentment, jealousy, and fear — had overwhelmed him.

When he got back to Emily's, he told her he'd be leaving for a few days but that he'd come back and stay with them before returning to Philadelphia. Emily was genuinely sad to see him go so soon, but he explained his need for some solitude and he thought she understood.

$-\!\!\!\!\sim 10 -\!\!\!\!\sim$

Tuesday morning, Manny drove east past Montpelier and north into New Hampshire and the White Mountains. At a quiet campsite, he set up his tent and found a nearby stream for fishing. The forest literally sang with music, creating an idyllic setting. The air was mild and warm, yet refreshing, and the sky, bright with sunlight, looked clear and pure. The sound of water rushing over rocks, the fresh smell of greenery, and the cool shade made him think of heaven.

In contrast, the past few days defined a life of futility, a kind of existential hell. Everyone involved had good intentions, but each — even Manny — had managed to sow distrust and resentment. Here, alone by the side of a rocky mountain stream, life felt simple. A few hours back in time lay the reality of a world of suffering. Was there an answer? He wasn't even sure of the question. He knew only that life was a lot more complex than fishing, and fishing was complicated enough.

Manny caught three trout and was preparing them back at his campsite when a car pulled up to the clearing across from his. He watched as two women set up their tent, then he stepped across the camp road to introduce himself.

"I don't want to intrude, but I caught some trout this afternoon and there's too much for me. I'd be grateful if you would join me for dinner. I hate to see fresh trout go to waste."

The two women shrugged and smiled. "Thank you. That would be very nice," said the taller of the two. "We've been driving all day. The last thing we expected was to have someone volunteer to make us dinner."

"You're at the right place at the right time," Manny smiled. "Come on over as soon as you're ready."

The two arrived at Manny's campsite bearing a plastic bowl of potato salad, a six-pack of beer, and two folding chairs. They introduced themselves. The taller, and perhaps older of the two, was Paula. Joan was slightly shorter, with longer, graying hair tied in a ponytail.

After dinner, they helped him clean up and make a fire. Over beer, Manny learned that Joan and Paula planned to do some hiking and birding, as well as photography and painting. Paula had been a professional photographer for many years and was only now pursuing painting in a serious way. Joan had been an established painter for more than two decades. Manny, who always had trouble estimating women's ages, guessed that both were in their early 50s. Paula explained that she and Joan had been college roommates; the camping trip was an annual ritual that ensured time to catch up on the year's events. They didn't get to see each other often enough — Joan lived with her boyfriend in Boston, and Paula had her studio in Bucks County, Pennsylvania.

Manny mentioned only that he was divorced, and had made the trip from his home in Philadelphia to visit his two daughters and grandchildren in Vermont.

"Philadelphia," Paula exclaimed. "That's only an hour from where I am. What do you do in Philly?"

Manny said he taught modern literature at the University of Pennsylvania, and Paula asked if he was familiar with some of the galleries in the city where she had exhibited her photos.

"To tell you the truth," he admitted, "I've been so busy trying to take in all of the performing arts that I haven't gotten into the gallery scene at all. I know almost nothing about them, although I'm aware of First Friday, when the galleries stay open late."

Both Paula and Joan urged him to go. "There's a lot of good art to see. No matter what your individual taste is, much of what's there is very interesting."

The next day, while the women went off for a hike, Manny spent the morning reading, then explored a different spot for fishing. When he returned empty-handed, Paula and Joan invited him over for some cheese and wine, then asked him to stay for dinner.

"We're making pasta with peas and tuna fish," said Joan.

"I guess we had more luck fishing than you did," Paula joked. She could affect a kind of goofy smile and had a playful sense of humor.

Manny was happy to have their easy company. After dinner, sitting around a fire and sipping tea, Manny absorbed the silence, the smell of wood smoke, the popping and crackling of the flames, and the contentment of a full belly.

"This is a beautiful moment," he said. "I feel very peaceful." He looked across the fire at the two women. "I had come up here for some solitude, to get away from ..." He paused, uncertain of how much he wanted to divulge. "Tension, I suppose. When I heard your car drive up yesterday, I thought, oh shit, there goes my peace and quiet. But, being with the two of you has been like being with old friends — sitting, talking about nothing important, sharing thoughts and feelings. It feels very comfortable. I want to thank you for your company."

The women looked at him, slight smiles upon their faces, and voiced similar feelings of comfort and gratitude.

Manny recalled his friends from childhood, high school, college, and graduate school — the affection, intimate camaraderie, playful competitions. In particular, he thought about his boyhood friend Jimmy. He visualized them as boys, hunting, fishing, playing war, building tree houses, sharing fantasies. Something about Paula — her tomboy comfort in the woods — enabled him to picture her there with them when they were 10 or 12 years old. Then he realized that, of all the women he had known or loved, Elaine had been the only one he had considered his best friend. *Just goes to show you.*

Manny spent another two days at the campground, rising early, napping later in the day, reading, fishing, or hiking with Joan and Paula. When the weather changed on Saturday morning, he decided to head back to Emily's. The two women said good-bye and headed to Boston. It started to rain as he drove west back into Vermont, and it was pouring heavily when he pulled up in front of Emily's house. She and Rosemary stood on the covered front porch as he ran across their lawn and up the steps.

"I'm glad to be here in one piece," he said, breathing heavily from the exertion. "The visibility on the road was terrible. It was coming down in sheets in places."

"I can imagine. It was like that here too. Come on in."

Rosemary stretched her arms up for Emily to carry her and Manny held the door open.

"I'll get my stuff later. Hopefully, it'll let up."

Mark was in the living room watching the news on television. He looked up. "Says it's raining out," he announced deadpan.

"Oh, really?" Manny said.

"Mark was going to barbecue, but …"

"I've been eating outside for four days, it'll feel good to sit down at a table no matter what we're having."

"We've got burgers and baked potatoes and salad," Emily answered.

"Sounds great," said Manny.

"And a beer, if you want," Mark offered.

"If you'll join me. I hate to drink alone."

"You're very persuasive," said Mark. "You should be in sales."

Manny sat down on the sofa and Mark got them each a beer. Rosemary climbed into her father's lap while Emily went into the kitchen to make dinner.

"How was the fishing?" Mark asked, turning off the TV.

"Good," said Manny. "I caught a few trout. It was very restful, very peaceful, and the weather was perfect up until this morning. It was exactly what I needed. All of this business with Elaine — it was too much for me. I guess I'm getting old, but I've come to need my peace and quiet."

Mark smiled. "While you were in the wilderness, all hell broke loose down here in civilization."

"Oh?"

"Your ex-wife got herself into some serious trouble."

Manny wondered what Elaine could do, cooped up in her house, recovering from the assault by Abigail.

Mark sat Rosemary closer to the TV and turned on a cartoon channel. "I really hate to do that, but sometimes it's just too damn convenient. Once in a while won't hurt her."

"Tell me. What happened?"

"You were here when the husband of that woman who attacked Elaine filed for divorce and for custody of their son, right?"

Manny thought. "Yeah, that must have been Monday, the day before I left."

Mark frowned, trying to accurately recall the details. "It was a couple of days later, Thursday, I think, that the woman, Abigail, got released on bail."

So Frank did what he had to do. I wonder if he had to put his house up for collateral.
"Then what?"

"Apparently, Elaine was so pissed that she got herself into her car to go over to this Gambon fellow's house to give him a piece of her mind."

Manny knew Elaine could be unreasonably headstrong.

Mark continued. "She had to drive through town to get to Gambon's place and, right in the middle of town, right across from the Inn, she spots Gambon and his daughter crossing the street. Next thing everybody knows, she plows right into the two of them. They're both in the hospital. Rose was out in front of the Inn and saw the whole damned thing. Elaine claimed it was an accident, but there's talk she could be arrested for attempted murder. Can you believe it?"

"Both Gambon and his daughter are in the hospital?"

"Yeah, over in Burlington. He has a broken leg. I'm not sure what else. His daughter has a severe concussion plus some other stuff. The paper said she cracked her head on the pavement and was in serious condition. Can you imagine? Talk about a fucked-up family."

"And all of this happened on Thursday? The day before yesterday?"

Mark nodded distractedly, one eye on the cartoons. Manny sat back and drank from his bottle of beer. Everything inside him was suddenly made of lead. He took no pleasure at all in Elaine and Frank's misfortunes. And Frank's daughter — what a mess, and what a mess for her poor little boy. Manny considered going back to the solitude of the White Mountains, but the drenching rain made that an impossibility. Christ, all of this made Philadelphia feel like a haven.

"Where's Elaine now?"

"I'm not sure, but I think she's home, out on bail. I'm not sure. Emily probably knows."

The mention of Em's name made Manny think of Rose. He could only imagine how she might be gloating. And she witnessed the entire incident. Manny recalled how he had once seen a boy on a bicycle get hit by a car. Both bike and boy somersaulted through the air in slow motion for 15 or 20 feet before falling back to earth. The boy hadn't been killed, but his body lay mangled, twisted and twitching on the gravel shoulder of the road with blood trickling out the side of his mouth. Manny had stopped briefly to see if he could help, but others on the scene were much more qualified. He had been unable to forget the accident for quite some time, almost as if it had happened to him. He assumed Rose would be similarly shaken up. When Emily came into the room, he asked her about the accident, but she didn't know anymore than Mark did.

"I feel like Elaine is the *Titanic* and I'm lucky to have had my reservation canceled," Manny said.

"I don't know about that," Emily protested. "All of us have suffered because of her."

Manny wanted to argue the point, still feeling that Emily and Rose's difficulties were mostly his responsibility. Yet, in light of everything that had happened, he couldn't deny Elaine's role in it. It had not all been his fault.

After dinner, Manny gathered Rosemary onto his lap. She was content with him and, even when she tired and wanted to go to one of her parents, she let Manny tease and persuade her into staying. He recalled doting on Emily at this age and wondered if he had been an adequate father, if he could have done better. At one point he caught Emily looking at them, a sweet smile on her face.

"She reminds me of you," he said.

"Does she?"

"She has your happy personality. The two of you must get it from your mother. I understand I was a real sourpuss when I was this age."

Emily studied him. "I'm surprised to hear that. You're certainly not a sourpuss now."

"Maybe not. But I feel like one sometimes."

"Even Ro has her down moments."

He smiled, focusing on his granddaughter. "That's hard to believe. She's so happy. It's like she's all full of bubbles, giggles, and kisses."

The next morning, after enjoying a leisurely Sunday breakfast, Manny telephoned Laura.

"I understand your mother is home on bail, and I was wondering about stopping by. I thought I'd better check with you first to see if that would be all right."

Laura was glad to hear from him again. "It's a good thing you called here first. Mom has agreed to stay with me for a while, until she's really on her feet. If you want to come over, that would be fine."

They talked for a little while longer and he agreed to stop by later in the afternoon and stay for dinner. He made a promise to himself to remember to pick up some wine and flowers to bring with him.

Next, he called the hospital and confirmed that Frank Gambon was still a patient there. While waiting to be connected to Frank's room, Manny briefly questioned why he was calling. On one hand, he was glad that he was not directly involved in this ongoing melodrama. On the other, he experienced a complex identification with the man; they were both founding members of a select brotherhood and he felt like a lucky voyeur, observing a suffering victim who could have been him.

Frank was glad to hear from him and said he'd welcome a visit. Manny asked if there was anything he could bring with him and Frank asked if he remembered how to get to his house.

"The back door will be open. I'd appreciate it if you could go upstairs to my room and get my robe and slippers and my shaving stuff and maybe a couple of shirts or something. I can't stand these goddamned hospital gowns. I can't think of anything more ridiculous or humiliating. Oh, and maybe bring an old pair of pants. I expect to get out of here soon and I'll need something to cover my ass."

Manny said he'd be there within a couple of hours.

"Looks like all you're doing up here is visiting people in the sick bed," Emily commented.

"I feel like it could have been me."

"Except you were smart enough to jump ship."

"I guess," he mumbled, wondering if that is what he had done — or if he had been thrown overboard.

At Gambon's house, Manny parked his car and walked around to the back, where he found the remains of last year's garden and a brick patio surrounded by azalea bushes and flowerbeds. He hadn't expected such homey surroundings from a rough-edged guy in an unhappy marriage.

Manny went through the kitchen to the stairs leading up to the bedroom. In Frank's closet, he found an old pair of jeans and a shirt, which he stuffed into a small duffel bag. The top dresser drawers contained the wife's belongings, but he found Gambon's underwear and socks in the lower drawers. In the bathroom, he found the shaving materials and pajamas and a robe hanging behind the door. He gathered everything up, and looked around to see if there was anything else. He stuffed a comb and brush into the bag and left.

Manny found Frank propped up in bed, reading the newspaper.

"You don't look too much the worse for wear," he said.

Frank put the paper down. "I really appreciate your going out of your way for me."

Manny put the duffel bag next to the bedside table and sat in the empty chair.

"This may sound crazy, but there but for the grace of God ..."

"Funny how things work out sometimes."

"How are you feeling?"

"Not too bad. Got my leg broken," he said, rapping the groin-high cast, "along with the ankle and the knee. It's going to be a pain in the ass getting around for the next six weeks or so, but I guess I got off lucky."

"How is your daughter doing?"

"She's been unconscious since the accident. She got her skull fractured, and a broken arm. The doctors are optimistic. Most people recover, they say. I think she'll be OK. I haven't seen her, of course," he said, again pointing to his cast. "Do you know what's happened to Elaine?"

Manny shook his head. "All I know is that she's staying with Laura. I'm going over there for dinner."

Frank cocked his head and fixed Manny with a stare. "Oh?"

"You have a problem with that?"

"*Moi?* No. Should I have?"

"Not at all. It's only a social call. I can't help but feel that all of this is some kind of crazy dream. I feel like I'm watching a disaster film."

"Yeah. Well, we'll survive. We all will."

"I'm glad you feel that way, but I'm not so sure how I'd be taking it if I were in your place."

Frank turned his head. "I don't know. Maybe you had your disaster and you're already past it."

Manny studied him, wondering if Frank had seen inside him to understand how hopeless he had felt that night five years ago.

"Maybe," he said. "So tell me, what exactly happened?"

Frank lowered his chin into his chest. "Let me see — did you hear about Abby's husband, Lenny?"

"You mean his filing for divorce?"

"And custody of Todd. Can you believe it? What a prick. I never liked that guy. I can't understand why she ever married him." He paused, then continued. "After that, I had no choice. I had to try to get Abby out on bail. Lenny would win if we didn't fight him. I put my house up as collateral for her bail and she got out Wednesday. I brought her home with me. Thursday morning, we went over to her place to get some things. Lenny made a big deal about allowing her in to get her stuff. I threatened to call the cops and he backed off. When we left there, we were both pretty rattled. I thought we'd stop in town and have lunch, sort of a way to cool off.

"We were crossing Main Street, down by the Inn. When the light changed, we started across and I saw a car come out of Park Row and make a left onto Main. I thought the car looked like Elaine's, and then I saw her staring right at us. At first, I assumed she'd stop and let us continue across, but then I noticed she wasn't slowing down. I grabbed Abby to pull her back out of the way and the car smacked right into us. The front tire ran right up my goddamned leg.

"The next thing I know, I'm lying in the street with the car half over me. Everybody is rushing around. I heard somebody yell, 'Call an ambulance!' and 'She's alive!' but then everything went foggy. Apparently, Elaine got out of the car and somebody made her get back in and back off of me. I kept thinking I'm glad I'm not wearing my good suit, lying here in the street." He chuckled. "Did you ever hear of anything so stupid?

"Then, of course, I thought about Abby and I was told she was unconscious. Somebody got a blanket to put over us. People can be so kind sometimes. People kept telling me to be calm, that the ambulance was on its way, and everything would be all right. I couldn't stop shaking. Adrenaline, I guess.

"And then I saw Elaine. She stared at me, didn't say a thing. Her bandages were off. Her face was all swollen and discolored. She kept shaking her head from side to side, but she didn't say anything. When I heard the siren, I thought, Christ, we're blocking all of Main Street and everybody will be pissed at us. Stupid thoughts you have at a time like that. The cops pulled Elaine away and I didn't see her again."

"What do you think? You think she drove into you deliberately?"

Frank raised his eyebrows and his hands. "Who knows? I'm sure she saw us. We were looking right at each other. I don't know what was in her head. I don't know what happened. Maybe she went to stop and her foot slipped off the pedal. How should I know?"

"Is that what you told the police?"

"What do you think?"

"I think you probably lied and told them you didn't see a thing."

Frank smiled.

"I thought so," said Manny. "You're still caught between a rock and a hard place."

"To coin a phrase."

Manny heaved a sigh of disgusted exasperation. "What about all the other legal problems, with your daughter?"

Frank hadn't talked to Abby's lawyer in a couple of days, so he wasn't sure what, if anything, was happening legally with Abby or Elaine. He was to be discharged the following day to a nursing home, until he was able to make arrangements for someone to help him at home.

Manny said he planned to return to Philadelphia in the next day or so. "If I don't see you again, I wish you and your daughter good luck and a complete recovery." They shook hands and Manny left.

He was glad to get back outside, into the warm June air. Breathing deeply, he took in the sunlight and fragrant smells of springtime. On the way to Laura's, he stopped and bought a bottle of wine and some flowers; he wasn't sure if they were for Laura or Elaine, and he decided not to try figuring it out. He found a big dump truck for Kyle that he wished he could play with himself. Then, considering the marvelous weather, he decided to take the local roads back to Laura's.

Kirk's pickup was out front, next to Laura's car. Manny assumed Laura must have driven her mother there. Perhaps Elaine wasn't allowed to drive. He parked his car next to the truck and, gathering up his packages, approached the house and climbed the stairs to the porch. As Kyle opened the door for him. Laura was right behind him.

"Hi, Manny," she said, reaching out to give him a hug. "What have you brought? Flowers?"

"For you and your mother," he mumbled. "And some wine for dinner — and," he took the box from under his arm, "this for my grandson."

Kyle reached up for it and immediately plopped down on the floor to rip off the wrapping.

"What do you say, Kyle?" Laura reminded him.

"Thank you, Grandpa."

Manny watched his eyes light up as he pushed the truck around the floor. "Enjoy it," he said. "I may get one for myself."

Manny noticed Laura watching her son. Now that Manny knew her paternity, her resemblance to Gambon was obvious.

Elaine must see it all the time.

Laura went into the kitchen and got a vase for the flowers. "Thank you, Manny, they're beautiful. Mom's in the den, if you want to go in. I've got some finishing touches to take care of in here."

Manny put the wine on the kitchen counter and went into a comfortable room at the back of the house. A large picture window looked out toward the wooded hills that were just springing to life with pale green. Elaine was seated by the window, a book in her lap. Her long hair, which he remembered as luxurious and vibrant, hung limp and frizzy. Her face, still swollen and purple, reminded him of bruised fruit.

"Hi," he said.

"Hello, Manny. Laura said you'd be coming over."

As he stepped closer, he saw the reddened scars reaching across both cheeks from the corners of her mouth. Her jaw and neck were a horrible swirl of dark colors not done justice by the term *black and blue.*

"How are you feeling?"

"Terrible," she said.

"Are you still in pain?"

"Not physical as much as emotional. You heard about the accident?"

"Yeah," he said, sitting down across from her.

"I feel so damned terrible about what happened. Abby is still in a coma."

"I saw Frank this afternoon." He paused. "He asked about you."

"What did you tell him?"

"Only that I knew you were here and that I'd be coming over for dinner."

From her raised eyebrows, Manny surmised that she wanted to know Frank's reaction to that bit of news. He decided to indulge her.

"I got the impression he was wondering if I was going to make a play for you."

A smile tentatively made its appearance on her lips, then immediately hid itself.

"I told him it was merely a social call," he added.

"How is he?"

"Full of piss and vinegar, I'd say. He's supposed to be discharged tomorrow to a convalescent home until he can make other arrangements. His leg is broken, and his ankle and knee. He'll be out of commission for at least six weeks."

"Did he say anything about me?"

"Only to ask how you were."

Elaine looked away. Laura came into the room and asked if she could get them anything. Manny felt his throat drying up. "A beer if you have one, otherwise anything will do."

Elaine opted for a glass of water.

"How's the recovery going? Can you eat yet?"

"It's still quite sore. I have antibiotics and pills for pain and pills to help me sleep, and antidepressants. I feel like a walking pharmacy. But at least it's loosening up and I can chew a little and talk more clearly, although, as you can tell, I still have this stupid lisp."

"I guess you'll lose that in time."

"I hope so. I sound like a four-year-old."

Laura brought their drinks and Kyle came over for his share of attention. It wasn't until a few minutes later, when Laura returned to the kitchen and Kyle went outside to play with his new dump truck, that they had a chance to speak again.

"Can you tell me what happened?"

Elaine's eyes widened and grew moist. "To tell you the truth, Manny, I'm not sure anymore. I remember what I thought then, when it happened. But now, looking back, I don't know."

Manny waited for her to continue.

"I remember making a left turn from Park Row onto Main Street and, as I did, I saw Rose, your ex-wife, standing outside the Inn, talking to someone. I thought she saw me. I think we made eye contact and I was debating whether to beep the horn or wave, then all of a sudden there were these two people right in front of me. I jammed on the brakes, but not in time."

She paused. "That awful, dull thud. What a horrible sound. I heard a scream. I honestly don't know if it was me or Abby or someone else. I didn't even fully realize it was them until I got out of the car. When I look back, I think I might have recognized them right before I hit them, but I'm not sure if I'm imagining that or not. I never expected to see Frank in town, especially with Abby. I was on my way over to his house." She stopped and drank some water.

"I shouldn't have been driving. I'm sure my pain medication must have slowed my reaction time. I can't tell you how many thousands of times I've made that turn. And, of course, I was preoccupied. I was in a terrible state, really. God, I feel so stupid. Wretched."

Manny was not used to hearing Elaine berate herself. Usually, she was too proud or vain to admit any wrongdoing. She looked old, worn and weary.

"Did you get feedback from any witnesses who saw the accident?"

"Someone said I aimed straight for them as they were waiting for me to pass. I don't know how that's possible, although I should have seen them. I thought I had glanced away to look at Rose for only a second, but it must have been longer. I don't know anymore. Obviously, it's my fault, but it was an accident. I didn't deliberately run them down like they're saying I did."

"What will happen? Legally, I mean. Do you know?"

"I have an attorney. I called Martha right away. You remember her?"

Manny did remember Martha, Elaine's lawyer in both of her divorces.

"She recommended someone from Burlington. Laura is taking me to see him tomorrow. This whole business is all so sordid. I don't know how I can ever show my face around here again." She gave a little laugh, "Especially being the way it is. I can hire myself out on Halloween."

"It does sound like a soap opera. The whole mess is hard to believe."

"I know. It's preposterous."

"Your scars will fade — the physical and emotional scars. So people will talk. That never stopped you before."

"I'm not sure what you mean. I was always been discreet. I never flaunted what I did."

"I know. I'm just saying that you never let public opinion dictate how you lived your life."

Elaine relaxed. "Still, I'm the talk of the town, the entire county, and not in a good way. I may even lose my job, for all I know. I don't know what I'm going to do."

"You'll get through it, one day at a time, one step at a time."

Elaine gently blew her nose and dabbed at her eyes. Manny sat back and drank his beer. What had happened? It was like a tornado had come to town and left these people devastated: Elaine, Frank, his wife and daughter. Everything turned topsy-turvy, including his own life. He glanced at Elaine. She was looking out the window, crying, and he thought back to that night, which he pictured as the fulcrum on a seesaw: One moment he was up, and then he was down. Only now, as he looked back, knowing all that he knew, he saw it as exactly the opposite: Before that night, he was down, and now he was up — free, outside the storm system.

"Elaine," he said softly. "What about you and Frank?"

She looked away again. "I don't know. It's bad enough that I drove into them, especially if he thinks I did it intentionally. But I'm afraid I went too far in demanding that he refuse to support Abby. I was so angry at that daughter of his, and at him. My whole life was ruined, and all he could think about was defending her. I couldn't tolerate it. I still can't. I still can't forgive him for that. It feels like he's condoning what she did to me. How can he do that?"

"Elaine, do you really believe that? You can't possibly."

She stared at him, horrified. "Look what she did to me."

"I know. But you can't really believe he condoned it. You can't possibly believe that of him."

Elaine shook her head. "His family, his wife and daughter, always came first. I was always an afterthought, the mistress who's supposed to understand that he has responsibilities, family obligations."

"But surely you can see that he feels a duty to help his daughter, especially now that her husband has left her and is suing her for custody of their son."

"She brought that on herself. That's her problem, not mine. Frank should be with me. I need him."

Manny felt like he was seeing her for the first time, her pig-headed selfishness. She had a buried grudge against Frank that went back to when she was pregnant with Laura. He decided he wasn't going to argue with her about it. If she chose to persist in making Frank a bad guy and herself the wronged woman, he wasn't going to try to stop her. In any case, he knew, it would be a futile attempt. He shrugged and finished his beer.

"Did I ever tell you about how my father left my mother?" she asked.

Manny thought for a few moments. "I remember you told me they split up when you were little, and you stayed with your mother mostly."

"When I was six, he left us to live with his girlfriend. My mother referred

240

to her as 'that bimbo.' My mother was always a little loopy. I imagine she wasn't much of a wife. Still, she was absolutely destroyed when she found out he'd been having an affair for three or four years. That last day he was home, I remember them yelling at each other. The screaming was awful. And then he came into the kitchen where I was sitting at the table, making believe I was coloring and hadn't heard anything. And he stopped and leaned over and said, 'I'm sorry, Princess.' And then he walked out. I remember the screen door closing behind him, squeaking, giving that extra little bump when it swung shut. And I went to the door and watched him walk away. He never looked back. I gave him a little wave anyway. I never saw him again.

"He and his girlfriend moved away. I don't know if he's dead or alive. I guess he doesn't know if I'm dead or alive. I was destroyed when Ken did the same thing to Laura. Poof! Just like that, gone. I'm sure Laura felt the same as I had, like worthless shit."

Elaine turned to face Manny. "I felt that way with you, too, when you said you couldn't bear to be with me anymore, and had to move far away. That's how you made me feel then, like worthless shit. I want you to know, so you will appreciate how much it means to me that you made a point of coming here. It means the world to me, Manny. I want you to know."

Manny didn't say anything. She didn't need him to say anything. He smiled gently at her. "I'm going out to the kitchen. Can I get you some more water or something?"

She barely shook her head.

"Where's Kirk?" Manny asked Laura when he was in the kitchen.

"In the barn, working," she answered.

"On a Sunday? Doesn't he ever stop?"

"He can't keep still. For him, it's play. He really enjoys what he does, building things."

"I think I'll go out and say hello. Anything I should bring out?"

"No, he's got a stocked fridge out there. He's very self-sufficient."

Manny grabbed another beer from the refrigerator and went out to the barn. Kyle saw him and tagged along, pushing his new dump truck ahead of him. In the barn, Manny found Kirk building a wall unit that would be installed in a house he was building. Kyle aimed his truck toward a heap of scrap lumber and proceeded with his own construction job.

"Be careful of nails," his father warned.

"How're you doing?" Manny asked.

"Good. You?"

"I'm fine." Manny was thinking how relieved he was to be out in the fresh air.

Kirk explained what he was working on and some of the special features he was building into the unit.

"How do you like having your mother-in-law with you?"

"We stay out of each other's way."

"How about Laura?"

"It's tougher on her. She's got her hands full as it is. The two of them get on each other's nerves. They always rub each other the wrong way, setting off sparks. I keep myself busy. I don't expect her to be here all that long. Neither of them will be able to tolerate it."

"You have any thoughts on the accident?"

Kirk stopped what he was doing and looked up at him. "Between us?"

"Yes. Just between the two of us."

"I think she deliberately ran them down. I don't have any doubt about it."

Manny was shocked by his definitiveness. "How can you be so sure?"

"Elaine is one of the most purposeful, deliberate, and stubborn people I've ever known. She wants something, she goes after it. Nothing stands in her way. Look at her doctoral program, as an example. She's been pursuing that degree for how long — seven, eight, nine years? And she's gotten extension after extension. Until all of this happened, she was planning on having her oral exam this coming year. And my guess is, she won't let any of this stop her. No, I don't think Elaine does anything she hasn't planned long and hard to do. *Accident* isn't in her vocabulary. No way."

Manny sipped his beer and contemplated what Kirk had said. He wouldn't have put it quite so strongly, but he had to agree that Kirk had her sized up pretty well, if maybe a little oversimplified.

"She says it was an accident."

"I know. It's never her fault, is it?"

"I agree with most of what you've said, but I'm wondering why you're so negative about her."

242

"I see how she affects Laura, that's all. I'll tell you the truth, Manny, I don't know how you stayed married to her for eight years."

Manny was unprepared to hear that. "I saw her differently, I guess."

Funny how you can love someone and others see that person in such a different light.

"Well, I'll be getting back in the house. I only wanted to say hello and see your workspace out here."

Kirk stopped what he was working on and shook Manny's hand. "It's my home away from home," he said, his eyes laughing. "You come on out here any-time, Manny. Anytime."

Manny went back into the house, nodded to Laura as he left his empty bottle on the kitchen counter, and returned to Elaine in the den. They made small talk about Kirk's perfectionism, and then Elaine raised her eyebrows questioningly and said, "You haven't told me anything about the women in your life."

"Not much to say."

"Oh? That's not what I would have thought. You always had a pretty big appetite for women."

"I've gotten older."

"You've given up looking? I'm surprised at you, Manny. I find that hard to believe."

"I don't have the stomach for it any more."

"For what? Sex? Companionship?"

"For the games, Elaine. You know, I thought the two of us had something beautiful. It's not only that I was in love with you and believed you were in love with me. I really did believe we were totally open and honest with each other. I believed in you."

He laughed. "Big fucking joke. No, I simply can't do it anymore. I don't have that trust. The women I've dated, they're no better than you, Elaine. Every-body lies their damn head off. Nobody is honest. I don't understand how two people are supposed to have a relationship. I don't know anymore if I even think it's possible. A woman is the last thing I need in my life."

"Don't blame your problems on me, Manny. I didn't create the world the way it is. People lie. If you want to live alone because you're too afraid of being hurt, that's your problem. That's your decision. Me? I don't want to be alone, although with this face, I probably won't have any choice."

"Christ, Elaine, don't you have any guilt at all?"

"Guilt? For what? For creating the eight beautiful years we had together? Would you really have preferred that I told you the truth from the beginning? Do you really wish we didn't have those eight years together? Be real, Manny. Be honest with yourself and stop blaming other people for your problems."

Manny shook his head.

"You're some piece of work, Elaine. Yes, at the time, those years were wonderfully lush. But looking back, the view isn't so great. It might have been better to have skirted around what I see now was a swamp. A swamp that you and Frank are still mired in. For me, well, I've had my run at wearing my heart on my sleeve. It doesn't work if it's one-sided. Maybe you and Frank have been more honest with each other than you were with me, but I doubt it."

Elaine drew in a deep breath. "You're really happy to see me in this condition, aren't you? You really do hate me."

"No, Elaine. Seeing you like this, physically, and in this legal mess, doesn't make me happy at all. I get no pleasure from your misery."

"Now who's not being honest?"

"Believe what you want, Elaine. I'm telling you the truth. Yes, I'll admit I'm still pissed at you for lying to me all those years. But I'm not happy that any of this has happened. I'm just glad to be out of it. I'll tell you straight, I do not hate you. But I don't love you anymore, either." Manny paused to let it sink in, and in that split second decided. "I'll be leaving tomorrow to go back to Philadelphia. I never thought I'd be happy to leave Vermont and go back to the city. But Jesus, this lifestyle you folks have up here is way too intense for me. I feel 10 years older than I did two weeks ago."

Laura called and they went into the kitchen. Dinner was pleasant, except for the usual tension between Laura and her mother. Kyle kept staring at his grandmother's scarred and distorted face and Elaine wanted Laura to make him stop looking at her as if she were a grotesque monster. Laura tried to be diplomatic, but was adamant in defending her son. Kyle spent the rest of dinner with his face buried in his plate. Kirk remained silent, alternately focusing on eating or exchanging furtive glances with Manny or Laura. To break the tension, Manny talked about his home in Philly and people in his department. He was relieved to hug everyone good-bye, and drive away.

Manny found Emily and Mark in the living room watching TV with Rose. "Hi, Rose," he said.

"Hi, yourself. I hear you've been gallivanting all over Vermont today."

"Kind of, I guess. I went into Burlington and then over to Laura's for dinner."

"How is everyone doing?" Emily asked.

Manny told them about Gambon's injuries, his daughter's skull fracture and resulting coma. Rose asked how Elaine was taking it.

"She says it was an accident, that she didn't see them in time. As a matter of fact, she said she saw you outside the Inn, talking with someone. I guess she took her eyes off the road for a second. I was wondering how it might have affected you, seeing a couple of people getting run over by a car right in front of you."

"It was awful. I was talking to my friend Hazel and I saw Elaine's car drive right into those two people. I had no idea who they were. I didn't know it was Elaine until she got out of the car. But there was this sudden squeal of breaks and then that soft thump and those two people thrown to the ground. I must have jumped and let out a scream. I was shaken the whole rest of the day. Every little thing and I'd jump out of my skin. Scared me to death."

"What do you think? Do you think she deliberately drove into them?"

"How should I know?"

"You saw it," chimed in Emily. "How did it look to you?"

Rose became a little flustered and looked from one to the other. "Well, yes, I saw it, but I wasn't really paying attention. I was talking to Hazel and sort of looking out onto the street and it took me by surprise. I don't know. I'm sure it was an accident. I mean, she stopped right away. She didn't drive off or anything like that."

Mark asked what Gambon thought. Manny hesitated for a moment. "He said he told the police he didn't see the car coming until it was too late. But all three of them were wound up emotionally. I'm not sure if any of them were paying attention to what was going on around them."

Manny didn't want to say anything that might lead people think it was a deliberate act on Elaine's part. As far as he was concerned, that was between Elaine and Frank.

Emily asked, "What do you think will happen if Abby doesn't come out of her coma? Or if she dies?"

Manny shrugged his shoulders. "Your guess is as good as mine," he said.

Mark asked, "Isn't vehicular homicide the same as manslaughter? Or reckless endangerment? I think I saw something like this on TV."

"I guess the lawyers will figure all that out," said Manny. "In the meantime, I hope the girl recovers. Frank said the doctors are optimistic."

"They always say that," said Mark.

"It's a wonderful hospital," said Rose. "She couldn't be in a better place."

Emily stood up. "We have chocolate ice cream and I'm going to get a dish. Anybody else want some?" Everybody said yes and Mark went into the kitchen to help her.

"How is all of this affecting you, Manny?" Rose asked when they were alone.

"Oh, I don't know. I feel sorry for them, even Frank's wife, Anita. I didn't even know her but I feel sad for her too; and the daughter having to find her like that. But on the other hand, I'm detached from it all. No, more than that — I need to get some distance from it. I don't want to be part of this mess. It's like a Greek tragedy with everybody killing or maiming everybody else. The only thing missing is the poison and the chorus. I feel like I'm looking at a group photograph that once contained my picture — except my face has been cut out. And everyone else in the photo is either dead or wounded, and here I am, safe, looking at the photograph. Does that make any sense?"

Rose shrugged. "That sounds creepy to me. I can't imagine what that's like. But I am glad you're no longer with that woman. She's trouble, that's all."

Manny chuckled. "Rose, you have always had a talent for understatement."

— 11 —

M anny took four days to get home. He went west from Vermont and
camped in New York State for a couple of nights and then drove south
into central Pennsylvania before finally heading home. By the time he
got back to his house, he felt rested and relaxed, although he was looking forward to sleeping in his own bed again. Being back in the relative anonymity of
the city was strangely comforting. The world of Elaine and Frank felt distant
and baffling. He took his time, savoring the leisurely simplicity of shopping for
food and washing laundry. He picked up his mail from the post office and pe-
rused catalogues and stacks of junk mail without considering the time it wasted.

At the office, he caught up with messages and the comings and goings
of his colleagues. Ed and his wife, Signe, were in Europe and wouldn't be back
until the end of summer. Emails on his computer numbered into the hundreds,
and he idled among them as if he were strolling through a park. It was a pleasant
way to float comfortably through the remaining summer days.

He even bought a second-hand bicycle and began riding in Fairmont
Park, lazing along the Schuylkill River, reading and girl watching. He found
himself getting aroused and was astonished to realize how long he had been
without any conscious sexual feelings. He felt reborn, interested again in the
energies of the life that surrounded him.

It was in such a state that Manny received a note from Paula. She en-
closed an announcement of the opening of an exhibition she was having in
Philadelphia in a couple of weeks, and invited him to see her work. He responded that he was pleased to hear from her and excited by the opportunity

to see her work. A few days later, she emailed that she was in the city making arrangements with the gallery owner, and perhaps he would be open to meeting for a drink.

"That sounds like fun," he wrote back, and suggested a café across from Rittenhouse Square. "If the weather is nice, we can sit outside and enjoy a view of the park. Not quite the White Mountains, but it'll have to do."

Manny was relaxing at one of the sidewalk tables when Paula came into view. He immediately recognized her long strides and had an image of her in the woods of New Hampshire. She smiled when she saw him, and he took a secret pleasure in observing her as she approached.

"It's good to see you again," he said, realizing that he really meant it. He felt like he was meeting an old friend.

They caught up on recent events, and Paula described the activities involved in setting up a gallery exhibition. After two gin and tonics, Paula commented that he looked more relaxed and less distracted than he had in New Hampshire.

"I probably am. There was a lot going on up there with my ex-wife." He didn't know if he wanted to get into the gory details. "It's peaceful leaving all of that behind."

"I guess former spouses can be something of a mixed blessing."

"I don't recall your mentioning a former husband."

Paula laughed and made a funny face. "Never had one," she said.

"You've never been married?"

"Never wanted to. Never wanted to have kids, either. I guess that's been a kind of mixed blessing too."

"Everything is," Manny agreed. "I once thought of a bumper sticker that read: Sacraments are a mixed blessing."

Paula chuckled. "I enjoy my nephews, my brother's sons, but I'm glad I didn't have to raise them as my own, even though I love them dearly."

Talking about their own families of origin, and Manny's children and grandchildren, the conversation flowed easily. Manny realized he was enjoying a level of comfort he hadn't had with a woman in a very long time. Allowing himself to notice her physical attributes, her perky haircut, the sweetness of her smile, the mischief in her eyes, the curves of her body, he was again caught off guard by a stirring within himself. He had relegated Paula to the category of old friend or camping buddy. Now that was changing.

As dusk approached, Paula said she had to get back to her studio. Manny threw out a subtle hint that she could stay over if she wished, but she let it go over her head and he didn't pursue it. They walked together to her car and exchanged a friendly hug and peck on the cheek.

"I really enjoyed seeing you again. I'm looking forward to attending your opening."

Paula gave him one of her patented goofy smiles. "If you'd like to come up to Bucks County and see my studio, you won't have to wait until then."

Manny felt the grin spread across his face. "That would be great!"

They made plans for him to drive up.

"I'll email you the directions," she said. "I'll show you my work, and we can either go out or I can fix us something to eat."

Manny was amazed at how giddy he felt. "I'll bring some wine," he said.

"Good," she said, her voice filled with enthusiasm as she got into her car. "I'm looking forward to it."

A couple of days later, Manny received an email from Laura.

I tried to call you a few times, but you were never in and I hate to talk to answering machines. I finally decided to write and bring you up to date on what's been happening since you left.

Mom stayed with me for about two weeks and we managed not to kill each other, so perhaps we're both maturing. Her face has healed about as much as it's going to. All of the swelling and discoloration is gone, but the scars will remain quite noticeable for a long time. Eventually, they're supposed to grow fainter and makeup will probably cover most of them.

Abigail remains in a coma or vegetative state, whatever the technical term is. She was moved to a nursing home and, since she poses no flight risk, the bail requirement was dropped, although the charges against her for assaulting Mom remain open. To be pursued with vigor, I assume, if she ever regains consciousness. If she dies, Mom may face charges of vehicular homicide, and Lord knows what will happen then.

In the meantime, Lenny, Abigail's estranged husband, is suing Mom for $10 million! It has her really frightened — and furious, as you might imagine. Even Kirk and I feel sorry for her. Her auto insurance is denying any responsibility, which, of course, is ludicrous, but it has Mom going bananas. If she were a different sort, I'd worry about her being suicidal, but that's not her way. Would you believe she's living with Frank? Well, she is! For the past two weeks.

249

One day she got herself all prettied up and borrowed my car. I had a hunch where she was going. I have no idea how she managed it, but she came back here later that day all smiles and told me she was moving back to her place.

―――

Elaine stood in front of the bathroom mirror. She wasn't at all happy with what she saw, but she realized it was true, as both Laura and the doctor had told her: Except for the scars, her face was back to normal. All of the swelling had subsided and the discoloration had mostly faded. The scars themselves, grotesque red ridges, were still as noticeable as they were the previous week. She knew they would grow fainter with time, maybe months or even years. Resigned, she spent a long time applying makeup and chose her clothing carefully, then asked Laura if she could borrow the car for a few hours. Laura asked if she wanted her to drive, but Elaine smiled and said it wasn't necessary.

She arrived at the nursing home less than an hour later, and asked at the desk for Frank's room number. She found him sitting in his wheelchair in the dayroom, his left leg propped up stiffly in front of him. He was reading when she approached him.

"Good morning," she said pleasantly.

Frank looked up and his eyes widened. "Well, I'll be damned."

"You look shocked to see me."

"I am."

"How are you?"

"OK," he said, gesturing to his immobilized leg, "about as well as you can expect."

"I'm so sorry, Frankie. I really am."

Frank met her eyes. Finally, he asked, "Why, Elaine? Why did you do it?"

"It was an accident. I didn't mean to run into you and Abby. Honestly, I didn't see you."

He challenged her. "Elaine, I was looking into your eyes. You were staring right at me. I know you saw us."

"Maybe at the last second, after it was too late. I didn't see you in time, is what I meant."

"Elaine, we were there in the crosswalk waiting for you to pass. There was no explanation for your hitting us. You aimed right for us."

"No! Don't say that. I would never do that. I didn't even know you were there. I only glanced away for a second."

Frank shook his head and continued to stare at her. Elaine turned away from his gaze.

"I saw Rose, Manny's ex-wife, standing in front of the Inn. She was talking to someone, a woman, and looking my way. I remember wondering if she recognized me and I was debating whether I should beep or wave or something. And then, all of a sudden, I saw two people in front of me. I had no idea it was you. You have to believe me. I would never do anything to hurt you. How could you even think that?"

"Maybe it wasn't me you were aiming for."

"I could never do that. Of course, I was angry at Abby. But I would never deliberately run her down." Frank raised his eyebrows. "You have to believe me, Frank. I would never do that."

"But you did."

"Not on purpose! It's not like I saw her and deliberately aimed the car at her!'" Frank gave her a questioning look.

"Believe me, it was a terrible accident. I admit it was my fault entirely. I know now that I shouldn't have even been driving, what with all of the medication I was taking at the time. That, plus my emotional state. I was heading over to your house to see you."

"So I heard."

"I read that morning in the newspaper that you had put up bail and Abby was out of jail. I was furious with you. I admit that. I'm still having trouble with that. I wanted to confront you. I couldn't understand why you were turning your back on me. On us."

She let her gaze wander to the window. "I felt so betrayed. I couldn't understand why you'd abandoned me. It made me question if you'd ever loved me. So I decided to drive over to your house and confront you. I needed to know if you loved me."

She looked at him and waited. Frank met her gaze with silence.

"Do you?" she finally asked.

"Christ, Elaine, at this point, how the hell am I supposed to know what I feel? You deliberately ran me over and then parked your fucking car right on top of my leg. My knee will probably have to be replaced. God knows about the ankle. Even my hip is sore. And let's not forget Abby. She's still unconscious,

Elaine. She may never regain consciousness. She's as good as dead. You know that, right?"

"Yes."

"You've taken my daughter from me."

"I hope not. I hope she recovers. Really." Elaine paused and looked away. "I never wanted to take either of your daughters from you."

Frank heaved a sigh. "Yeah, if you say so."

Elaine turned abruptly back to him. "What do you mean by that?"

Frank shrugged. "I don't know. It's just sometimes I've wondered if she was really mine. Maybe she was Ken's after all. How do I know for sure?"

Dumbfounded, Elaine staggered to a chair. "I never knew you doubted. Frank, you knew you were my first. I never let Ken ... until afterward. You knew that."

"I know. I'm only saying that all of this craziness makes me wonder, that's all." After some silence, he continued. "Even if Laura is my daughter, I didn't raise her. I never knew her the way I knew Abby. Maybe they're both my daughters, but I'm Abby's father. And your recklessness has changed everything. Jesus Christ, Elaine, don't you have any remorse for what you've done?"

Her eyes grew fiery and her jaw stiffened. "Yes," she said. "I feel terrible about what I've caused, both to you and to her. If I could undo it, I would. But at least my destructiveness wasn't intentional. I was at fault. I was responsible, but I didn't mean to do it."

"That doesn't undo the damage, does it?"

"Maybe not, but your daughter did this to me deliberately. She meant to cause me harm. I nearly died because of her. She nearly killed me."

"Elaine, it's all the same. Don't you see? When she picked up that knife, it was because it was there, in her hand. She didn't have time to think about what she was going to do. The knife just happened to be in her hand when she struck out."

"You believe that? You actually believe she didn't come over to my house to verbally and physically attack me? Why the hell do you think she came over in the first place? To get my recipe for brownies? She came over to avenge her mother's death because she blamed me."

"Maybe she did come over to give you a piece of her mind, to accuse you. But I don't believe she ever gave a moment's thought to physically harming you. That's not who she is. Abby has never hurt anyone. Never."

"So I'm her first victim, so what. She still did it. She tried to kill me and you're defending her." She shook her head and looked out the window again, her eyes glistening, her scars enflamed.

When he finally spoke again, his tone was softer. "Elaine, if I believed for one second that she deliberately tried to kill you or that she consciously wanted to cause you permanent injury, then I don't think I could defend her." He paused and pondered for a moment. "I don't believe what she did was intentional. I really believe it was an accident, an impulsive gesture with tragic consequences. If I really thought she did it intentionally, then I don't know. As much as I feel an obligation to support her, I'm not sure I could." He looked directly at her. "How could you ever believe otherwise?"

"You don't think she's capable of this," she said, gesturing to her face, "even though you were there? Even after seeing that crazed, maniacal smile on her face afterward? Even after those bizarre statements she made to the police about wanting me dead? And yet, you can believe I would deliberately run you down? How could you?"

Frank lowered his head and played with the raggedy edges of his cast. "Maybe being the victim gives a different perspective. Maybe if I had been in the passenger seat next to you as you ran into two other people, I might react differently. I might see your point of view. Maybe if Abby had slashed my face, I might feel differently about her intentions. I don't know." After a moment, he added, "Maybe it doesn't make any difference. What's done is done. Nothing is going to change what happened."

"No," she said. "Nothing is going to change what happened." They sat silently for a while, and then Elaine spoke. "That's part of the reason I came over today."

"Why?" he asked, turning to her again.

She took a deep breath. "I was hoping we could make a fresh start. I know I'm still furious with you and Abigail. And I know you still want to blame me. But I also know that I miss you, Frank — terribly. Sometimes I do want to beat some sense into you. I admit it. But I still want you. I still love you."

Frank sighed and looked away.

"Frankie, please forgive me."

He stared at her. "Do you really think we can move on after what's happened?"

"We've come this far, Frank. We've gotten past everything else. It would be stupid for us to stop now, when we actually have a chance to be together. Frank, don't abandon me now."

Elaine leaned closer and reached out to grasp his hand. His fingers curled around hers and then gripped them firmly. She pulled a tissue from her purse and wiped her eyes.

She gave an embarrassed laugh. "And I was so careful putting on my makeup this morning. Now it's all ruined."

"You never needed makeup, Elaine."

"I do now."

"No," he said evenly. "Not even now. The scars don't make a difference. You're still you."

Elaine heaved a big sigh, then put her arms around his neck and kissed him.

"Let me tell you what I was thinking," she tried to tame the excitement in her voice. "I thought either I might come over to your place or you could stay with me in mine. No, let me finish. I know you need someone to help you around the house until you're more mobile. Oh, Frank, I'm so sorry I did this to you."

"I know."

"I want to take care of you. And I can't stay at Laura's any longer. You know how we are with each other. She takes offense at everything I do or say. I'm ready to go home. A visit for a couple of hours is fine and I love Kyle, but I can't stay there any longer."

... Mom moved Frank — it's always Frank now, never Mr. Gambon — into her little cabin. His cast won't come off for at least two more weeks and then they'll figure out the next step (is that a pun?). He will probably need more surgery. His school let him go so he's now retired, and can devote his full attention to holding Mom's hand as they do battle with Lenny and the insurance company. Mom keeps me posted on a daily basis and I know much more than I want to, which is why I'm vomiting this into the computer so I can send it off into cyberspace and perhaps be rid of it forever (I wish).

Mom said she and Frank want to have us over for a cookout. Can you imagine? It makes me feel creepy. What do you think? I know he's the man in her life, and I guess I'm glad he's there. If she had no one, I'd really be in the hot seat. But there's something about him that feels strange. I don't know why. I never felt that way with you. I'm not sure why I'm telling you this, but if you have any thoughts, I'd like to hear.

Well, that's the news. I didn't even ask you about you. How are you doing? What are you doing? Have you recovered yet from your visit here? Has this email caused a relapse? I hope not.

Love,

Laura, et al.

Manny thought long and hard about his response.

Laura,

I believe that the relationship between your mother and Frank is a very complicated — even a tortured — one. I hope, and must believe, they have brought each other great happiness. To stay together this long, through so many difficulties and so much pain, there must have been great intensity and passion. One thing we both know is that your mother is not a masochist. She wouldn't have persisted in that relationship with such determination if she weren't getting a great deal out of it. I've found that when two people care about each other, they also care about who and what is important to the other. Although that may not have been true for your mother — I doubt she ever developed a sincere interest in Abigail — I do believe it is true of Frank. I think it's only natural that he has a deep and genuine interest in you and your family, precisely because he truly loves your mother and those who are important to her. I think he means well.

I don't know if their bond was forged in heaven or hell. It is an understatement to point out that theirs is not an easy relationship. I hope Abigail recovers and doesn't face any prison time. I hope Frank and your mother escape the prospect of financial ruin. But that's all in the future. Right now she needs him and she also needs you in her life. And it sounds like it's important to her for you and Frank to meet each other. There's no law that says he has to like her daughter or that you have to like him. But, as you said, he is the man in her life, and you would be selling everyone short if you didn't have the opportunity to get to know each other. Then, if you don't feel comfortable, you can at least say you tried it. Like broccoli.

It looks like I may have found someone to spend some time with. Actually, we met during those few days in June when I was camping in New Hampshire. I feel like I've known her my whole life. She's a photographer and I'm driving up to Bucks County this weekend to see her studio. She's exhibiting her work here in Philly the following week. I'm excited about the prospects. It feels good to be alive again, kind of like bobbing up to the surface after a very long period of submersion. Wish me well!

www.ingramcontent.com/pod-product-compliance
Lightning Source LLC
Chambersburg PA
CBHW031106260626
47172CB00001B/239